GH00759492

THIS WAS IVOR

CLAUDE HOUGHTON OLDFIELD was born in 1889 in Sevenoaks, Kent and was educated at Dulwich College. He trained as an accountant and worked in the Admiralty in the First World War, rejected for active service because of poor eyesight. In 1920 he married a West End actress, Dulcie Benson, and they lived in a cottage in the Chiltern Hills. To a writers' directory, Houghton gave his hobbies as reading in bed, riding, visiting Devon and abroad, and talking to people different from himself. He added: "I like dawn, and the dead of night, in great cities." He disliked fuss, noise, crowds, rows, and being misquoted, or being told how much he owed "to some writer I've never read."

Houghton's earliest writing was poetry and drama before turning to prose fiction with his first novel, *Neighbours*, in 1926. In the 1930s, Houghton published several well-received novels that met with solid sales and respectable reviews, including *I Am Jonathan Scrivener* (1930), easily his most popular and best-known work, *Chaos Is Come Again* (1932), *Julian Grant Loses His Way* (1933), *This Was Ivor Trent* (1935), *Strangers* (1938), and *Hudson Rejoins the Herd* (1939). Although he published nearly a dozen more novels throughout the 1940s and 1950s, most critics feel his later works are less significant than his novels of the 1930s.

Houghton was a prolific correspondent, generous in devoting his time to answering letters and signing copies for readers who enjoyed his books. One of these was novelist Henry Miller, who never met Houghton but began an impassioned epistolary exchange with him after being profoundly moved by his works. Houghton's other admirers included his contemporaries P. G. Wodehouse, Clemence Dane, and Hugh Walpole. Houghton died in 1961.

MARK VALENTINE is the author of several collections of short fiction and has published biographies of Arthur Machen and Sarban. He is the editor of *Wormwood*, a journal of the literature of the fantastic, supernatural, and decadent, and has written the introductions to Valancourt's editions of volumes by John Davidson, Forrest Reid, Michael Arlen, R. C. Ashby, Claude Houghton, and Russell Thorndike.

By Claude Houghton

The Kingdoms of the Spirit (1924)

Neighbours (1926)

The Riddle of Helena (1927)

Crisis (1929)

I Am Jonathan Scrivener (1930)*

A Hair Divides (1930)

Chaos Is Come Again (1932)

Julian Grant Loses His Way (1933)

Three Fantastic Tales (1934)

This Was Ivor Trent (1935)*

The Beast (1936)

Christina (1936)

Strangers (1938)

Hudson Rejoins the Herd (1939)

All Change, Humanity! (1942)

The Man Who Could Still Laugh (1943)

Six Lives and a Book (1943)

Passport to Paradise (1944)

Transformation Scene (1946)

The Quarrel (1948)

Birthmark (1950)

The Enigma of Conrad Stone (1952)

At the End of a Road (1953)

The Clock Ticks (1954)

More Lives Than One (1957)

CLAUDE HOUGHTON

THIS WAS IVOR TRENT

With an introduction by
MARK VALENTINE

VALANCOURT BOOKS

This Was Ivor Trent by Claude Houghton
First published London: Heinemann, 1935
First Valancourt Books edition 2013

Published by Valancourt Books, Kansas City, Missouri
Publisher & Editor: James D. Jenkins
20th Century Series Editor: Simon Stern, University of Toronto
http://www.valancourtbooks.com

ISBN 978-1-939140-11-1 *(trade paper)*

Set in Dante MT 11/13.5

INTRODUCTION

CLAUDE HOUGHTON enjoyed brief acclaim in the interwar years as the author of a handful of powerful and profound novels, amongst them *This Was Ivor Trent*. They typically evoked, indirectly, an enigmatic figure, charismatic and mysterious, as seen by his friends and rivals, who have more human failings. Houghton's admirers thought him a major visionary. In *The Bookman* it was claimed that spiritual archetypes stalk his books, bringing us a clear, strong vision of the mystic destiny which is shaping for humanity. The *New York Times* spoke of him as "the foremost, if not the most widely known, exponent of the metaphysical attitude in fiction" whose books were "the finest and most firmly thought-out exposition of the spiritual problem of modern times".

Thomas Masaryk, the President of Czechoslovakia, was an enthusiast, and Houghton visited Prague as the guest of the government there. Hugh Walpole, Clemence Dane and Henry Miller were also ardent about him, and wrote appreciations. His novel *I Am Jonathan Scrivener* (1930, also available from Valancourt) was a best-seller in its time, and much talked about. He was translated into many European languages. Yet he has largely disappeared from view in the last fifty years and his work has remained almost completely out of print. There has never been a full study or biography, and there are hardly any essays on him.

His full name was Claude Houghton Oldfield and he was born in Sevenoaks, Kent, in 1889, and educated at Dulwich College (P. G. Wodehouse's alma mater). He trained as an accountant and worked in the Admiralty in the First World War, rejected for active service by poor eyesight. In 1920 he married a West End actress, Dulcie Benson, and they lived in a cottage in the Chiltern Hills. To a writers' directory, Houghton gave his hobbies as reading in bed, riding, visiting Devon and abroad, and talking to people different to himself. He added: "I like dawn, and the dead of night, in great cities." He disliked fuss, noise, crowds, rows, and being misquoted, or being told how much he owed "to some writer I've never read". Those whose influence he did acknowledge included Swedenborg, Balzac, Flaubert and "the great Russian novelists". Contemporaries who had helped him, as well as Walpole and Dane, included Phyllis Bentley, Compton Mackenzie, J.B. Priestley, James Hilton and Arnold Bennett, an interesting roll-call of the most commercially successful "middlebrow" writers of the period: but his work was nothing like theirs.

His earliest writing was poetry and drama, described (by a champion of his, Geoffrey West) as "just a little too consciously exalted", though with "undoubted verbal beauty and dignity of thought". Though they may be studied for glimpses of his later visions, his verses are perhaps for the completist. It is the novels that claim our attention.

They began in 1926 with the extraordinarily brooding, Kafkaesque *Neighbours*, an erotically-charged study of a split personality, a sort of psychological doppelgänger story. The protagonist, taking an attic room high above London, records in minute detail the artistic and sexual affairs of another lodger, in rooms opposite. This character, a fevered and fervent would-be author, is passionately evoked, suggesting he is partly autobiographical. As the book unfolds, the reader feels uneasy about the obsessive voyeurism of the narrator. But then the realisation grows that we are really witnessing two aspects of the same man: a staid, dulled observer, trapped in the world of appearances, and a fervent, flaming visionary soaring too high towards the sun. The denouement is not entirely unforeseen but still strongly conveyed and thought-provoking. It provides the pattern for many of Houghton's subsequent books, in which we only see the central character through the eyes of others.

Houghton achieved some fame and popularity in his early forties with *I Am Jonathan Scrivener* (1930). In sum, it sounds simple. We hear about the title character from many people, but never directly see him. He has had a profound impact on other lives, yet we do not really know who he is, or the source of his power. He is a storm cloud from which many strange trees and plants have been watered, but remains himself dark, ethereal, a distant presence looming above the other figures. "At the end of the book," Houghton wrote about the fate of the title character, "I deliberately had a query suspended in my mind—and I still have". So does the reader—and that can be frustrating, or it can be admired as existentially true. Michael Dirda has described the book as "a highly diverting, philosophical novel of considerable merit", and compared it to the work of G. K. Chesterton, Evelyn Waugh and Charles Williams.

A book that followed, *Chaos Is Come Again* (1932) is perhaps the most fraught with the ferment of the Thirties—"a microcosm of modern civilisation in collapse" as West has it, shown through the manoeuvres of an eccentric, fraying family. A young man agrees to become the tutor to a bright invalid boy, since he feels the need to work, to be useful, though he does not need the money. Dexter, the protagonist, has read a description of civilisation "as merely an increased capacity for receiving impressions," and thinks that the world of the Thirties is testing that to the limit:

> Events, thoughts, theories, ideas beat nowadays upon the delicate screen of our consciousness like a perpetual rainstorm. The world seethes on the threshold of our minds. Distance has been abolished—and science has destroyed silence . . . half our vitality is expended in rendering ourselves immune to the clang and clamour of a world which is rapidly becoming one gigantic factory.

The new interest in his work resulted in an essay on him by the critic Geoffrey West in *The Bookman* for November, 1932, which remains one of the acutest studies of his books. Even then, West noted, Houghton had still not had all the attention he deserved, "as one of the two or three most profoundly imaginative writers of his generation". The critic admitted some weaknesses; "He can be gaudy in description, at times merely clever in dialogue" and is sometimes over-ambitious, his effects daring long-shots that only just about succeed. But all his work, West says, is written from a "spiritual—though never doctrinal—conviction". His characters are on "an inward Odyssey" towards a revelation of the true nature

of the world. The turmoil of the time he was writing, the Thirties, with its mass unemployment, depression, political extremism,
the rattling of the chains of the dogs of war, Houghton attributes
in part to the lack of spiritual maturity. West quotes a "gnomic
phrase" of Houghton's that he says is a keynote of all his books:
"Where no gods are, spectres rule". To understand it fully, says the
critic, one must read the books.

West concludes with a litany of Houghton's merits: "He is
richly inventive, he continually exhibits the ingenuity of imaginative daring, he has humour, wit, a memorable brilliance in phras-
ing, real spontaneity, and with it all both human and spiritual
understanding".

Houghton's next novel, *Julian Grant Loses His Way* (1933) was
exquisitely described by Marguerite Steen as "lovely and hideous".
It was not a book "for a lonely house and a windy night and no
company save one's own. There is not one single conventional
thrill in it; but something is at one's shoulder as one reads". The
protagonist is already dead at the opening of the book, but is still
wandering in Piccadilly. His after-life hovers between glimpses of
the mortal world, still carrying on its noisy, flurried, bustling way,
and of another world where figures glide as if in a dream.

To stoke the interest in his books, in 1935 his publisher compiled
a booklet of appreciations by two then popular fellow-authors,
Hugh Walpole and Clemence Dane. The former, always generous in supporting other authors, wrote that Houghton was "one
of the most important novelists now writing in English" and
praised "his odd mixture of reality and fantasy, his gifts of drama
and of philosophy, his unusual and significant and courageous
themes". Clemence Dane, the author of *Legend*, used imagery to
convey Houghton's work better: "There is a slow accumulation
of significant details, significant conversations, significant themes.
These are piled up by the skill of the author into a card house
of extravagant height. Then, on the final page, a door opens, a
cold draught comes whistling in, the edifice collapses and you turn
from that slight, important wreckage to face for the first time the
real problem of the book—the stranger who opens the door and
lets in that dramatic thought."

This Was Ivor Trent (1935) was Houghton's next novel. It has
a very effective opening on the Embankment in a London fog,
where the majestic author of the title, haunted by the potentiality
that man might evolve into another form of spiritual being, suddenly comes face to face with a hooded figure which seems to be
just such a being: the image precipitates a nervous collapse and we
do not see Trent again until the last section of the novel. But we do
see a swarm of characters, lonely and damaged by the world, who
talk about their encounters with Trent and the inhuman power
he possesses over others. There is one highly memorable character, a valetudinarian misanthrope with utter contempt for virtu-
ally all he meets, whose brittle conversation and mannerisms are
brilliantly portrayed. Others include a vaguely Buchanesque main
protagonist, a hollow-eyed artist's model, a young woman in flight
from her boorish family, a vain and self-pitying critic lamed in the
war, a youth who thinks he is a reincarnation of Nietzsche. Their
lives hold a morbid interest for the reader but we are waiting as we
witness them for the re-emergence of Trent and a resolution of
the hooded figure vision.

This we do not quite get, but Houghton just about manages
to hold the novel back from anti-climax. His aim, he told Henry
Miller, was that he wanted the reader to feel "Ivor Trent, at the
end, being reinforced by a greater vision and fuller powers". Whatever chaos and futility there may be here below, there are still,
Houghton suggests, higher influences that we may bring into our
lives. Some inkling of this is indeed conveyed, but perhaps a little
too elliptically. Though ultimately it may seem unresolved, *This
Was Ivor Trent* has a bitter and brooding power which conveys well
the disillusion, the weariness of the Thirties, and the expectation
that something massive was needed to shatter the dismal order of
things. When the Common Sense Englishman character puts in a
half-hearted defence of the masses against the vituperative invalid's contempt, the latter hisses, "You think the nations are slowly
climbing back to the pinnacle of 1914, do you?", prophetic words.

Like Arthur Machen, whom we know he read, Houghton saw
this world as the outer husk of a far greater world beyond. His
maxim is, "The Temporal is the shadow of the Eternal". There are

various means for us to gain insights into the rarer realm, including mysticism—in aspects of all faiths—and literature. But, just as Machen saw a certain quality as necessary to make true literature—he called it "ecstasy"—Houghton avers, "Art is spiritual biography, or it is nothing." And he was sure that some people could access, or develop, what he called "an added consciousness", though only at great risk to themselves. It was their duty to harness this power, but without losing their essential humanity—he had no time for the idea that such visionaries were superior beings; they were still fully human, and vulnerable.

It's important to note that Houghton's philosophy did not draw him towards any of the noxious political movements of the Thirties, proclaiming the advent of the overman. His sight seems to have been fixed well beyond the politics of the day. And in his books, where a figure has achieved higher (mystical) powers, it is a matter for humility and care, for these are elusive and potentially perilous: "The soul in each of us is like a seed in that only in silence, in darkness, and in secrecy can it begin its ascent towards perfection."

Henry Miller was introduced to Houghton's work in 1941 by the bookseller Ben Abramson. The latter had written an appreciation of Houghton's novels in 1937, and often urged them upon his friends. "Every line that he writes throbs with a strange excitement," he claimed, with pardonable hyperbole, ". . . Houghton's reach for the reality behind the symbol gives an edge to every incident and a significance to every action". This may stand as a good example of how strongly Houghton's work struck certain readers then.

At first, Miller was unconvinced, but then a character caught his attention, and he became an enthusiastic convert: "he is an aristocrat, a man, who if not to be called an 'initiate' is definitely on the threshold. . . . I like the trend of his mind. I admire his ability to delineate character with hatchet strokes," he proclaimed. He quickly read more of his work, and wrote a long, fervent letter to Houghton in 1942 to "pour out" all he had found in the books. Houghton, always a passionate and charming correspondent, replied by return. Miller compared Houghton to Algernon

Blackwood, particularly his book *The Bright Messenger* (though he thought this overcrowded with characters). And he echoed back to Houghton the idea of how those with new spiritual powers must mute their outward signs: "They have learned how to *radiate* their extraordinary powers without drawing attention to themselves".

This had also been one of the themes of the novels of Ronald Fraser, a contemporary of Houghton. His first book, *The Flying Draper* (1924) showed what happened when an unassuming character (a Primrose Hill haberdasher) gained higher powers that he could not conceal. In later, subtler books, such as *Flower Phantoms* (1926, also available from Valancourt), *Rose Anstey* (1930) and *Marriage in Heaven* (1932), the influence of those who glimpse the beyond steals more softly over those they know and the wider world. Though Fraser's style and vision are much gentler than Houghton's, there are certain preoccupations in common—particularly the survival of the spiritual in troubled times.

Though he may not have known it, and may not have agreed with the assertion, Houghton had reached his apogee with *Julian Grant* and *Ivor Trent*. The novels that followed often had a similar theme and pattern, but they begin to be less fantastical, more solemn. While there are always passages worth celebrating in his work, his reputation is likely to rest on the Thirties novels.

During the Forties and Fifties it is undeniable that Houghton's work suffered an eclipse. The predominant literary vogues were for kitchen-sink realism and the seasoned despair of existentialism. Houghton can be observed adjusting somewhat to these trends: his later books often depict marital and emotional discord and abandon his more outré visions. He still had his followers, and publishers willing to take his work, but he was gaining no new ground.

Even his more metaphysical books had always had a strong element of suspense in them, and his new publisher, Collins, saw fit to emphasise this element more, presumably in a bid to make his work appeal to a wider, popular readership. But the result was that Houghton's taste for melodrama in plotting (murder, suicide, revenge, fatal love affairs) came more to the surface, and was not always sufficiently balanced by other, subtler qualities. He remained even in his last books a master of psychological tension, the creator of strong and flavourful characters, and an explorer of the outré, and no Houghton book will ever disappoint the reader in quest of the bold and curious, but it is fair to say that the vast flourish of his Thirties fantasies had faded.

After Houghton died in 1961, Henry Miller wrote to his widow: "I stood before the desk at the Savage Club where I was told Claude Houghton wrote some of his books and I communicated with him silently wherever he is. I miss him." But his passing was not otherwise greatly noted: his books by then may have seemed part of another, pre-war era, and his passion for spiritual verities an embarrassment in a greyer world. His books went into the shadows for a while.

Yet Houghton is clearly a writer whose reputation deserves to be much higher, who has somehow gone astray in the citadels of literature, a spirit wandering the corridors and ante-chambers, whereas he ought to be a watchman on one of the high and lonely turrets, a companion of the gargoyles, the weather-vane and the lightning-rod, his visions flickering as richly and quickly as the tongues of the scarlet gonfalons flying above.

MARK VALENTINE

January 15, 2013

THIS WAS IVOR TRENT

CONTENTS

PART I

APPARITION

I

A YELLOW fog brooded over the city like a curse.

It was about six o'clock of a Sunday evening in October, 1933.
For over an hour Ivor Trent had stood by the undrawn curtains
in his sitting-room, looking down on desolation. No one was visible: every sound was muffled. The church bells seemed to be sum-
moning the ghosts of a forsaken city to worship.

Some minutes passed, but Ivor Trent remained motionless.
Anyone entering the room would have been startled by this immobility, which was that of a waxwork. But moments of deep interior
intensity have a physical reflection, and such a moment now possessed him—elevating him to an eminence from which the pattern
of his life was clearly discernible.

And Ivor Trent saw that he had reached a final frontier: that
he stood, not on a high-road, but at the end of a cul-de-sac. The
future would hold only repetitions, not unique experiences. He
would become the plagiarist of his own past.

But his will rebelled against this discovery. His plans had been
made, and he decided to execute them. His friends believed he was
leaving England, to write another book, and that in all probability
he would not return to London for a year. Every detail had been
arranged—he had let the flat for nine months; letters were to be
forwarded to his bank; the luggage was now piled in the hall. He
was leaving almost immediately.

The flat was at the top of a comparatively modern block near
Cork Street, and Trent lived in it only when he was not working. He
had never written a line in it. Each of his books had been created
in very different surroundings, for, although his friends had been

5

told he was leaving England, and although they believed he always went abroad to work, it was nevertheless a fact that every one of his books had been written in a house quite near the flat—a queer, dilapidated house, which became more strange each time he visited it. It was in Chelsea, and stood at the end of a street which ran down to the Embankment. The river could be seen from the upper windows.

Ten years ago this house had been the home of an experiment. A number of writers and artists had decided to live a communal life in it. Each had taken a room, or a couple of rooms, decorated and furnished them, rents being assessed according to the size and desirability of the accommodation selected. The communal element had been provided by the dining-room on the ground floor and a library, next to it, to which anyone could go at any time in search of companionship.

This experiment had demanded a capitalist to finance it, and eventually someone had discovered a Captain Frazer. He was an odd, proud, nervous man—then about thirty—who had been badly wounded in the war and had recently recovered from a serious nervous collapse. He had just married a strong, vigorous woman, five years his junior, who had nursed him through his illness.

For some curious reason the experiment had appealed to Captain Frazer, and he invested every penny he possessed in it. Possibly he felt he must do something in the world, and realised that he was incapable of doing much. Perhaps he believed he was serving the higher aspirations of humanity. One thing is certain, however—the idea of owning an ordinary lodging-house would have dismayed him. His ideal was to be military and extremely correct. But this hive of geniuses was entirely different. It flattered him with the promise of a reflected immortality.

Of course the experiment failed. In less than a year the house was a miniature Bedlam. Quarrels and disputes were perpetual. Wives ran away with lovers: one husband committed suicide: rents were months in arrear. Eventually, the inmates decided to sub-let their rooms, selling their furniture to the new tenants, with the result that a number of persons—in no way related to the higher aspirations of humanity—began to invade the house. Finally, only two of the original pioneers remained: Ivor Trent, and a man in a small room on the first floor, who believed he was a reincarnation of Nietzsche.

So Captain Frazer discovered that he was the owner of an ordinary lodging-house. One effect of this degradation was to make him even more military in his bearing; another was that he disassociated himself entirely from the establishment, explaining to those who did not know the facts that the venture was an eccentric whim of his wife's. The latter, however, welcomed the failure of the experiment and directed her great energy and practical ability to the task confronting her. The house was their only asset—it must be made to yield them a living. She transformed the dining-room and the library into bed-sitting rooms, letting the former to a commercial traveller and the latter to the manager of a local picture palace. She then revealed to Nietzsche her opinion of him, which had been maturing for many months. He disappeared a few hours later, owing sixteen weeks' rent.

Eventually, the only remaining traces of the experiment were the decorative effects in the various rooms, and numerous pieces of furniture which—having had a succession of owners—finally became Mrs. Frazer's property. These latter were allocated to different apartments, where they stood in gay isolation, like ambassadors from a happier world, surrounded by drab pieces from a second-hand dealer which had been bought to supplement them.

This was the house to which Ivor Trent was going on this particular Sunday in October. Ten years ago, he had taken two rooms at the top, facing the river. He still had them—and every one of his books had been written there.

II

"The taxi is waiting, sir."

Trent had not heard the servant enter the room, consequently the sound of her voice startled him. He went into the hall, put on his hat and overcoat, then looked round the flat for the last time. Just as he was about to leave, the telephone-bell rang. He told the servant to say he was away, then followed the luggage out of the flat. When it had been loaded on to the taxi, he tipped the porter and dismissed him, then gave the driver the Chelsea address, asking him to tell Mrs. Frazer that he would arrive at about nine o'clock.

The taxi drove slowly away, leaving Trent on the pavement.

The fog had descended. It drifted through the streets, or eddied round the buildings, like fine yellow smoke. Blurred patches of light defined the immediate obscurity, but the intimate character of everything was obliterated. All was shrouded in fantastic anonymity. The recognisable had become a grotesque counterfeit of the familiar.

Trent started to walk automatically, careless of direction, fascinated by the phantom aspect of the streets. Each slowly emerging scene might have been the work of an artist who had subdued the actual to his own chaotic vision. In Piccadilly, the traffic was almost at a standstill: the headlights of buses and cars probed the drifting gloom like eyes of invisible monsters. Electric signs blazoned their legends from the void. Shouts and cries rose intermittently, and once—in the near distance—he heard the crash of glass.

He walked to Piccadilly Circus, crossed Leicester Square, only to find himself a minute later in a chaos of obscurity. For nearly an hour he groped about, becoming progressively irritable, till at last he emerged in the Strand.

A number of questions then besieged his mind simultaneously. Why had he not gone to Chelsea with the luggage? Why had he decided to dine out? And what in the name of God had induced him to lose himself in this desert of desolation! He had been ill recently, and a return of that illness would undermine every plan he had made. It was imperative to escape from himself; to work month after month on his novel; to identify himself so wholly with the creations of his imagination that his own name would convey less to him than that of one of his characters. This, and only this, was deliverance—and he was jeopardising it by wandering about fog-shrouded streets like a somnambulist!

He began to walk rapidly towards Fleet Street, having remembered a venerable tavern where he could dine, and where the risk of encountering anyone he knew—on such a night—was negligible.

The Strand was deserted. Every now and again he emerged into an oasis of clarity, but Fleet Street was a drifting darkness, and he had great difficulty in discovering the narrow alley leading to the tavern. At last, however, he detected an ochreous blur which proved to be the solitary light over the entrance.

He went into a room, the character and furniture of which has remained unchanged for centuries. It had heavily-timbered grimed windows, a low-planked ceiling, a floor covered with sawdust. Flames flickered merrily in a projecting fireplace. On one side was a long oak table: on the other were high stiff-backed partitions, sombre with age—resembling old-fashioned pews, with hard cushionless seats—which boxed off half-a-dozen diners to each ancient table. The room was as brown as an old meerschaum and rich with the aroma of ages. It is said that Charles II ate a chop here with Nell Gwynne.

The place was empty. Trent chose the inmost seat of the first partition on the left, the back of which was surmounted by a brass rail from which hung a short green curtain. Immediately behind him was a box, designed for greater privacy, containing a table for four.

Whether it was the result of wandering through wraith-like streets, or the effect of the time-haunted atmosphere of the tavern, or the beginning of illness, he was unable to determine, but gradually his surroundings seemed remote and he experienced a strange mental isolation which alienated him even from his memories. He dined, feeling like a man who knows he is dreaming, then—just after the waiter had brought his black coffee—he heard two men enter the box immediately behind him.

Something unusual in the sound of their movements arrested his attention, but this was soon explained, for he heard one say to the other:

"Bit of a tight fit. Can you manage? Give me those things. That's more like it."

Evidently his companion had crutches. A moment later he sank heavily on to the bench. He had chosen the corner seat, consequently only the green curtain separated him from Trent.

"That's better! Put my crutches in the corner. Not surprised the place is empty. It's a hell of a night. We'd better have a drink, Rendell."

The two men continued to talk, but Trent ceased to listen. He felt ill and irritable. Then, just after the waiter had served them with drinks, he heard the crippled man say:

"Well, when are you going to tell me why you, of all people, have suddenly become interested in Ivor Trent?"

The sound of his own name seemed to widen, like an expanding circle, till it filled the room.

"It's like this, Marsden. As you know, I'm a consulting mining engineer—I've done very well out of it in my day. I've no need to work, and, anyway, there isn't much doing. So I draw retaining fees nowadays while waiting for things to get going again. I tell you that to show you that I've leisure. But the essential fact is this: I lost my wife nearly a year ago and——"

"My dear fellow, I'm dreadfully sorry! I'd no idea——"

"Nearly a year ago," Rendell repeated. "I had a pretty bad time and I'm having a pretty bad one still. Well, in June, someone gave me Trent's last novel. I was in Germany. I read a good deal, but I don't read fiction as a rule. Anyway, this book rang my bell. I've read it three times and I'm interested in the man who wrote it. That's why I sent you a line after all these years. I knew you'd know everything about him."

"Don't you believe it. I know all about his *books*. Oddly enough, I've just attempted a critical study of him as a novelist, but I don't know him really well as a man."

"I thought you'd known him for years?"

"So I have, on and off. I suppose, nowadays, we meet about once a year. I owe him a lot, but that's another story. Incidentally, I rang him up to-night, hoping he'd be able to come along, but he's away. Anyhow, this is what I want to know. Why did Trent's last novel interest you so much?"

After a long pause, Rendell said slowly:

"I suppose it was this, really. The man who wrote that book knows all about loneliness."

Marsden laughed.

"Only as the result of observation."

"That may be," Rendell replied doggedly, "but he knows all about it nevertheless. I've been down the road and I know the scenery."

There was a long silence, then they began to discuss what they would eat, consulting the waiter at some length.

Trent remained motionless in his corner. Had he been well enough, he would have paid the bill and gone. It would be simple enough to leave unobserved. But he felt dizzy and knew, from recent experience, that the slightest additional exertion might have unpleasant results. To stay, and to overhear, were therefore inevitable. Marsden was, literally, only a few inches from him. So Trent remained, huddled in his corner.

A few minutes later, Rendell asked:

"What sort of age is Trent?"

"About forty."

"What's he look like?"

"You'd notice him anywhere. He's tall, dark, powerful—broad forehead, and odd penetrating eyes. But a physical inventory only describes him, it doesn't convey him. Directly you see him, you feel he's exceptional."

"Does he know a lot of people?"

"Oh yes, no end." Then, after a pause, Marsden added: "Did you say you'd read only one book of his?"

"Yes, the last one."

"Well, as you're interested in him, you'd better get his first novel. That tells you all about him till he was twenty-one. It's called *Two Lives and a Destiny*."

"That's an odd title."

"It's an odd book. Roughly, this is the story. Ivor was an only child. When he was seven he was told that his mother had died. She was very lovely and he had worshipped her. The description of their last meeting is one of the best things in the book. But that's by the way. The legend of his mother's death held good till he was twenty-one."

"The legend!" Rendell exclaimed.

"Well, these were the facts. She had gone to Italy with her lover.

It ended disastrously, for, three years later, she died in poverty. She wrote to her husband on her deathbed, begging him to come and to bring Ivor. He did not answer the letter. She died—and a year or two later her lover committed suicide."

"Good God! And what sort of man was the husband?"

"You'll find a first-rate portrait of him in *Two Lives and a Destiny*. He was fifteen years older than she was. He must have been about forty when she left him. He was a distinguished-looking man, rich, independent, and proud as the devil."

"Did you know him, Marsden, or are you quoting the novel?"

"I knew him, but my knowledge of him comes from the novel. Ivor and I were at school together and I often spent part of the holidays with the Trents, as my people were in India. Old Trent was devilish impressive: cultured, aristocratic, self-sufficient. Seemed to look down on life, if you know what I mean. No use for emotional people. But I'll say this for him: he had great physical courage. There's a description in the novel of how he stopped a bolting horse in the Row when Ivor was ten. We thought he was God Almighty when we were kids."

"But do you mean that he never referred to Ivor's mother for fourteen years?"

"Never! There wasn't a photograph of her in the house. He cut himself off from everyone who had known her. He moved to London after she left him. Before then, they had lived in Suffolk. He took the most elaborate precautions to ensure that Ivor should not learn the truth. And he did everything to widen and deepen his influence over him. Above all, he instilled his own contempt for women into him. And he did it with great subtlety."

"To prejudice Ivor's reaction to the facts when the inevitable disclosure came?"

"Yes. Ivor learned the facts when he was twenty-one. That was in 1914. They had spent the last two years abroad. You read the description of the scene between the father and the son in *Two Lives and a Destiny*. It's amazing. As Trent told Ivor the history of his marriage, he became a stranger—a spiteful, writhing, humiliated being. Fear, hatred, tortured pride, and above all sexual jealousy, were the realities behind Trent's façade. The fact that it was

APPARITION   13

fourteen years ago; that she was dead; that he was talking to her son—counted for nothing. He flung insult after insult at her, used the foulest language, stamped and gesticulated like a madman. And behind this frenzied figure Ivor saw—in a kind of vision—the woman whose loveliness had haunted his childhood."

"How did it end?"

"There was a terrible quarrel between them. Ivor cleared out. A few months later the war came. His father refused to see him when he left for the front. And before Ivor had been in France a month, Trent fell dead in the street."

"And that's the story of *Two Lives and a Destiny?*"

"That's the story, Rendell. The book ends with an analysis of Ivor's sensations on going into action for the first time. But the significant fact is this. When he was twenty-one, he was confronted by two crises in swift succession: he discovered that the man he believed his father to be was a fake; and a few months later he found himself in the inferno of the war."

"But you said just now——"

"Here's the food," Marsden interrupted. "Let's eat. I don't know about you, but I'm starving."

They spoke only in isolated sentences during the next twenty minutes. Trent remained in his corner, a crowd of memories stampeding through his mind. Gradually, however, an unreasoning hatred of Marsden possessed him although, simultaneously, he was amused by the discovery that Marsden was one man with his own friends and another with him. There was an independence, a hint of patronage, in his attitude to Rendell which were unknown in their relations. But what chiefly disturbed Trent was the knowledge that he was still unable to leave the tavern. Any attempt to rise instantly provoked a sensation of dizziness. But one thing was definite—he had no curiosity. He knew the limits of Peter Marsden's knowledge.

"Well, what do you think? Just coffee?"

"That's all I want," Rendell replied. "And now I'm going to revert to Ivor Trent."

Marsden laughed.

"You're very interested in him."

"So are you," Rendell retorted bluntly.

"I'm very full of him at the minute, I admit. But then I've been doing nothing but read and re-read his books for the last few weeks."

"Yes, but apart from that," Rendell insisted.

"He's an interesting person, of course," Marsden replied irritably, after a just perceptible pause.

"You said, earlier on, that you owed him a lot. Any objection to telling me in what way?"

"No, I've no objection, but I'd rather you kept it to yourself. It began like this. I've told you that Ivor and I were at school together. Well, he delivered me from a bully. I don't know if you've any idea of the fanatical devotion that inspires in a schoolboy?"

"I can imagine it."

"No, you can't. It's one of those things you have to experience. Ivor became my hero. I thought God must be exactly like him. But it was not only that he delivered me—it was the way he did it."

"Don't understand," Rendell said abruptly.

"It was like this. The bully was twice Ivor's size, but the latter simply obliterated him by the might of his spirit. He gave him a look, told him to clear off—and he cleared off. It was astonishing. I became a fervent believer in miracles."

"And that was the start of your friendship?"

"Yes. A year or two after the bullying incident we drifted apart. I suddenly became pretty burly and mad-keen on games. Eventually I went up to Cambridge while Ivor was travelling all over the place with his father. I didn't see him for a hell of a time. In fact, not till 1923—just after *Two Lives and a Destiny* had been published."

"What happened to Trent in the war?"

"He was decorated for bravery and was slightly wounded in 1917. Our next meeting was rather dramatic. I'd been badly smashed up just before the Armistice. Since then I'd had treatment of all kinds, operations, and God knows what. Finally, I was told that I'd go on crutches for the rest of my life. It's probable that I should have done myself in if I hadn't run into Ivor again."

"You'd not seen him for years?"

"Not since we left school. I ran into him one night in Regent

Street, quite by chance. I was just getting out of a taxi with great difficulty as Ivor emerged from a restaurant with a woman—an imperious lady with a disdainful stare and a magnificent figure. He put her in the taxi I had just left and let her wait while he talked to me. She was very impatient and clearly resented the delay. I believe it amused him to keep her waiting. Anyway, he soon discovered that I was at the end of things. I told him I was living in a cottage in Surrey. A few days later he came down and stayed with me.

Marsden broke off and remained silent for some moments, then added:

"I admit I was flattered by his visit, Rendell. Ivor was then thirty, very handsome, very much in demand. *Two Lives and a Destiny* had just been published and had had an instantaneous success. But the real point is this: he brought me back to life!"

"Brought you back to life!"

"Yes. He stayed some weeks. He talked a lot about literature and read a number of books to me. He's a first-rate critic. I'd always read a fair amount but he opened another world. He revealed the spiritual structure of the books we read. Well—to cut the story short—he eventually got me a job as a publisher's reader. Later, I became a reviewer. And now I do a good deal of free-lance journalism."

"You certainly owe him a lot, Marsden. Everything—it seems to me. I suppose you see him pretty frequently nowadays."

"No, I don't. I told you, about once a year. For one thing, he frequently goes abroad for long periods to work. He writes a book every two or three years, and, when he's working, no one hears a word from him."

"I take it his work means everything to him?"

There was a long silence, then Marsden said slowly:

"I'm damned if I know."

"Why? What do you mean?"

"I sometimes think, Rendell, that his books are only a by-product of an intense interior activity. He never discusses them and he does not mix with literary people. You hear queer odds and ends about him occasionally."

"What sort of things?"

"Oh I don't know! They are probably all nonsense. I doubt if anyone knows more about him than I do—and I don't know much."

"Do you know many of his friends?"

"Scarcely any. I met a woman, quite by chance, a year or two ago in Paris, who knew him. I told her very much what I've just told you. Her only comment was that I had a greater gift for fiction than Ivor Trent."

Marsden laughed, then added:

"And now *you* tell me that Ivor's an expert in loneliness. That's quite a new angle on him. I can only repeat that he knows lots of people in all sorts of worlds. Also, he's rich and famous."

There was a long silence, then Rendell said deliberately:

"I've a question to ask, but I doubt if you'd like it."

"I'll risk it."

"Are you jealous of Trent?"

"Not in the least."

"You're certain?"

"Certain!"

"You're resentful then."

Marsden's attempt at a laugh was a failure. Evidently he recognised it, for there was no bravado in his tone when he asked:

"How did you guess?"

"So it's true?"

"Of course it's true! I told you just now about that bullying incident, but I only revealed what it meant to me at the time. I've regarded it from a less romantic level for a number of years."

"I don't know what you're driving at, Marsden."

"I believe Ivor was concerned wholly with himself—not with me."

"I still don't follow you."

"I didn't think you would. Well, let's put it this way. To Ivor, that bully was an opportunity to test himself. He wanted to prove the power of his own will. The fact that I was being knocked about was entirely secondary."

"How the hell can you know that?"

"I don't know it," Marsden replied with intense irritability. "I'm telling you what I feel. And I feel it, too, about that visit of his to my cottage. It was another opportunity to demonstrate his power. Here was a man at the end of things. It interested Ivor to identify himself with my state—and then deliver me from it. I believe he regards me in exactly the same way as he regards a character he's created in one of his books."

Rendell gave a short laugh.

"Well, you've certainly made me want to meet him. The trouble is, I should probably bore him to death."

"I doubt it," Marsden replied slowly. "He's been faithless to many of his ideas, but he's always stuck to one of them. And it makes him interested in everyone to some extent."

"And what's that?"

"It's rather uncanny. He's convinced that man contains the potentiality of a new being. I'll repeat that in order to emphasise it. He's convinced *that man contains the potentiality of a new being.*"

Rendell made some reply—but Trent did not hear it. To remain an instant longer suddenly became impossible.

He rose unsteadily, hesitated for a moment, then left the tavern unobserved by Marsden and Rendell.

III

THE character of the fog had altered. It no longer drifted through the streets like pestilence made visible, but infested certain areas with a static and pall-like gloom. Everywhere was dripping desolation. The City had become its own caricature.

Trent stood irresolute for some moments, surprised to discover that all trace of physical weakness had vanished. He began to walk rapidly, unconscious of direction, aware only of a necessity for movement. Ten minutes later he found himself on the Embankment.

Again he hesitated. Sentences from the conversation he had just overheard drifted through his mind, but they seemed to relate to a stranger. He felt that a new consciousness possessed him—a luminous awareness hitherto unknown. Thought, emotion, and will had attained a flame-like unity which illuminated new and mysterious horizons. The landscape of his old life was vanishing.

Almost immediately, however, fear captured him. He rebelled against the dominion of this consciousness which reduced all experience to a dream. It must be the herald of illness, and he would combat it by clinging to the concrete and the known.

He walked on quickly.

In order to re-establish the normal, he began to recapitulate his plans. He was on his way to the Frazers. For many months he would live in his rooms, converting night into day, while he wrote the novel which had challenged his imagination for nearly a year. He would cease to be Ivor Trent. He would become the instrument of that mysterious power which could create a world more real than that of actuality. This was his programme. And yet, the more he analysed it, the less substantial it became. It was what he had planned, but it was not what was destined to be. He had reached a final frontier. Either he would never write again—or he would write a book different in kind from any he had written.

He made an angry gesture. Why did every thought turn traitor to his plans? What was happening to him? It was perilous to surrender to weakness. If illness menaced him, he must confront it with the whole might of his will. But, now, he must be patient. The first essential was to escape from these spectral streets into the seclusion of his rooms.

He looked round in search of a taxi, but the Embankment was deserted, and after a few moments' hesitation he hurried on in the direction of Chelsea. More than once he entered a region of deeper darkness, emerging later into relative clarity, but—as he approached his destination—the fog's dominion became more generally established, and it was only intimate knowledge of this part of the Embankment which enabled him to identify it. Finally, he stopped opposite the street leading to the Frazers' house.

He leaned over the low Embankment wall and gazed into the vapoury void below. Several minutes passed, but he remained motionless, listening to the life of the swiftly-flowing invisible river. In the near distance, the blast of a siren suddenly gave desolation a voice. A moment later, a ruby-coloured light slowly emerged, glowed for a second, and vanished. Then all was still and dark again.

Gradually, a deep hypnotic stupor possessed him, depriving him of all sense of personality. An interior indolence lulled him to yield to this trance-like state in which only dreams had substance. But the remnant of his will rebelled, and he sought to regain contact with actuality by recalling the conversation he had overheard in the tavern. To his dismay, however, he discovered that he could only remember Marsden's final sentence:

"He's convinced *that man contains the potentiality of a new being.*"

The words circled in his brain till repetition robbed them of the last vestige of meaning. Then, with a final effort to attain normality, he turned abruptly, determined to seek sanctuary in the Frazers' house.

Instantly he gave a cry.

He saw a shrouded figure confronting him. The face was fully revealed and Trent knew—with a certainty deeper than knowledge—that this was the countenance of a new order of being. It reflected thoughts and emotions unknown to present-day humanity. The glance of the eyes transmitted a secret wisdom. The forehead was crested with serenity.

Trent knew that a man from the Future confronted him.

It seemed to him that they stood facing each other in the timeless realm of destiny.

Then terror overwhelmed him like an avalanche, till he was conscious only of the necessity for flight. He started to run towards the Frazers' house, and continued to run until he reached the top of the steps. Then he glanced fearfully over his shoulder. Nothing was to be seen but the drifting chaos of the fog.

Nevertheless, terror swept him again and he began to beat with clenched fists on the door.

It was opened almost immediately by Mrs. Frazer.

"Mr. Trent! You are ill!"

He just heard the words, saw the white blur of a face, then fell senseless at her feet.

Part II

AT 77 POTIPHAR STREET

I

"Hullo, Rendell, you here! Damn it, you don't mean to say you're still in the Club?"

"Obviously. You'd better have a drink, Jordan. What's it to be?"

"Pink gin. But, look here, you told me——"

"Wait till we get the drinks. What's happened to everybody? This bar's usually crammed at six o'clock."

"Just a fluke. Damn it, I can do with a drink. Ah, here we are! But I say—seriously—you're not going to stay here much longer, are you?"

"I can't. I've got to go to-night. You know the rule here? I've had my room for the maximum period. My suitcases are with the hall-porter and he's waiting for me to tell him to get me a taxi."

"Where are you going?"

"I haven't the slightest idea."

"You're not serious?"

"Perfectly."

Jordan gave a boisterous laugh. It was well known in the club and it rasped the nerves of the more sensitive members. He was an overblown florid man, who assumed that he was immensely popular and invariably acted on the assumption. Owing to his initiative, certain rather suggestive paintings hung on the walls of the bar. He now surveyed these with heavy satisfaction for some moments, then said jocularly:

"Well, you're a damn fine feller, Rendell! Been a member here for years, never put a foot inside it, and yet for the last few months you've haunted the damn place. And now you've got to leave— and you can't think of anywhere to go."

20

Jordan paused, then added, indicating Rendell's glass:

"Better have the other half of that."

"Right, but it's my last."

Jordan gave an order, then turned to Rendell. "What the hell did you do yesterday? Sundays in London are the devil if you're on your own."

"I dined with a man I hadn't seen for years—a man I don't like."

Again Jordan's laugh jarred the room. As he spent the whole of his leisure with his mistress, the devices of others to cheat loneliness always amused him.

"Dined with a man you don't like!" he echoed. "Who the hell was that?"

"A fellow called Marsden."

"Never heard of him. What did you dine with him for if you don't like him?"

"You often talk to a man you don't like if you're lonely, Jordan."

After a perceptible pause, Rendell went on:

"Also, I wanted to discuss a man he knows—who happens to interest me."

"Who's that?"

"Ivor Trent."

"Never heard of him either. Well, damn it, I'll have to go. Dining at home to-night—worse luck! Still, I've cut it down to twice a week. You know the old saying about wives: get 'em young, tell 'em nothing, and treat 'em rough. Don't like leaving you on your own, though. Here! I'll tell you what! I'll give you my paper. Save you sending for one. Here you are! Two more winners for Gordon Richards. Well, so long."

Rendell took the paper mechanically, then watched Jordan's exit, noting his attempt to hide unsteadiness under a swaggering gait.

When he had disappeared, Rendell muttered to himself:

"Jordan! God! Am I down to that?"

He turned over the paper, scarcely glancing at it. Suddenly a name at the top of a short paragraph made him start. He flattened the paper on the bar and read:

"MR. IVOR TRENT"

"Last night, Mr. Ivor Trent, the eminent novelist, was taken ill suddenly. He is now at 77, Potiphar Street, Chelsea, in a delirious condition."

Rendell read the paragraph again.

Last night! . . . taken ill suddenly! . . . So, while he was talking to Marsden about Trent——*Where* did it say he was?

He glanced again at the paper.

77, Potiphar Street, Chelsea—in a delirious condition.

It was the oddest coincidence, why——

Suddenly an idea came to him.

He hesitated. Doubts, objections, advantages surged like an unruly crowd across his mind. A bit absurd, perhaps. And yet, why not? He'd got to do something. It might be interesting. Anyhow it would be a minor adventure. Yes, why *not?*

He strode out of the bar, ran down the stairs, got his overcoat, then said to the hall-porter:

"Get my things, Johnson, will you? And I want a taxi."

"Yes, Mr. Rendell." He struck a bell. . . . "Page! Get Mr. Rendell's things—and look sharp about it. Then get a taxi."

Two minutes later the boy returned.

"Taxi's waiting, sir."

"Right! Thanks. I'll have to change a cheque. Tell the driver to go first to 77, Potiphar Street, Chelsea. Then I'll want him to take me on somewhere afterwards. I'll let him know where later."

II

IT was a blustering night. Winter raged on the heels of autumn. News-posters fluttered; shop signs swung violently to and fro; pavements were thronged with people hurrying to escape from a wind bristling with the menace of icy rain. The lights of Piccadilly shone hard and clear with a steely fixity.

Rendell put his feet up on the little seat opposite, then lit a cigarette. He was acting instinctively, and surrendered himself to the luxury of this knowledge. In all the major crises of his life—and he had encountered several—instinct, not reason, had prompted his actions. Then, as now, he had had no programme. An inner impulse was in command and he obeyed its orders.

Regarded rationally, his decision to go to 77, Potiphar Street was ridiculous. It would lead nowhere—and would solve nothing. He would ask some servant how Trent was, and then he would have to decide where to go and what to do. It was a trick to evade a problem which had long baffled him. To inquire about a man he did not know and had never seen! Nothing could emerge from such a futile expedition.

But although Rendell allowed these strictures to drift through his mind, he did not react to them. Three facts of deeper significance were operative in him. A book of Trent's had impressed him more than any he had read for years. Last night he had dined with Marsden only to learn something about its author. And, now, he had discovered that, while they had been discussing him, Trent had been taken seriously ill. And he—Rendell—had happened to see a paragraph in the paper which gave not only the fact of Trent's illness, but also his address.

Somehow, though illogically enough, this sequence seemed an indication to Rendell that Trent was destined to enter his life.

As the taxi spun along Sloane Street, Rendell remembered that he had been to Chelsea only twice previously—and that ten years separated him from his last visit. He had no memories of the place, consequently, when the taxi turned into the King's Road, he looked out of the window with some curiosity.

Before they had proceeded many yards, however, the driver slowed up, pushed back the glass trap, and inquired:

"You said Potiphar Street, didn't you?"

"Yes—77."

"Don't happen to know which side it is, I suppose?"

"Haven't an earthly."

"Ah well, never mind, we'll find it," the man replied, with that large tolerance concerning time and space which characterises taxi-drivers, but which is seldom possessed by their fares.

At the Town Hall the taxi stopped and the driver indulged in a series of speculations and questions with a youth whose face resembled a map of vacancy. After which, he cross-examined a street vendor, who gave a lengthy list of the streets with which he was familiar, ending with the announcement that, if there were a Potiphar Street in Chelsea, he would very much like to know where it was. Finally, at Rendell's command, the driver—most reluctantly—asked a policeman, who supplied the information instantly.

"I knew it was somewhere down there," he said contemptuously to Rendell, with an attempt to recover professional prestige. A minute or two later they turned down a street, along which trams were crashing, then to the left down the Embankment. Rendell caught a glimpse of an old church, but almost immediately another turn to the left brought them into Potiphar Street.

It was a narrow street and his glimpse of the houses was not invigorating. They belonged to the later Victorian age, and seemed mutely to protest against their survival. At the end of the street, and facing it, stood a tall house with a flight of steep steps leading to the front door.

The taxi drew up with a jerk of finality.

"Here you are!" the driver exclaimed, as if he had materialised the house to gratify an eccentric whim of Rendell's. "Here you are. Number 77."

"Good!"

Rendell got out, then said:

"Wait, will you? I don't suppose I'll be long."

The driver fumbled for his pipe.

"Right you are, sir."

Rendell ran up the steps, then gave three resonant blows with the knocker.

III

A MINUTE passed, during which he regretted having knocked so vigorously. He had forgotten that the house held a man who was seriously ill. But when another minute had passed, the necessity for knocking again presented itself. Rendell raised the knocker and gave three timorous taps which evoked no response. After a suitable interval, he knocked again, then—later—again. Nothing! Finally he became exasperated. "After all, I might be the doctor for all they know," he muttered to himself, then seizing the knocker he gave a series of resounding blows.

A minute later the door was opened by a man, but as the hall was dimly lit, Rendell could not see him distinctly. He was about to inquire concerning Trent, when the man said irritably:

"My wife's out. I know nothing about the rooms. That's her business, not mine—thank God! Now you've arrived with your luggage, and she's not here. Well, I can't help it. It's nothing to do with *me*."

"When will your wife return?"

"Oh, don't ask me! Always dragging me into her wretched affairs! This letting rooms is a ridiculous hobby of hers. I'm far too busy with important affairs to give it a thought. Far too busy, I assure you. And *she* won't be letting rooms much longer. Fine activity for Captain Frazer's wife!"

He became very erect as he uttered the last sentence in a tone of hysterical intensity.

Rendell said nothing. Curiosity and astonishment contended within him for supremacy. But Captain Frazer went on almost immediately:

"Well, you'd better come in, I take it!" he exclaimed with remarkable irritation. "I suppose you know which your room is, don't you? It can only be this one here. All the others are let, she tells me. Not that I want to know."

"Very well, I'll come in."

"You'll want your luggage, I take it?"

Frazer's tone would have been insolent if a quaver of weakness had not deprived it of every positive quality.

"I'll tell the driver to bring it in."

Rendell turned and walked to the taxi. He was about to enter the house under false pretences—and was duly elated by that knowledge. The possibility of adventure stirred him. He'd take a room in the house in which Ivor Trent was ill—and see what happened.

Two minutes later his luggage had been deposited in the first room on the right. Rendell paid the driver, and then found himself alone with Captain Frazer.

The latter's appearance interested him. He was tall, thin almost to emaciation, with a narrow worn-out face and scanty mouse-coloured hair. Dark eyes looked spitefully at the world from the cavernous depths in which they were buried. His suit was old and shiny, but evidently it was tended with sedulous care. Prominent creases of Euclidean exactitude triumphed down the trousers. His bearing was immensely military in moments of dignity, but during relapses he made a number of staccato gestures which served to emphasise his irritability.

Also, Rendell soon discovered that on occasions Frazer developed a nervous facial contraction. When especially agitated, his right eye produced a series of very rapid and highly disconcerting winks.

"Well, I can discuss arrangements with your wife later," Rendell said at last. "In the meantime, I want to know how Mr. Trent is."

"How did you know he was here?"

Frazer shot the question at him.

"It's in the paper."

"Have you got one? Where? Let's have a look."

He seized the paper and scanned the brief paragraph eagerly.

"Ah, that's all right," he muttered to himself. "*That's* all right. Trent!" he exclaimed, drawing himself to his full height and regarding Rendell with motionless dignity. "He's just the same."

"You mean, he is still delirious?"

"Raving. He's worse to-night."

Rendell was about to ask another question, when a gramophone of peculiar virulence was put on in a room above. Simultaneously someone in the upper regions began shouting instructions to a man who was noisily descending the stairs.

"Swine!" exclaimed Frazer, banging the door violently. "I tell you it's impossible for me to go on living in this house—impossible!"

"Are these noises normal then?" Rendell inquired, feeling that he might as well know.

"Oh, there's always a hell of a row. Damn the place! *Damn* it!"

"But don't these people know that Trent's ill?"

"Trent? Oh, he's at the top of the house. He's all right. He's got his own rooms up there—had 'em for years."

"For years!" Rendell echoed.

"Yes, why not?"

"There's no reason, of course."

Silence ensued. Rendell said nothing, as he was thinking intently. He wanted to learn all that Frazer knew about Trent and was considering the most efficient technique for eliciting it. Frazer remained silent, as he was scrutinising Rendell with great curiosity.

Now, in appearance, Rendell was everything that Frazer would like to have been. He was tall, powerful, with bronzed features and fearless eyes. His clothes were of excellent quality. Independence and a general atmosphere of purpose and assurance invested him.

The form that Frazer's admiration assumed was a desire to impress Rendell with his own importance. He decided that to reveal his knowledge of a distinguished man like Trent was the quickest shortcut to this end.

"Trent's had rooms here for years. In fact, he's written all his books in them."

"Are you certain of that?"

"Certain? Of course I'm certain! You don't doubt my word, I take it."

"I asked the question," Rendell said slowly, "because I dined with a man last night who has known Trent for a very long time, and *he* told me that Trent had written every one of his books abroad."

"It's a lie! Absolute lie! I tell you that on the honour of an officer." An impressive pause. "Trent's had those rooms at the top of the house for ten years at least. He comes here to write. He lives alone up there for a year or more, turns night into day, writes his book—and clears off. Then, about two years later, he comes back to write another."

"That's extremely interesting. You see——"

"Oh I know a lot of interesting people—a lot, I can assure you! Don't bring 'em here though. Not to this *hole*. I used to mix with writers and artists—till my wife suddenly took it into her head to turn the place into a common lodging-house. Yes! A common lodging-house!" He shouted the words. "That's what she's brought me to. Till then, I mixed only with distinguished people. This house was full of them."

Then, after a very brief pause, he added in a confidential whisper:

"Excuse me. I must go and telephone a man. It's most important. I—I shan't be very long. You don't mind, I take it."

"No, that's all right. See you later, perhaps."

"Certainly—certainly. Matter of only a few minutes, you understand. But important—important!"

He disappeared with remarkable celerity.

Rendell welcomed privacy. The events of the last five minutes had been so unexpected, so intriguing, that he felt he was in some strange region where the improbable was the usual. But, discovering that so many mysteries clamoured for attention simultaneously, he decided to dismiss all of them in the hope that, eventually, they would range themselves in order of significance.

He took off his overcoat, then looked round the room.

It was large, high-pitched, and had a bay window. Most of the furniture was ancient, battered, but solid. It had evidently encountered a number of second-hand dealers, and seemed depressed by the premonition that—at the next visit—its value would be assessed, not as furniture, but as wood.

There were exceptions, however. The carpet, though faded, had clearly been bought by someone who demanded a correspondence between their aspirations and their surroundings. The same quality distinguished a little red chair whose jauntiness time had failed wholly to obliterate. Also, by the wall farthest from the window stood a divan. The majority of the furniture seemed to demand a brass bedstead, in order to rivet the apartment to the category of a bed-sitting-room in a lodging-house, but the presence of the divan triumphantly asserted individuality. Altogether, the room represented a compromise between dead orthodoxy and the spirit of revolt.

Rendell assessed it pretty accurately. He had lived in all sorts of surroundings in all parts of the world and so was an expert in his degree.

"Not too bad—for a week or so," he said to himself. "Draughts— certain. Mice—probable. Anyway, it will do. That is, if it's vacant. Have to see what Mrs. Frazer says."

He struck a match and turned on the gas fire. No hiss of escaping gas greeted his listening ear. He blew out the match, then sought— and found—a meter. He produced a shilling and inserted it.

"The last tenant was clearly no altruist," he muttered, then sat in an arm-chair and reviewed his situation. His summary dealt only with facts.

Here he was in a room on the ground floor of 77, Potiphar Street, Chelsea. Ivor Trent was seriously ill in a room at the top of the house. He, Rendell, had impulsively decided to take the room he was in—if it were free. Also, and above all, he had learned certain facts from Captain Frazer relating to Trent which were in direct opposition to those given him last night by Marsden. And Frazer, like Marsden, had known Trent for years!

Here was mystery—definite mystery—but he had no time to explore it now. For the moment, he accepted Marsden's account as the true one. Frazer was clearly eccentric. Possibly Mrs. Frazer's arrival would provide additional data. In the meantime——

But at this point Captain Frazer returned.

"I talked to my man. Satisfactory, quite satisfactory! I have a business deal with him—just a little idea of mine, but it came off, it came off. I'd have been back before, but I ran into the doctor——"

"Trent's doctor?" Rendell interrupted.

"Yes, yes. He's just gone. Trent's still delirious, but has lucid moments. That was the doctor's phrase—lucid moments. Trent refuses to be moved from here. That's very good—excellent in fact. They wanted to take him to a nursing home. Damned nonsense!"

"Does the doctor think he's dangerously ill?"

"Didn't say—doesn't know. Says Trent keeps raving about some man he's seen. Nerves, that's all, just nerves."

Frazer paused, then added explosively:

"Why, I myself—do you know—sometimes suffer from nerves. Not often, but sometimes."

He looked down at Rendell, his features tense and his right eye winking with remarkable rapidity.

"Well, I suppose we all do at times," Rendell said calmly, imagining he would pacify him.

"No—we—do—*not!*" Frazer exclaimed. "But, if one is humiliated, day in, day out, *then* one does suffer from nerves. You understand, I take it. Why, I——"

He broke off, made a movement enjoining silence, then went swiftly to the door, opened it a few inches, and listened.

"Ah, here she is! Always punctual! Always to the minute! She isn't a woman—she's an alarm clock. I'll clear out. Say you don't know where I am."

He slipped out of the room and almost immediately the front door banged.

Two minutes later Mrs. Frazer came into the room.

IV

RENDELL rose and they surveyed one another for some moments in silence.

Mrs. Frazer was a total contrast to her husband. She was sturdily built, still handsome—although her features were coarsened by overwork and worry—but resolution and capability surrounded her like an aura.

Her scrutiny of Rendell evidently culminated in a favourable impression, for her first remark did not relate to his presence.

"Was that my husband went out just now?"

"Yes. You must wonder who I am and what I'm doing here. It's like this. I came to inquire about Mr. Trent and——"

"How did you know he was here?" she interrupted.

"It's in to-night's paper."

He picked it up and showed her the paragraph.

"I see," she said at last. "That's my husband's doing."

"I'm afraid I don't understand," Rendell replied, greatly mystified.

"He's friendly with an out-of-work journalist. He must have

told him about Mr. Trent. And now he'll share with him whatever the paper paid for the paragraph. Did you tell him it was in to-night's paper?"

"Yes, I told him."

"I see." There was immense resignation in her tone. After a pause, she added: "And did he go and ring someone up soon after you had told him?"

"He did," Rendell replied.

"That was the journalist. And now he's gone to meet him—to drink the money. Well, if there's trouble, it's not my doing."

"I'll be frank with you, Mrs. Frazer. My name is Rendell. I'm a mining engineer and am at a loose end at the moment. I came here to-night to inquire about Mr. Trent. Your husband imagined I had booked a room and had come to claim it. I had done nothing of the kind, of course. But, finding this room vacant, it would—as it happens—suit my plans to take it. That is, if it's available, of course—and if you are agreeable."

She looked at him narrowly for some moments before she asked:

"Are you a friend of Mr. Trent's?"

"No. I've never even seen him. I'm interested in him, that's all."

"Well, the room's free, and you may as well have it as anyone else."

They discussed terms and arrangements. Finally Rendell said:

"That's settled then. I don't know how long I shall be here. And now, if you're not busy for a minute, I'd like to ask you one or two questions about Mr. Trent."

"What do you want to know?"

"Were you expecting him last night?"

"Yes. He was coming here for several months to work."

"Does he always come here to work?"

"Yes, always," Mrs. Frazer replied. "He's had the rooms at the top of the house for years and years. He's written all his books up there. Why do you want to know?"

"For two reasons. I'm interested in his books—and I was told that he always wrote them abroad. What—exactly—happened last night?"

Mrs. Frazer looked over her shoulder towards the door, then took a step nearer Rendell.

"I never had such a shock in my life—never! It must have been about nine o'clock—somewhere about. I happened to be in the hall—luckily. Suddenly, I heard someone beating on the front door, beating desperately with clenched fists. I was frightened, and I'm not easily frightened."

She broke off, but almost immediately she went on breathlessly:

"I opened the door. He looked like a ghost with great staring eyes. I said something—I don't know what—and he fell to the ground, senseless. I thought he had dropped dead."

"Well—and then?" Rendell asked, after a long pause.

"Two of the men in the house carried him up to his room and put him on the bed. He began to rave. I couldn't make out what he said. Something about a man he had seen—some man who had appeared out of the fog on the Embankment. I didn't know what to do. I was afraid to leave him. He was terribly excited. Kept wanting to go to the window and look out. He leapt about till I thought he'd have a fit. So I stayed with him—and got someone to telephone the doctor. It was terrible."

"You'd better sit down, don't you think?"

She sank mechanically into the chair Rendell placed by her side.

"All to-day it's been the same," she went on. "I *had* to go out a quarter of an hour ago—but it was the first time to-day. The doctor wanted him to go to a nursing home, but the mere idea made him terribly angry. So the doctor has sent in a nurse. She's with him now."

"Has he ever been ill here before?"

"Never! I can't believe it! I never thought to see him like this."

"I can understand you're upset," Rendell said slowly. "After all, you've known him a long time."

"He's been a friend to me. More than once I should have been sold up if it hadn't been for him. My husband invested all the money he had in this house and filled it with a lot of crazy people—artists, and I don't know what not. A year later, we were nearly ruined. Mr. Trent stayed on, and helped us out, else we shouldn't be here now."

Then, with a swift return to her normal methodical manner, she rose, looked keenly round the room, then said:

"Now, are you sure you've everything you want? If not, just tell me. And I'd better explain that several of the lodgers here are not *my* choice. But nowadays, you take what you can get—or what you have to. All of them are in arrears with their rent—and some of them haven't paid a farthing for weeks. And what can I do? Throw them out—and get others like them?"

She paused, then added:

"If my husband asks you to pay him the rent—or to lend him money—please don't do either. Can I rely on you for that?"

"You can count on me."

She walked towards the door, then paused and turned to him.

"You can't blame him, really. It was that war that did for him. Only his body survived it, if you know what I mean. There's plenty like him—more or less."

The door closed behind her.

Rendell began to pace up and down the room. Finally, he decided to go and dine at a local restaurant and think things over.

V

BEFORE Rendell had been at 77, Potiphar Street, for twenty hours, he found it difficult to believe that any doctor could allow a man who was seriously ill to stay there—however determined his patient might be to remain.

A number of incidents, none conducive to Rendell's personal comfort, created this opinion. Most of the lodgers were noisy, some presumably never went to bed, and two returned home in the small hours, having either forgotten their latch-keys or being in no condition to manipulate them. It seemed to Rendell that hardly had peace descended when it was rudely banished by certain early risers who clattered about their rooms, then rushed down the stairs, and finally banged the front door behind them as if to indicate that they had left the house for ever in a furious passion.

Half an hour after the last of these Lear-like departures, a maid was heard continually ascending the stairs bearing breakfast-trays. More than once she paused to shout details of certain forgotten articles towards the abyss of the basement. Rendell soon learned that her name was Mary, for a gentleman in the upper regions shouted it twice, then inquired in no half-hearted manner as to the likely time at which he might expect his shaving water.

At nine o'clock a gramophone in the room above emitted a colourful lament in a tone of impressive richness, power, and volume.

From ten o'clock onwards, various persons delivered a series of blows with the front-door knocker. These summonses were ignored, usually, by the inmates of No. 77—a fact which inspired the person on the doorstep to a more variegated and a more strenuous performance.

As the window of Rendell's room afforded an intimate view of the steep steps leading to the front door, he was able to study the appearance of the person demanding attention, while, simultaneously, he was deafened by the anvil-like blows of the knocker. On several occasions, in desperation, he went to the door himself, imagining that by dismissing the disturber of his peace it might return to him.

He found, however, that it was only necessary to open the front door of No. 77 in order to find himself confronted by victims of the economic earthquake. One ex-Service man wanted to sell him a writing-block. Another produced an album containing specimens of Christmas-cards which—Rendell was assured—were bankrupt stock, and so were going considerably under cost. Finally, an ex-officer appeared who was hawking ladies' underwear. The man was about Rendell's age, belonged to the same class, and was obviously entirely genuine. He explained briefly that he was doing this as it was literally and absolutely the only activity he had been able to find.

Rendell gave him a ten-shilling note—and let the next comer knock, till the man's arm refused to perform that function any longer.

But at twelve o'clock, when Rendell happened to be standing at the window—watching three little girls dancing with perfect enjoyment to the strains of a barrel-organ—a large car drew up. Instantly a man leapt out of it, ran up the narrow stone path leading to the house, sprang up the steps, and gave three brisk authoritative raps with the knocker.

Rendell felt instinctively that this visitor must not be kept waiting. He went to the door.

"I answered your knock," he explained, "as they're not too good here at attending to visitors."

The man glanced down the narrow hall, then at Rendell, in considerable perplexity.

"Care to come into my room for a minute?" Rendell suggested, feeling it incumbent on him to make an effort to placate this visitor, who was clearly an important one.

"Yes. Thanks! Shan't stay long—too much to do. Ah, your room's just here, is it? Good! Most kind of you. Thanks!"

Rendell glanced at his companion, while waiting for him to state his business.

He was above middle height and had scanty carrot-coloured hair and grey luminous eyes. A great domed forehead bulked impressively above a lined mobile face. He was not still for a moment, but Rendell felt that this man possessed real and remarkable ability of some kind.

"Now, I've not long," he began. "What's all this about Trent? But, first of all, you must know that I'm Bickenshaw, head of Polsons." A pause. "You know, the publishers—the publishers!" he added, swiftly and irritably, as the light of comprehension and admiration had not dawned in Rendell's eyes.

"Oh yes, of course," the latter said quickly. "You publish Trent's books, don't you?"

"Yes, yes! Well now, look here—what's happened? Is he better, or is he still delirious?"

"I believe he's still delirious."

"Must have collapsed in the street," Bickenshaw said briskly, "and so they brought him in to this hole. Why, God bless my soul, he was lunching with me a week ago and never looked better. Told me he was just going to start his new book. I thought he'd have left England before this. Well, anyway! Do you know him?"

"No, I don't, but——"

"Never mind! Directly he's better, you go and see him. Tell him I called. Say I came in person. Don't forget. And mind you tell him this *from me*. What's wrong with him is blood-pressure. Everyone has it—I've got it myself. And it plays queer tricks at times. But you tell him—from me—not to worry. Just say that I said it's only blood-pressure."

He turned swiftly to Rendell and demanded:

"Have you got it?"

"No, I——"

"You've probably got it—and don't know it. Heaps of people are like that. It's my belief that *everybody* has got it. Now, I must get on."

He turned, walked swiftly out of the room, followed by Rendell. At the top of the steps, however, he paused.

"You live here, I suppose? Right! Then tell him—from me—to get out of this hole. I know a first-rate nursing-home. Tell him that, will you? Thanks very much. He must get out of this hole just as soon as he can. That's essential. Tell him I said so."

Bickenshaw sprang down the steps, ran to his car, leapt into it, and flashed away.

Rendell returned to his room and began to pace slowly up and down. It seemed to him that his primary need, at the moment, was to obtain some degree of mental perspective. Ever since his arrival at No. 77 last evening, impressions, discoveries, mysteries, and distractions of all kinds had so enveloped him that he was wholly unable to separate the significant from the trivial. His mind was chaotic and, in the hope of introducing some principle of order, he kept repeating to himself that it was less than forty-eight hours since he had dined with Marsden and cross-examined him concerning Ivor Trent.

But the iteration of this fact only increased his perplexity, for it seemed to him that he had been at No. 77 for at least a week, and that the week had contained an extraordinary number of remarkable incidents. One thing was definite, however—his curiosity concerning Ivor Trent deepened hourly.

At this point someone began to knock on the front door, but

Rendell decided that he had had enough adventures in that region. So he continued to pace the room, speculating on the possibility that—if he stayed long enough—he might become so accustomed to the knocking that he would not hear it. He encouraged himself in this hope by recalling that once, in Sydney, he had become so inured to cats wailing all night and every night in the yard outside his room that, when a new-comer complained, he was amazed to discover that these nocturnal activities remained a fact.

He was interrupted in these memories, however, by a sharp rap on the window. This was a new form of technique, and a challenging one. Rendell decided that its originator was a person of resource and so worth his attention.

He went to the front door, opened it, and announced briskly—indicating the window of his room:

"That is *not* the servants' room. It happens to be mine."

"I'm most awfully sorry, but I've been here so long, and I really am in a hurry. Still, I do apologise."

The man's voice was attractive. Rendell capitulated.

"That's all right," he said, then, glancing at the visitor, he added: "Have you come to inquire about Trent?"

"I have. How did you guess?"

"Well, I've been in all the morning and I suppose a dozen people have battered on that door. I can now spot those who have come to sell things—and those who want to learn about Trent. Come in to my room for a minute."

"That's most kind of you."

"As you see, it's near the front door. Now, what can I——"

"My name's Voyce. I'm Trent's literary agent. I was terribly upset to see the news in the paper. I live in the country, and only saw that paragraph in the train going home, or I should have come last night. How is he?"

"Much the same, I'm afraid. The doctor has sent a nurse in."

"But what's *wrong* with him? That's what I want to know. I saw him a few days ago and he seemed perfectly well. And what on earth is he doing *here*?"

"It's the first time you've been here then?" Rendell inquired.

"Yes, of course. And it's the first time *he's* been here. Don't want to be rude, but, frankly, this is not exactly Ivor Trent's setting. He's got a perfectly good flat of his own near Cork Street."

"Oh, he's a flat off Cork Street, has he?"

"Yes, had it for years. He must have been taken ill in the street. Incidentally, have you been here long?"

"No, I only came last night."

"Only last night?" Voyce hesitated. "Don't think me inquisitive, but do you intend to stay some time?"

"Well, I think I can say definitely," Rendell replied, with some emphasis, "that I shall stay here as long as Trent does."

"Then do me a favour, would you? Give him this letter, when he's better, and ask him to write me his opinion. I've got to go away, but his letter would be forwarded."

"Very well. He shall have the letter directly he's better."

"It's really good of you. I'm damnably upset about this collapse of his. I can't understand it."

They walked together to the front door.

Just as Voyce was about to leave, Rendell said:

"By the way, Bickenshaw called about half an hour ago."

"Did he? But of course he would! What's he think is wrong with Trent?"

"He thinks it's blood-pressure."

"Oh, Bickenshaw's got blood-pressure on the brain! Good-bye, and many thanks."

Rendell returned to his room. The information that Trent had a flat near Cork Street, had had it for years, and, nevertheless, had written all his books at 77, Potiphar Street, so bewildered Rendell that sanity seemed to depend on ceasing to speculate any further on the mystery of Trent.

Consequently he deliberately began to analyse Voyce's last remark—that Bickenshaw had blood-pressure on the brain—trying to determine whether authoritative medical opinion would accept the statement as a scientific one.

Arriving at no conclusion, he decided it was time for luncheon. He glanced out of the window. A sunny autumn day—he would not need an overcoat.

He took his hat and stick, went to the front door and opened it.

He was confronted by a telegraph-boy, whose hand was raised in a frustrated attempt to seize the knocker.

"Trent?"

"Oh, go to the devil!" Rendell shouted, then brushed past the astonished youth, nearly falling down the steps in his eagerness to escape—if only for an hour—from the mystery of Trent.

VI

RENDELL had no definite ideas as to where to lunch, but, finding himself on the Embankment, and discovering a restaurant with three or four tables gaily displayed on the broad pavement in front of it, he decided that luncheon in the open air was desirable, the day being mild.

Consequently he joined the half-dozen rather self-conscious persons already seated, and instantly acquired the slightly defiant air which characterised them, and which seemed to assert "one does this in Paris, so why not in London?"

Traffic shot and crashed down the Embankment, trams trailed monotonously over Battersea Bridge: tugs fussed up and down the sparkling river, wailing mysterious intentions to the initiate. An impish breeze frisked about, fluttering the table-cloths and whisking odd scraps of paper to dizzy altitudes, then incontinently abandoning them.

Two young men, at the table next to Rendell's, were engaged in an endless and highly technical conversation, largely monopolised by the lankier of the two. On the rare occasions when he was forced to pause, the less lanky seized the opportunity to demand: "What about Flaubert?" And, as the more lanky consistently ignored this question, it was repeated perhaps a dozen times by the less.

Rendell, eventually finding this somewhat monotonous—and not wishing to revert to private speculation—transferred his attention to another table in his immediate vicinity.

Two young women were seated at it. The more talkative had a countenance vaguely suggesting a snapshot of winter, but this was compensated for to some extent by the kindred virtue of a polar clarity in her speech. She was explaining, in the briefest and clearest of terms, such mysteries as commodity prices, inflation, deflation, the gold dollar, and certain economic theories held by the U.S.S.R. Each sentence was delivered with revolver-shot precision. Her companion—a rosy-cheeked, athletic girl of about twenty— kept interpolating enthusiastically: "Oh, is *that* what it means? I've often wondered."

Soon, Rendell bought a newspaper from a passing youth, but as the lunch edition had not yet reached Chelsea, it contained only racing information—in which he was not remotely interested.

So, his coffee being cold, owing to exposure, he rose, having decided to have a stroll round Chelsea before returning to No. 77.

He wandered about, indifferent as to direction, interested or fascinated by a number of things. He encountered Chelsea Pensioners who, swiftly glimpsed, resembled moving pillar-boxes: little old-world shops nodding drowsily in the sunshine: a wooded public garden with Carlyle's statue in the middle of it—leaves drifting idly down past the unseeing eyes of the sage. Then he lost himself in a labyrinth of little streets, now catching a glimpse of a porch of breath-taking beauty; or a charming interior with decorative people, remote and removed from the rigours of the age; or a dreaming house with an overhanging tree, surrounded by green lawns and a grey wall, serene and mature in the mellow October sunlight.

Later he found himself confronted by a tiny edifice of remarkable individuality. He paused to study it. Observing his interest, an old gentleman with silver hair and dark benevolent eyes, who wore a black velvet smoking-jacket, informed him that it was reputed to have been Henry VIII's shooting-box, and that many earnest people hoped it was haunted.

On leaving this urbane and cultured individual, Rendell wandered on till, turning a corner, he found himself threatened by the maelstrom of the King's Road.

He glanced at his watch. A quarter to three. He would return to No. 77 and, if possible, have an hour's sleep—to compensate in part for a very disturbed night.

VII

THE house was quiet on his return. He lit a cigarette, then, gradually, became aware of something oppressive in the atmosphere. Dismissing this sensation, by attributing it to the unwonted silence, he stood by the window, vaguely deliberating whether a view of the river was obtainable from Trent's rooms at the top of the house.

Several minutes passed, then, being mentally idle and therefore interested in details, he noticed a taxi approaching down a deserted Potiphar Street.

He watched it aimlessly till his interest was quickened by the fact that it drew up outside the house. But although it became stationary, no one alighted. Nearly a minute passed. He saw the driver turn his head to address an invisible fare. Then the man pushed his arm back, turned the handle, and flung the door open.

A woman got out slowly. Hardly was she upright on the pavement when she glanced up at the house, then to the right, then to the left—hesitated—and finally made a movement which suggested that she was about to re-enter the taxi and drive away.

The driver, however, shut the door, and jerked twice with his left forefinger in the direction of the house.

Slowly, unwillingly, the woman approached it, pausing half-way to look again in each direction, then with sudden determination she almost ran to the top of the steps.

Rendell heard a single timid knock. If a mouse had been in the hall, it would have ignored it.

"This has got my number on it," Rendell muttered to himself, and went into the hall.

He opened the door. Instantly an exclamation broke from him.

A beautiful but terrified face with great hunted eyes confronted him. For an endless second they stared at each other, then she began to tremble so violently that Rendell thought she was going to collapse.

Instinctively he caught her by the arm.

"Steady! It's all right. Take your time. You'll feel better in a minute."

She made a lightning movement with her hand, indicating that she wanted the door closed. Rendell shut it with alacrity, then, still holding her arm, guided her to his room.

"You'd better sit down, don't you———"

"Trent—*Trent!* I must see him. Now—immediately!—do you understand?"

The intensity of her tone, no less than her convulsive movements, so astonished Rendell that he stood hypnotised, staring at her.

She came nearer to him, moving her arms up and down, her fingers writhing in a frenzy of impatience.

"He's here—he's still here—isn't he?"

"Yes, he's still here, but———"

"Then go! *Now!*"

"But I tell you no one is allowed to see him. The doctor has sent in a nurse and———"

"He's not *still* delirious?"

"Yes, he is———"

Rendell broke off. She had sunk into a chair and now began to rock to and fro, her face buried in her hands.

"Delirious . . . delirious . . ."

She repeated the word as if it held her death-sentence.

By now Rendell was seriously alarmed and, which was worse, felt totally inadequate to the situation. Simultaneously, in the hinterland of his consciousness, he was dimly aware of a very disturbing quality in this woman's beauty.

"Look here," he broke out at last, "you can't let yourself go like this. I tell you what you'd better do," he went on, having no idea as to how he would end the sentence, "you'd better—well—you'd better have a drink, or something."

A pause.

Then a laugh rang through the room. It was so unexpected, so musical, that Rendell started as if it had been an explosion.

When he recovered, he found that she was on her feet—her

eyes scrutinising his features with embarrassing intensity.

"You must be a nice person. Only a nice person could have said something so stupid. Listen, listen! I've got to trust you. There's something you must do for me. But promise—*promise*—you'll never tell anyone."

"I do promise."

"Get me a piece of paper—and a pencil. Quick!" She scribbled a word and some numbers—then tore the paper to shreds.

"No! Tell him—directly you can—that he *must* ring up Rosalie Vivian. *Directly!* Tell him it's terribly urgent—terribly!"

Again she sank into the chair and buried her face in her hands.

"Oh no, no, no!" she moaned, "that's no good. He's delirious —delirious! My God, I can't stand this—I can't stand it another second—I——"

"For God's sake——"

But she was on her feet again, quivering from head to foot.

"They don't take any notice, do they—doctors, nurses!—of what a man says in delirium. They don't, do they? They know it's all nonsense—lies—don't they? *Do answer!*"

"Yes, of course they do."

She seized his arm and gripped it with a sudden nervous strength that amazed him.

"You—they—you haven't heard—they've not told you anything he's said——"

"No, no, of course not! You need not fear that. Doctors and nurses are used to all that. It doesn't interest them."

"You're *certain?*"

"Certain!"

A long silence, which reminded Rendell of a respite during a thunderstorm. He stood, braced and taut, believing himself to be prepared for anything.

"What's your name?"

The tone was nearly a normal conversational one. Rendell reeled. He had not been prepared for this.

"Rendell—Arthur Rendell. I only came to this house last night. I don't know Trent. But do believe that you can trust me. I'd—I'd help you in any way I could. Please believe that."

"I do believe it."

There was a deep resonant note in her voice. The words might have been spoken by a serious child—giving the whole of her confidence to someone who had earned it.

A long silence followed.

She had sat down again and was leaning forward, her elbows on her knees, her chin resting in her hands.

Possibly she was thirty—dark, lithe, and deceptively frail-looking. Her hands and feet were perfect. She had large very blue eyes, which, in moments of tranquillity, looked at the world with an expression of frightened wonder. But, as Rendell had seen, they could flash with extraordinary power when she was emotionally moved. She had the rare quality of creating—by her mere presence—a sudden tension in the atmosphere surrounding her. Rendell was aware of it now, as he stood looking down at her.

She seemed to have forgotten time, place, and circumstances as she sat, leaning forward, staring into vacancy with bewildered eyes. This swift alternation from hysteria to inertia was so mysterious to Rendell that it reduced him to impotence. He stood like a slave awaiting the next demand of a capricious master. He had not to wait long.

The sound of footsteps descending the stairs stabbed broad awake in her that spirit of passionate hysteria which had so suddenly become quiescent.

In a second she was on her feet.

"Who's that?"

"Only one of the lodgers."

"Lodgers!"

"Yes, didn't you know that this was a lodging-house?"

She stared at him incredulously.

"Then why is Ivor here? I saw him on Saturday," she raced on, "only Saturday! He was well. He was going abroad the next day to work. I must see him! I *must*, I tell you! I'm in terrible trouble. And he's here—delirious! You don't know what that means to me."

A pause, then on again, the words rushing from her in a torrent:

"I did not sleep for one second last night. I read that paragraph in the paper again and again. I couldn't believe it. I *daren't* believe it. And then, to-day, I couldn't get away to come here. I had to come, although I was terrified of coming. And yet I ought not to be here. Anything might happen. And I'm telling you all this—you, a stranger! I shall go mad to-night when I think of it. But I can't stay—not another minute! And God alone knows when I shall be able to come again."

Tears blinded her eyes and she was trembling violently.

"Look here, you really can't go on like this," Rendell announced firmly. "You'll make yourself ill."

"Ill!"

"Yes—ill! And that won't help. I promise you that, directly I can, I will ask him to telephone you. I'll do anything else I can."

"Wait, wait! I must think. Suppose someone saw me come in here? You'd say that I was a friend of yours. You'd do that? You remember my name? Rosalie Vivian. A friend of *yours*. You understand? And you'd tell them that I did not know Ivor was here. That's what you'd say, isn't it—isn't it?"

"Yes. I'll say that. How can I convince you that I only want to help you?"

"I believe it—now I'm here with you. But, when I've gone—to-night?—alone? Wait, wait!"

She went to the mirror, dabbed her eyes with a diminutive handkerchief, then studied her reflection critically.

"Yesterday seemed like a month. To-day has been a year. I shall soon be old."

"Things will come out all right and——"

She turned and looked at him—and his platitudinous phrase died in middle age.

"How nice you are," she said slowly. "Now please get me a taxi."

Rendell stared at her.

"Well," she went on, "is that such a very extraordinary request?"

"But—but——" he blurted out, "the one you came in is still waiting."

"Oh, is it? That's all right then. Please see me into it. And, remember, I came to see *you*."

"Shall I see you again?"

"I don't know—I don't know anything."

"I'll tell you what I'll do. I'll be in at three o'clock every day for the next week."

With a swift movement she took his hand, pressed it, then turned, and he followed her out of the room.

They walked in silence to the taxi. Rendell watched it till it disappeared, then returned to his room, haunted by the image of a lovely face with frightened eyes.

VIII

Out of the maze of conflicting thoughts and emotions created by Rosalie Vivian's visit, one fact eventually emerged—Rendell had become involved. Till his meeting with her, he had been a spectator—one whose curiosity had deepened hourly—but no more. At any moment he could have given up his room, returned to the normal, and regarded his adventures at No. 77 as amusing or intriguing incidents in a comedy which he had abandoned before its end.

This was so no longer. A tragic shadow had fallen across the comedy—and he had ceased to be a spectator. Even in terms of time, he was committed. He had promised to be in his room every day at three o'clock during the next week, but—apart from that— he was involved emotionally. He was convinced that her need was desperate, and that she had no one in whom to confide. Also, and more strangely, he was certain she was married, though, as she had not removed her gloves during her visit, this certainty was wholly intuitive.

Gradually other—and more obvious—certainties presented themselves. She was Trent's mistress. Why, otherwise, had the knowledge that he was delirious made her hysterical with fear? As Rendell saw it, the governing facts were clear enough: she was married; she was Trent's mistress; Trent was delirious; and therefore she was terrified.

But what was far more important, to Rendell, was the personal fact that she was unique in his experience. Till his marriage, women had been only a physical necessity, but, on that level, he had had many adventures. He was still deeply sensitive to a woman's physical being, and yet, although Rosalie Vivian was beautiful, he could evoke no image of her figure from his memory. Her attraction was psychic, not physical. Nevertheless, Rendell made an essentially male mental note that—should he see her again—he would study her figure in detail. At present, he could remember only face, feet, and hands—and her amazingly blue, frightened eyes.

He had reached this point in his deliberations when he stumbled across a fact, hitherto overlooked, which instantly attained primary importance.

It was just understandable that Trent had lied to Marsden, to his publisher, and to his agent when telling them that he always went abroad to work. But it was far less understandable that he had told Rosalie Vivian—who was almost certainly his mistress—only last Saturday that he was leaving England the next day. She, then, like the others, was ignorant of the fact that Trent had had rooms at 77, Potiphar Street for years and had written all his books there.

"One thing's definite," Rendell said to himself, "if I ever see her again, the first thing I shall find out is—how long has she known Trent? The answer will tell me whether he's an occasional liar or an habitual one. And a thing like that is always worth knowing."

But at this point he was interrupted by a light knock on his door. "Come in."

A nurse appeared and said apologetically:

"I'm sorry to disturb you, sir, but do you happen to know where Mrs. Frazer is?"

"No, I don't, I'm afraid, but I'll find her for you. But, tell me, how is your patient? I've several excellent reasons for wanting to know."

"He's still very excited."

"Not delirious?"

"Very excited, I should say."

"Well, it's like this. His publisher and agent were talking to me this morning. Is it possible to give Mr. Trent a letter—and a message?"

"Oh no, quite impossible, I'm afraid. The doctor forbids him to see anyone or to have any letters. He was very definite about that."

"Very well. I've done all I can. Would you let me know directly there's a change in the doctor's orders?"

"Yes, certainly."

"Thanks very much. It's awkward for me, having letters and so on. Wait a minute!" Rendell exclaimed. "I think that's Mrs. Frazer in the hall."

The nurse went out, and a lengthy half-whispered conversation ensued between the two women. Eventually Rendell, hearing the nurse ascending the stairs, called to Mrs. Frazer:

"Give me a minute, will you?"

She came into the room, looking tired and worried.

"I don't want to bother you," he began, "but, frankly, don't you think this house is a bit noisy for an invalid?"

"I hope you haven't been disturbed——"

"Oh, never mind about me! I'm all right—more or less. But what about Trent?"

"He has double doors and windows in his rooms," she replied. "The top floor is really a self-contained flat, so he's cut off from the rest of the house."

"I see. Well—as you asked if I'd been disturbed—I would like to know one thing. Does anyone ever answer the front door when people hammer on it?"

Mrs. Frazer made a despairing gesture.

"That front door will bring me to my grave! When I'm out—and I *have* to go out a lot—no one answers it. It's a mercy I happened to be in the hall the night poor Mr. Trent arrived. The girl says she's deaf and can't hear the knocking—and my husband won't open it. He's in nearly all day, but he just won't go to it. He's too proud. It's a wonder he let you in last night."

"That's how it is, is it? Well, it doesn't bother me much. I'll soon be used to it, and to the lodgers, too, I daresay—in time, of course."

Mrs. Frazer regarded him mournfully. Then, having turned to make certain that the door was shut, she said emphatically:

"Don't imagine that I'm satisfied with the lodgers, because I'm *not.* And that's a fact. You wouldn't believe it if you knew what I have to put up with. But what can I do? You've got to be thankful to get anyone nowadays. You know what things are like. They say they are better. Well, they may be—but not in Potiphar Street. And my husband, for all his fine airs and graces, is thick as thieves with the worst of them. I'm afraid you were very disturbed last night."

"Now don't you bother about me, Mrs. Frazer. I find it all very interesting. There's a little noise, of course, and a few visitors, but —I'm all right. In fact, I think I shall be here some time."

"I'm very glad to hear it. Anything you want, you let me know. And now I must go to Mr. Trent. I was a nurse myself once— though I've almost forgotten it—and I suppose I was the biggest fool ever born not to remain one."

Having made this oblique reference to her marriage, Mrs. Frazer paused, then—evidently prompted by her sense of justice—added impartially:

"Still, I will say this for him: he's made himself useful attending to people who've called to inquire about Mr. Trent."

As Rendell believed that this duty had devolved wholly on himself, her statement puzzled him, but he gave no indication of this fact when he said:

"Really! And when was that?"

"The last hour or so—when you were out. Several people called." She produced a number of visiting-cards from the pocket of her overall and handed them to Rendell for inspection. "And what with one or two of the newspapers ringing up, and I don't know what, he's been quite busy—for him."

Rendell said nothing. He was turning over the cards, as if mechanically, but actually with considerable interest. He detected several well-known names in the literary and social worlds, then, finally, one appeared bearing a name which startled him.

"Marsden!" he exclaimed.

"Oh yes, the crippled gentleman! My husband told me about him because he had such a job getting up the steps. And what's more, he was so certain that Mr. Trent would have asked to see him that he wouldn't take 'No' for an answer."

Marsden! Rendell totted up probabilities, while contracting and expanding the card between his right thumb and forefinger. Then he remembered that Marsden had told him—before they dined together on the Sunday—that he was staying in London for some weeks. Inevitably, therefore, he would call to ask about Trent. It was rather surprising he had not been earlier.

"Didn't say when he was coming again, I suppose?" Rendell asked at last.

"Well, now you mention it, as a matter of fact, he did. Told my husband he might come at six o'clock. And he said it in a tone which was as much as to say: 'And mind you don't keep me waiting!' My husband wasn't best pleased, I can tell you. That's why he mentioned it to me."

After a pause, she added:

"Well, I must be getting upstairs. You'll let me know if you want anything?"

"I certainly will—and many thanks."

She disappeared, and Rendell stretched himself on a sofa—whose appearance and personality seemed to defy anyone to subject its age to any such indignity—in the hope that he might sleep for a couple of hours.

Destiny granted half his desire, then, at about five o'clock, a single but resonant knock on the front door roused him to consciousness.

He rose, stretched and yawned simultaneously, then felt his way through the twilight of the hall.

"I'm sorry to trouble you, but is Mr. Trent better?"

The voice was richly modulated. She stood looking up at him, and in the half-light he dimly discerned a broad powerfully-moulded face with dark eyes under black brows.

"A bit better, I think," he replied. "Doctor won't let him see anyone, so the nurse tells me, but I fancy he's not as bad as he was yesterday. Will you leave your name? Then, later, I'll see that he's told that you called."

She laughed pleasantly.

"Oh no, thanks all the same. I'm no one. I just wanted to know how he was. That's all."

But this self-effacement was too attractive for Rendell to let it go at that.

"What do you mean—you're no one?" he demanded.

"I work in a bar in the West End. Mr. Trent used to come in sometimes. Not regularly, I don't mean, far from it. But just now and then, every few months, when he was in London. And——"

"And?" Rendell echoed, as she hesitated.

"Oh well, I don't know—he was always very nice to me. That's all. Always had a bit of a talk before he went. Sometimes told me a book to read—once or twice gave me seats at a theatre for my night off. That's all—but it helped. Gets a bit monotonous at times, serving in a bar."

"I'll bet my life it does!"

"You feel sometimes you'll have to hide under the counter to get away from all the faces opposite. Then you get all right again, and go on. But I mustn't take up your time like this."

"That's all right. What's your name?"

"They always call me Rummy."

"Why?"

"Oh, an old major who comes in a lot said some time ago he was going to call me Rummy because I was a rum 'un—and the name stuck."

"Which bar do you work in?"

"The long bar at the Cosmopolitan."

"Well, perhaps I'll look you up there one day soon and tell you how Trent is."

"Would you? I'd be grateful if you would. I must go now or I'll be late. Good night."

"Good night."

Rendell shut the door, and immediately remembered that he had not asked Rummy whether she knew Trent was at No. 77 or whether she, like all the others, had come there as that address had been given in the newspaper. Then, having decided that he would ask her when he went to the Cosmopolitan, he dismissed the subject, and began to pace up and down the room—trying to determine whether or not he should see Marsden if the latter turned up at six o'clock.

A volley of blows on the front door interrupted his attempt to reach a decision.

"That probably *is* Marsden—but, if so, he's a bit early. Anyhow, *I'm* not letting him in."

A one-minute silence, then another series of determined knocks.

"By God, I *won't* go!" Rendell exclaimed. "I'm damned if I do."

A few moments later he heard steps in the hall. Evidently someone had heard the summons and was responding to it. Almost immediately Captain Frazer entered the room, without the formality of a knock on the door.

"Sorry and all that," he began, in a tone that was an even blend of insolence and servility, "but there's someone else come about Trent. My wife tells me you've been good enough to——"

"Yes, I have," Rendell cut in, "but I can't keep on interviewing Trent's friends for ever. May go on for days."

"Quite—quite! Never mind. Don't you worry. I'll send my wife down. I've got to go out for five minutes. Important, you understand. But I'll send her down. Don't you bother."

"She's probably enough to do," Rendell replied bluntly. "As you put that paragraph in the paper, it seems to me that it's up to you to deal with its consequences."

Captain Frazer stiffened till he became completely rigid, his right eye winking convulsively. Then, still erect as a sentinel, he turned and marched out of the room.

A moment later the front door banged.

"God! he's gone! Hope the visitor's gone with him."

But Rendell soon discovered that the reverse was the fact. Frazer had evidently considered that the effect of his military exit would have been marred had he paused to close the door. It remained three-quarters open, and Rendell, who had begun to pace the room again, was not a little astonished suddenly to find that a woman stood in the doorway, regarding him with somewhat grim attention.

"I'm afraid I'll have to trouble *you*," she began in a collected manner, which, nevertheless, suggested one or two rehearsals, "to give me some information."

"Well, why not? I'm getting pretty used to it. In an honorary capacity, you understand."

"Is Ivor Trent still here?" she asked, with measured deliberation.
"He is."

"He's not still—delirious?" The last word was jerked out, despite a great, and obvious, effort at control.

"Very excited, is the phrase the nurse used—when I asked her this afternoon."

A long pause.

Rendell made no attempt to mask his scrutiny of her, as he considered that her method of entry, and her general manner, did not necessitate elaborate courtesy.

She was about twenty-four. Her broad face, with its strong regular features, would have been commonplace had it not been for the deep-set dark eyes. The eyes might have belonged to a fanatic. Unlike Rosalie Vivian, there was nothing elusive about her figure. It was sturdy, somewhat over-developed, and seemed to rebel against the restriction of clothes.

"Yes, that's what the nurse said some hours ago," Rendell went on, "'very excited,' were her exact words." He paused, then added: "Of course, he may be delirious again now."

A sudden determination to humble her made him add the last sentence. Her assurance was assumed—her manner was a pose. She had consciously adopted a method to create a definite impression. Rendell was certain of it, and so he had made that reference to the possibility of Trent being again delirious—in much the same spirit as he would have shown a whip to a dog that was putting on airs.

His success was dramatic, for she blushed a deep crimson. Her embarrassment was so extreme that he shared it.

She sat down limply and half closed her eyes.

"But in all probability," Rendell said quickly, "he's over the delirium for good."

"Why is he here?"

She asked the question lifelessly, with no trace of her former manner.

"Well," Rendell began, then hesitated. After all, why should he reveal Trent's secret? "I will only tell you that his publisher and agent were here this morning and they assume he collapsed in the street and was brought in here. Have you seen him lately?"

"No—not for months. I don't want to see him—ever! I only came because the paper said he was——"

She broke off and again there was silence.

"I'm afraid I'm not much help," Rendell said slowly. Then an idea occurred to him, and he added: "Do you know any of his friends?"

"I met one some time ago. A man called Denis Wrayburn." She moved uneasily as if her memories of him were not pleasant. Then she went on: "And I met another. His name was Peter Marsden."

"Marsden! That's odd, because he'll probably turn up any minute. Perhaps you'd like to see him."

"Why?"

"Well, he was here earlier and had a talk with Captain Frazer—that's the man who owns this house—so perhaps Marsden could tell you more definitely than I can how Trent is."

"I'm completely indifferent as to how he is," she replied. "Have I asked you once how he was?"

"Well, no, you haven't."

"If you had told me that he was dead, I shouldn't have cared in the least. I'd have been glad. I hate him as I've never hated anyone—and I'm not a bad hater. All I'm afraid of is that if he's—delirious—he might babble some infamous lies about—well—me, if you want to know."

"I didn't want to know particularly, or I should have asked. You volunteered the information."

She turned to him, and their eyes met for the first time. The dark intensity glowing in hers almost startled him.

"You are a friend of his?" she asked more humbly.

"I've never seen him."

"Read his books, perhaps?"

"One of them."

"I wish to God I'd never read a line he's written. Anyway, his books are all lies."

As Rendell said nothing, she went on:

"You don't agree, of course!"

"I don't know what you mean by all lies. I've read only one of his books, but I read it three times. To me, it was a revelation. But I'm not a critic, like Marsden."

She was about to speak, but Rendell silenced her with a gesture. He was standing by the window, listening intently to a minor commotion on the steps.

"That sounds like Marsden. I'll ask him in. That is, if you have no objection."

"Just as you like, I'm completely indifferent."

Rendell opened the door, but, finding that the maid who happened to be in the hall was about to respond to a knock, he said to her:

"If that's Mr. Marsden, show him in here, will you?"

A moment afterwards Marsden appeared. He stood in the doorway, supported by crutches, gazing from one to the other in considerable perplexity.

"You're Vera Thornton," he said at last. "I can understand your being here. But what on earth are you doing, Rendell—and whose room is this?"

"Mine," Rendell replied. "Let's take those things, then you can sit down and have a cigarette."

Marsden allowed himself to be relieved of his crutches, then sank into a chair and accepted the cigarette Rendell offered him. But during these operations his sharp little eyes did not cease to regard Rendell with a hint of disapproval.

"*Your* room!" he exclaimed. "What the devil are you doing in this hole? Why, good God! they can't even answer the door."

Rendell explained briefly the impulse which had prompted him to come to No. 77 the night before; the manner of his reception, and his sudden decision to take the room. In extenuation of his eccentricity in so doing, he pointed out to Marsden that his action was really no more than a sequel to their conversation during dinner on the previous Sunday.

He ended by saying:

"The fact that I dragged you out in the fog to dine and talk about a man I don't know was a pretty good indication that I was mentally and emotionally unemployed. Well, I still am. I had to clear out of the club: I came to inquire about Trent: I found this room vacant and I took it. It's not really as odd as it sounds."

Marsden immediately asked a number of questions—the answers to which only necessitated restatements of the explanation already given. Rendell made them mechanically, while secretly trying to determine whether or not to reveal to Marsden any of the strange information he had amassed during his brief residence at No. 77.

He had longer to ponder this problem than he could have anticipated, as Marsden suddenly transferred his attention to Vera Thornton. Rendell, therefore, continued his private deliberations, but even so, he did not fail to notice that Marsden possessed one manner for men and another for women. Vera Thornton's presence transformed him. He spoke in a higher key, with great animation, referred frequently to his literary activities, and generally represented his life as a brilliant and dashing affair—which brought him into intimate contact with everyone and everything worth while.

Rendell was amused, but grateful. He had time to reach a decision—subject to the answers to certain questions, which he now proceeded to ask.

"Your plans haven't changed, Marsden, I suppose? You're going to be in town for some weeks?"

"Yes, why?"

"I only wondered. So you'll be coming here to inquire about Trent pretty often, naturally."

"I shall be coming to *see* him. I've no doubt whatever that he's already asked for me, but they're in such a muddle in this house that I've not been told."

Rendell hesitated. Marsden would be visiting the house frequently. He'd learn Trent's secret from Captain Frazer or his wife. Well, then, *he* might as well tell him.

"Yes, they're very casual here," he said lightly. "But I expect you've known the house and its ways for a long time."

"Do you mind telling me—exactly—what you're talking about?"

There was lofty patronage in Marsden's tone. Although he addressed Rendell, he looked at Vera Thornton.

"I said that I expect you've known the house, and its ways, for a long time," Rendell repeated. "Not a very surprising statement—as Trent has had rooms at the top of this house for the last ten years."

"Why, you must be——"

But Vera Thornton had risen and was staring at Rendell.

"For the last ten years!" she exclaimed.

"Yes—he's written all his books here."

Marsden could restrain himself no longer.

"My *dear* Rendell, I don't want to be offensive, but you really *are* talking the most fantastic nonsense. Ivor Trent is an old friend of mine, a very old friend—as you know perfectly well—and I do really rather think I know something about his movements."

"Yes, I know you think you do," Rendell replied curtly, "but the point is—you don't."

"But, my *good* man——"

"I'm not arguing, Marsden. Ask Captain Frazer, or his wife, if you don't choose to believe me. You'll find one or other of them downstairs."

"But he told me himself, only last week——"

"That he was going abroad on Sunday to write his new book," Rendell cut in. "I'm quite sure he did. He told his publisher and his agent just what he told you. Well, it was a lie."

"Look here!" Marsden shouted, "Trent's a friend of mine and——"

"It was a lie," Rendell interrupted. "He was coming here. Every two or three years he comes here, and stays here for months—writing. They expected him to arrive about nine o'clock on Sunday night. He'd sent his luggage by taxi in advance. Well, he did arrive at about nine o'clock—and collapsed directly the front door was opened. Now, those are facts—which you can confirm. And you can make what you can of them."

They stared at him in silence. Fully a minute passed, then Rendell went on:

"I suggest you see Mrs. Frazer and cross-examine her yourself. You can see her here, if you like. I'm going for a walk and then I shall dine—and come back early. You'll excuse my leaving you, but I've had enough of Ivor Trent for one day."

He nodded to Marsden, bowed to Vera Thornton, then left them together.

IX

A SURGING wind which rose occasionally to a squall, hurtling drops of stinging rain, buffeted Rendell directly he left the house. He turned up the collar of his overcoat, then swung along, surrendering to the exaltation of physical exertion. Soon the rapid movement, the resistance of the wind—which attained almost gale intensity when he reached the Embankment—deprived him of all sense of identity. He ceased to be Rendell: he was a man fighting with the wind.

The Embankment was deserted. A low-lying moon—now hidden, now revealed by routed battalions of flying clouds—intermittently illuminated the scene. Whirlwind confusion claimed everything. Leaves leapt fantastically upward; lights quivered; houses cowered back in the shadows. The pulse of the sea raged in the turbulent river.

Rendell battled on through the derisive fury of the wind for half an hour, then, encountering a sudden onslaught of icy hail, he turned and was blown back to Chelsea in ten minutes.

He hurried into the first restaurant he found, which stood in a narrow street, a public garden being between it and the Embankment. He closed the door with difficulty, then looked round blinking—the sound of the wind in his ears, and the darkness of the night in his eyes.

Gradually the room ceased to be a blur. Objects began to emerge. First, several black tables lit by candles in silver sticks, then a warm-coloured floor, and finally white walls on which hung various brass articles reflecting the candle-light.

All the tables were occupied, but having caught a glimpse through a narrow archway at the back of the shadowy forms of other diners, he walked through the room—only to discover that the two or three tables at the rear were also occupied. Noticing, however, a corkscrew stairway leading to mysterious regions above, he mounted it—passing several candles, set in various nooks and crannies, each of which flickered wastefully in the draught.

A smaller room containing little black tables awaited him. Bare boards emphasised the sound of every movement. The lower half of the walls was covered with dark woodwork, the upper half being whitewashed. A waiter in a white coat—of the type sometimes worn by dentists—was standing in a corner surveying the diners with an air of benevolent detachment. His head was tilted back, and his tongue was making certain involved and highly technical explorations in the left region of his upper jaw.

Rendell, having observed these details, and having detected a small table near the window, crossed to it, sat down, and picked up the menu.

After an interval, the waiter strolled across, leaned lightly on the corner of the table, and studied the menu over Rendell's head in a manner which suggested that he had never seen it before, would never see it again, and was anxious to memorise its details.

"What's the steak and kidney pie like?" Rendell asked.

"I'd have it, if I were you. Tasty! Boiled and cabbage?"

"All right—boiled and cabbage."

The waiter turned, gazed at the stormy scene from the window for some moments, then crossed the room, picked up a newspaper, glanced at it impassively, and finally disappeared, rattling a pencil between his teeth.

Rendell surveyed the room and its occupants. The latter consisted of couples, or studious-looking solitary young men with books propped up against the heavy candlesticks. A cultured calm lingered over everything. Rendell decided that he liked the place. If the food were as good as the atmosphere was unique, he had made a useful discovery.

The food proved to be excellent, although the waiter placed it in front of him with an expression which implied that its appearance was a lucky fluke, and was by no means to be regarded as a precedent.

It is probable that if an incident had not occurred at this particular moment, Rendell would have engaged the waiter in conversation. His bony physiognomy, his rapt abstracted gaze, his attractive nonchalance which seemed to imply that his present activity, though temporary, was interesting—and that he derived deep inner satisfaction from witnessing its performance—all prompted Rendell to talk with him. But an incident prevented this.

A remarkable-looking individual appeared at the top of the stairs, then stood motionless and subjected each table to a searching scrutiny. He wore a light, and very wet, fawn overcoat and held a drenched soft hat in his left hand. A strand of black straight hair had fallen across a high, narrow forehead. A small moustache, and a dank little beard, contrasted oddly with the frail feminine features. The bony shoulders, too, seemed disproportionately heavy for the slender body. Grey eyes looked penetratingly out of the hatchet-shaped face.

His survey of the tables continued with great deliberation. Rendell's was the last to be reviewed. Consequently Rendell discovered that his features and general appearance were the subject of profound consideration by an odd-looking individual who stood motionless the other side of the room. One glance at this person created a sensation of intense aversion in Rendell, and an angry hope that he would not occupy the empty chair at his table.

The latter was destined to perish, for the unknown crossed the room with swift, long strides, halted opposite Rendell, and announced:

"Your name is Rendell."

Accepting the latter's look of astonishment as assent, the newcomer removed his overcoat and handed it, with his hat, to the waiter, and then proceeded to give him the most minute instructions as to the manner in which they were to be dried. Having specified the precise distance from the fire which they were to occupy, and the exact duration of their tenancy, he picked up the menu, tossed back his strand of errant hair, and studied the bill of fare with an absolute concentration.

When a minute had passed, the waiter made a suggestion.

The menu was immediately put down, the waiter regarded with passionless animosity, then this brief announcement was made:

"I will choose."

Rendell was surprised to discover that there was nothing in the least amusing about all this. It was hard and repellent. The atmosphere of cold isolation which enveloped this man was definitely the reverse of amusing. Rendell began to study his appearance in greater detail.

Everything about his clothes was incredibly neat. The fawn suit, the long-pointed soft collar, the dark tie, links—everything—suggested a deliberate choice—calculated to create a certain general effect. He looked like a fastidious student. He was probably about thirty.

Rendell's aversion increased. The narrow face with its dark pointed beard; the mauve vein clearly discernible on each temple; the slender hands with their tapering fingers, and, chiefly, the glacial aura which invested him, all contributed to foster Rendell's dislike. Also he objected to a mole on his right eyebrow—which he had just detected.

At last an order was given to the waiter. It consisted of eggs. Minute directions as to their preparation followed, and the waiter was not permitted to withdraw until his repetition of his instructions was correct to the last detail.

"My name is Denis Wrayburn."

The very articulate pedantic tone increased Rendell's irritability.

"I don't know that I'm particularly interested," he began, then broke off in obedience to a quick gesture from Wrayburn.

"Would you mind having *this* chair? It's in a draught." A pause. Then Wrayburn added, stabbing his right forefinger towards Rendell: "Say if you do mind, of course."

To Rendell's great astonishment, he rose, pushed his plate, etc., across the table, then seated himself in the draught Wrayburn had vacated.

"I have just come from 77, Potiphar Street," he announced, pausing between each word as if to suggest that every action of his had a special significance.

"From Potiphar Street!"

"To look for you. No—please!" A restraining hand was raised. "Let *me* explain. It will be quicker. I found there two extremely stupid persons: Peter Marsden and Vera Thornton. Both excited, both incoherent. By cross-examination I elicited that they were in your room, and that their information concerning Trent had come from you. They said you were dining out and returning early. I knew, therefore, that you would dine locally. I made them describe you, and then I came here."

"And why did you imagine I should be here?"

"They said you were going for a walk. In Chelsea, that usually means the Embankment. Anyway, does it matter? You are Rendell, and I have found you."

The coolness with which it was assumed that Rendell would not resent this intrusion lacked insolence, for it was absolute. Rendell was annoyed at not being irritated.

"I have not come to chatter," Wrayburn went on. "I'm not in the least interested in the fact that Trent's had rooms in that house for years without telling his friends. I leave that to Peter and Vera to discuss." He used their Christian names with withering emphasis. "I've come here to see just what sort of a person *you* are."

"Well, that's very thoughtful. I'm——"

But as Wrayburn actually writhed at such a commonplace attempt at satire, Rendell broke off, feeling a trifle stupid—greatly to his secret irritation.

Nevertheless, he looked sharply at Wrayburn, seeking legitimate fuel for his anger—and finding it. Wrayburn's attitude was offensive. He sat very upright, and, although his glance met Rendell's, his head was slightly averted. The effect was inquisitorial and Rendell resented it.

"If you would rather be alone," Wrayburn said slowly, emphasising each word, "say so now. Personally, I doubt it. You think you're a lonely person."

Rendell did not reply immediately. Wrayburn's remark showed clearly that he was determined to define their relations from the outset. He would sever them—or dominate them. It was for Rendell to choose, once and finally. And the latter was too interested in this odd individual to dismiss him.

"You said I was a lonely person, I suppose, because Marsden told you so."

"He did not tell me so. He told me that you had taken a room at No. 77 on impulse—although you do not know Trent. Well, that is the sort of thing a person does who thinks he is lonely. That is, of course, if he can afford it—which you can."

"I see. You're an expert in loneliness. Is that it?"

A flush passed over Wrayburn's features. It came—and went—instantly. His voice was even more controlled and even more pedantic when he replied:

"I am an expert in detecting people who think they are lonely. One moment! Here are my eggs."

A scrutiny of them, and a cross-examination of the waiter, followed. Then Wrayburn began to eat—in the manner of one performing an occult rite. Several minutes passed in silence. Eventually Rendell realised that Wrayburn had not the slightest intention of resuming conversation till he had finished.

He glanced at him again, though inwardly ashamed of the interest this odd person had created in him. Rendell had been to a lot of places and met numbers of people, but nowhere had he encountered anyone in the least like Wrayburn. Of that he was certain. Appearance, speech, personality—all were unique. Nevertheless, he disliked him, and felt uneasy in his presence.

To divert his thoughts, he looked out of the window. Through the rocking boughs of half-naked trees he caught a glimpse of the turbulent river. The moon was obscured, so all was darkness, except for a few street lights—and a lurid glow on the water which was the reflection of an advertisement in letters of crimson fire that adorned a building on the south side of the river. The wind still raged and—with increasing frequency—great rain-drops lashed the window-pane.

"I have finished eating."

The statement made Rendell start like a guilty schoolboy. He endeavoured to retrieve his dignity by offering Wrayburn a cigarette.

It was refused with a lightning flick of the hand. Rendell lit his cigarette then decided to assert himself. It was absurd to surrender to this stick of a man whom he could kill with one hand.

"How long have you known Trent?" he demanded.

"I have known him five years. Why?"

"Because I wanted to know," Rendell replied brusquely. "Do you know any of his friends?"

"I have told you that I know Peter and Vera," Wrayburn pointed out coldly. "I know others, of course. Why?"

"Well, damn it," Rendell exploded, "you came here to talk about Trent, didn't you?"

Wrayburn leaned forward, then, placing his elbow on the table and stabbing his left forefinger at Rendell, demanded:

"Do you really consider such questions and answers as *talking* about a man? Do you really? That's interesting, extremely interesting."

He regarded Rendell with genuine curiosity as if he were a species of half-wit hitherto unencountered.

"Do you mind," he went on, "if I prove that such questions are meaningless? Do say, if you do mind. I shall not be offended."

"Well, go on," said Rendell gruffly.

"You asked *how long* I had known Trent." Again the emphasis was withering. "And I replied: five years. If you'd asked Marsden the same question, and he had told you that he had known Trent for twenty years, would you have assumed that he knew him four times as well as I do? If not, I do not see the significance of the question."

Rendell felt there was an answer, but, as he couldn't discover it, he felt a trifle stupid.

"Do you think," Wrayburn went on—stroking his little beard as if to convince himself of its existence—"as a favour to me, you could avoid *cliché* remarks? Do you think you could?" he repeated, in the tone of an icy governess trying to coax a dull child into intelligence.

Rendell blew out a cloud of tobacco smoke.

"Perhaps it would be safer if I listened to you," he announced grimly. "That would settle it."

"That's an intelligent suggestion. But—just one minute!"

He extended his arm and, without turning his head, began to snap his fingers to attract the waiter's attention. As the snaps sounded like revolver-shots, he was soon successful.

Wrayburn held out a neat wrist-watch for the waiter's inspection, then tapped it with a finger-nail.

"It's time for my coat and hat to be removed further from the fire. *Not* nearer to it—further *from* it. You understand that? And in five minutes—*five* minutes—I want some weak China tea."

The waiter vanished.

"I want to know one thing," Rendell demanded, with a rising note in his voice, "do you invariably address people as if they were idiots?"

"Habitually—until they've submitted definite evidence to the contrary."

"I see. I only wanted to know."

Wrayburn ignored this comment so completely that Rendell felt he had not made it.

But it was evident that Wrayburn was pondering a problem. His glance was fixed on Rendell, his thin lips were pursed, and he drummed lightly on the table with his fingers.

"Yes, I think so," he said slowly. "I think this will convince you how stupid it is to ask a person *how long* he has known someone. Now, I have only just met you. An hour ago I did not know that you existed. Do you accept those statements as facts?"

"Certainly," Rendell replied, "I've every reason to believe they are facts."

"Excellent. I now propose to tell you what I make of *you*—having just met you. Then you can compare it with the knowledge of someone who has known you for years."

Rendell put his cigarette out and lit another. He did not anticipate Wrayburn's psychological diagnosis with equanimity.

"To begin with," Wrayburn said quickly, as if to have done with a platitude, "you are a natural man who has reached a state of considerable muddle and——"

"But, look here——"

"One moment!" Wrayburn's hand shot up in protest. "Do you propose to *interrupt*? Just say, if so—then I can adapt myself."

"I confess I rather wanted your definition of a natural man."

Wrayburn regarded him in a manner which soon convinced Rendell that he had sunk to the status of a quarter-wit, in his companion's estimation.

"I see how it is," the latter said to himself meditatively. "Only facts, I think—just simple obvious facts." Then, abandoning soliloquy, he turned to Rendell and said clearly and rapidly:

"You are about forty. You know your world well. You always knew what you wanted, and had the requisite ability to get it. You've travelled a lot—obviously. You've been in difficult situations, have had to handle men—and you have been successful because your instinct is more developed than your intelligence. You might belong to one of several activities. You might be, for example, the South American manager of a big exporting firm. You might be a mining engineer. Or, just conceivably, an explorer."

Wrayburn broke off. Again he extended his arm, and began to snap his fingers to summon the waiter.

"My weak China tea," he demanded, when that individual appeared, without glancing at him.

"Things went on pretty well with you till a few years ago, I imagine," Wrayburn continued in the manner of a lecturer. "Then you probably fell in love and it wasn't wholly successful."

"I married three years ago and—two years later—my wife died," Rendell said simply.

"I felt it wasn't wholly successful. Just one minute!"

The tea had arrived. It was inspected minutely—and eventually accepted.

"Since then," Wrayburn continued, as if no interruption had occurred, "you've found yourself in a world of which you know nothing—the *interior* world. You were only familiar with the external one." A pause, then he added: "Mr. Peter Marsden told me that a book of Trent's had interested you. That fact, and your going to Number 77, and your appearance makes what I've told you very obvious."

Rendell put his cigarette in the ash-tray, then stared uneasily at his companion. Wrayburn's analysis compelled respect.

"Look here," he said at last, "I may as well admit——"

But Wrayburn waved him into silence.

"Confirmation is of no interest. It's all very obvious—and rather tedious. I merely wanted to demonstrate that *how long* one person has known another is not remotely to do with anything. That had to be established before we could discuss Trent productively."

Rendell realised that he must surrender all hope of gaining the initiative in this conversation unless he could produce an analysis of Wrayburn as penetrating as the one just delivered by that psychologist. Recognising his inability, he said slowly:

"Couldn't say much about you, I'm afraid. Nothing positive, anyway. I could only say what you're *not*."

"That's intelligent—quite intelligent," Wrayburn replied, a sudden flush invading his countenance and vanishing instantly. "Just one minute! This tea is not right."

"Have some black coffee?"

"If I had one cup of *black coffee*, my good man, I should suffer certain peculiar physical disabilities for a fairly extensive period."

He had the tea removed, then, having asked Rendell, who was about to light another cigarette, whether this was an essential proceeding on his part and, if not, whether he would refrain—he proceeded to give a brief account of himself, which was a miracle of lucidity and detachment.

Wrayburn did not remember his parents, did not admit the existence of relatives, had no money, but had, nevertheless, acquired an extensive education by means of scholarships, and a clairvoyant faculty for detecting anything that was going for nothing. On coming down from Cambridge, this faculty—and a gift for organisation—had enabled him to make what he referred to as a "tightrope" living in a series of miscellaneous activities. He had served as a courier to a rich American family. He had been a lecturer, an interpreter, a translator, and a reviewer. He had travelled as a tutor with several distinguished families. He had catalogued private libraries, organised a medical conference, and generally held a bewildering number of appointments—all of a transitory nature.

Rendell watched him as he listened, amazed at the will of this fragile-looking man who narrated his experiences with the detachment of an onlooker. There was heroism and pathos in this creature pitting himself against the world and wresting from it a precarious and solitary existence. For Rendell was convinced that Wrayburn was solitary, although it transpired that he had numerous acquaintances. Also, it was very obvious that, physically, Wrayburn lived on the frontier of life. His references to his health, and to the many and involved precautions necessary "to enable him to function," were too numerous and detailed to leave a remnant of doubt. Finally, Rendell decided that only his eyes were alive, but in them shone the light of a cold implacable will. He had no illusions about himself, and none concerning the world outside him.

"I am a completely negative and wholly conscious person," he announced in conclusion, his right hand coaxing his beard to its maximum dimension. "I am outside life as it is lived. I know it. I accept it. People like me have to come to terms with actuality, once and finally. I have looked at life through the dirty windows of innumerable bed-sitting-rooms in many cities. My destiny is to observe. That's why your appearance told me a good deal."

"Told you a damned lot, in my opinion," Rendell admitted grudgingly.

Wrayburn regarded him intently.

"And—be frank, you understand—do you mean that *my* appearance doesn't tell you a good deal?"

"No, not particularly. Of course——"

But Wrayburn leaned towards him, then asked quickly, indicating his clothes with a swift gesture:

"This suit—for instance—tie, shirt, and so on. Wouldn't you *guess*, from their general neatness and all that—that this rig-out is the *only one* I possess? Wouldn't you—wouldn't you?" he asked, with lightning rapidity, the sudden flush invading his features and vanishing instantly. "You wouldn't! Really! If you happened to notice me in the street, you'd think—would you?—that I was more or less a normal person? Would you? Say if you wouldn't."

"Yes, of course," Rendell lied. "Why not?"

"That's all right, then. I only wanted to know. So, if you saw me in the street, you'd think—there's a student, rather a *neat* student. You would? That's all right then."

Rendell moved uneasily. Wrayburn was regarding him intently, although his right hand continued to supplicate his beard to greater endeavours. As Rendell saw it, this desire to be regarded as normal was significant. And it was pathetic.

Wrayburn made a swift motion of his hand, which was his method of indicating that another phase of their conversation had come to an end. Then he glanced at his watch.

"It's still early, but, nevertheless, I propose to go now. I am not very well. It's nothing. I know exactly how to deal with it. But, still, I think I shall go. I will meet you to discuss Trent shortly. Just one minute! I must think which day will suit *me*."

He withdrew into himself and remained motionless for some moments with closed eyes.

"Next Sunday. No! next *Monday*. After dinner. It will probably be wet, so you had better come to my room. I am at 4, Waldegrave Road, Fulham—for the minute. No, don't *remember* it—write it down. Here's a pencil and a piece of paper."

Rendell wrote it down.

Again Wrayburn's fingers snapped like revolver-shots—till the waiter brought his coat and hat. He made entirely certain that they were dry, then put on his overcoat, refusing the waiter's proffered assistance.

"Now, sir!" the latter exclaimed genially, turning to Rendell, who was waiting for his bill. "What shall we say? Three bob?"

"Very well," Rendell replied. "Three bob."

He gave the man three shillings and sixpence.

"I thank you. And now, you, sir——" the waiter went on. "Your bill is——"

"One and ninepence," Wrayburn interrupted in a tone of finality. "I did *not* have that extra pat of butter."

He gave the man one and elevenpence. Directly the waiter had retired, he turned to Rendell and said:

"Your bill was three shillings. Did you give the waiter sixpence?"

"I did. Why?"

"Fourpence would have been rather more than ten per cent. It's people like you who spoil waiters for people like me."

Rendell pondered this statement as he followed Wrayburn down the corkscrew stairway.

When they reached the pavement they discovered that it was raining heavily.

By a miracle, there was a taxi on the rank opposite. Rendell hailed it, then said to Wrayburn: "Could I take you as far as——"

"Jump in, jump in!" the latter exclaimed. "I'm getting wet."

Rendell got in, then heard Wrayburn say to the driver in a tone
of icy exactitude:

"Go, first, to 4, Waldegrave Road, Fulham. Then take this gentleman on to 77, Potiphar Street."

X

DURING the next few days Rendell made the commonplace discovery that until events cease to present themselves in a never-ending
sequence, leisure is lacking for an analysis of the more important of
them. Thus, although he made several appointments with himself—
at which he proposed to review his conversations with Rosalie Vivian, Vera Thornton, and Denis Wrayburn—he kept none of them
owing to new and unanticipated demands on his time and curiosity.

The first of these was the discovery of the extraordinary relations existing between Captain Frazer and his wife. Soon after his
arrival, Rendell had realised that these were far from normal, but
their actual complexity was not revealed till the morning following
his conversation with Wrayburn.

The manner of their revelation was somewhat dramatic, for
Captain Frazer—having had a bitter dispute with his wife during
breakfast—burst into Rendell's room at an early hour and straight-
way proceeded to narrate the long history of his wrongs with hysterical vehemence.

When Rendell could obtain a hearing, he attempted to suggest
that possibly Mrs. Frazer would object to the discussion of these
intimate details with a stranger. But he got no further, as Frazer
exclaimed:

"Never mind about her. She's all right. *She's* gone to the shops.
Yes, Captain Frazer's wife has gone to the shops—to haggle with
tradespeople, or to cajole them to wait a little longer for their
damned money! She's not got the pride of a rat! You're not married, I take it? Well, don't *you* marry out of your class. I did, and it's
dragged me down to this—to *this!*"

Quivering with indignation, he took a cigarette from Rendell's
case, which was open on the table.

"But I'll tell you something," he raced on, coming nearer to Rendell and speaking in a significant whisper, "this show of hers will go bust soon—and a blasted good job too! The sooner the better!"

Rendell said nothing. Frazer's exaltation at the imminence of an event which would involve his own destitution could only be witnessed in silent astonishment.

"She *lies*—do you know that? Take the lodgers here—will she admit the facts about them? Not she!" He laughed unpleasantly. "What about the woman in the room upstairs? Says she's a palmist and a clairvoyante. I ask you! Four or five men come very regularly to have their fortunes told. They must know them by heart. But *she* believes the woman's a palmist. Shall I tell you why?"

Rendell remained silent, so Frazer went on:

"Because she's about the only one who pays her rent regularly. That's why. There's sickening stinking humbug for you!"

But Rendell had had enough.

"Look here, Frazer," he said curtly, "I'm not too keen on discussing people in their absence——"

"I bet she discussed *me* in my absence! I bet she asked you not to pay your rent to me, or to lend me money. Yes or no?"

"Yes. And I said I wouldn't."

"I don't want any money out of this hole—and she knows it. I left here once—and I'll go again before long. I've some irons in the fire that would surprise Mrs. Basement."

Frazer paused, in order to allow Rendell time to appreciate that Mrs. Basement was a synonym for Mrs. Frazer, then he went on:

"I've friends—business deals—*she* knows nothing about. She thinks I'm a fixture here. I'll show her how much of a fixture I am before she's very much older."

"You left here once?" Rendell asked, curiosity overmastering him.

Frazer gave a shrill laugh.

"Yes I did! Well, when I say I left, it was more amusing than that. Here!" he exclaimed, seizing Rendell's arm. "Come downstairs. I'll show you something. You've time, I take it?"

Rendell allowed himself to be piloted down the basement stairs.

Eventually he was ushered into a small square room which looked out on to a neglected backyard.

"My study," Frazer announced.

Rendell looked round with some curiosity.

In a prominent position over the mantelpiece hung Frazer's commission in a narrow black frame. Suspended above it was a sword. A case containing three medals stood in the centre of a small table near the window. The walls were almost hidden by huge photographs of regimental groups—and nearly a dozen others, depicting a uniformed Frazer in a series of martial attitudes, his hand on his sword. Festooned round several of the frames were the dust-laden scarlet poppies of many Armistice Days.

The solitary chair the room contained was in the corner furthest from the fire, but at an angle from which a comprehensive view of these trophies was obtainable.

Frazer stood like a sentinel while Rendell examined these witnesses to his former glory.

"*This* is what I was. And you can see what I am—thanks to Mrs. Basement."

Rendell began to ponder the precise extent to which Mrs. Frazer could be regarded as responsible for the world war, when his speculations were interrupted by Frazer announcing:

"We'll go back to your room now. No objection, I take it. She may come back any minute. Not that she ever comes in here. I won't allow that."

When they had returned to his room, Rendell reminded the Captain that he had not revealed the circumstances in which he had left No. 77.

"I didn't leave—actually," Frazer cut in. "It was a trifle more subtle than that. I was left a little money a year or so ago. Not much, you understand. Well, I took a room here—and paid for it. And I insisted on being properly looked after. There was no doubt about that. They knew they had an ex-officer for a lodger, I can tell you."

Rendell stared so long at the gaunt emaciated figure that Frazer's right eye suddenly began to produce a series of winks with bewildering rapidity.

"But next time," he shouted, "next time I'm clearing out—and for good. Stay here with these nobodies for the rest of my life! Never—*never!* And I'll tell you something else. *She* won't, but I will. What about the great Mr. Trent, eh? What about him?"

"I don't follow you," Rendell replied truthfully.

"Don't you?" He came nearer Rendell, his face distorted by a leer. "Comes here to write his books—that's what you're told, aren't you?"

"That's what you told me."

"Bah!—only quoting her. She pretends to believe it. If it's true, you tell me this—why did none of his friends know he was here? Marsden didn't. I talked to him last night. He wouldn't believe that Trent had had rooms here for years. Neither would the woman who was with him, Vera Thornton. Fine woman that, by the way. Plenty of her—not one of these boys in skirts like most women are nowadays. Well, neither of them would believe it about Trent. They went to dine together to discuss it."

"And what is your explanation?" Rendell asked with simulated interest, for, actually, he was thanking destiny that Frazer had not interviewed Rosalie Vivian and knew nothing about her.

"Explanation! Obvious, my good sir. He used this house for his filthy affairs. There's a woman, an artist's model, who stays here sometimes, who knows more than she'll say. A red-haired beauty, who hasn't a farthing. But that's by the way. *That's* why Mr. Trent had those rooms all these years. And that Bible-punching wife of mine knows it. That's why our Mr. Trent bribed her by lending her money to keep the damned place going. Why——"

Frazer broke off abruptly. He was standing by the window.

"There she is! Mrs. Basement must have forgotten something. Bah! She looks like a servant. I'm getting out of this. I can't stand it for another second!"

He disappeared, and almost immediately the front door banged. But as, a moment later, Mrs. Frazer knocked on Rendell's door, it is probable that she had guessed the nature of her husband's activities during her absence.

"Come in," Rendell cried in response to the knock. "Oh, it's you, Mrs. Frazer. I——"

"He's not been troubling you, has he?" she asked tonelessly.

"Yes. He's been in here."

"Did he show you his room?"

"He did."

"I thought so. Always shows someone his room after we've had a row."

She stood motionless, holding a heavily-laden shopping basket with both hands.

"Did he mention Mr. Trent?"

"Yes, I'm afraid he did."

"Ah well!"

She put the basket on the floor with a weary movement.

"He's going to make trouble," she added.

"You mean that he's discovered that Mr. Trent's friends did not know he had rooms here, and——" Rendell hesitated.

"Yes, that's what's worrying me. He loves to think the worst. And he'll borrow money, if he can, from the people who call to inquire. He had some from Mr. Marsden last night."

Rendell turned a laugh into a cough, then said sympathetically:

"I'm afraid he gives you plenty to worry about."

"Worry!"

And then, mechanically and in a drab tone, she enumerated certain of the more quotable of her husband's activities. Rendell learned that, should a prospective lodger call when his wife was out, he would give him or her instant possession of a vacant room, providing something was paid there and then to him on account. Also, ignoring her entreaties, he would collect a part of the rent from the less reputable lodgers, giving a receipt for the whole of it. In addition, if a bottle of whisky was left out in any of the rooms, the Captain would help himself frequently and with liberality. And, finally, that in a number of ways—some of which Mrs. Frazer preferred not to mention—he conducted underground warfare against her, and the lodgers who were loyal to her, ceaselessly and with great cunning.

When she had finished, Rendell turned to her and said emphatically:

"Now, you listen to me, Mrs. Frazer. If you drift on like this, he'll bring you and himself to the gutter. Why don't you allow him thirty shillings a week on the express condition that he gets out—and stays out."

There was a long silence. Then, slowly, she raised her eyes till her glance met his. It told him that she loved her wreck of a husband.

"Good God," he said softly, "good God."

Then, fearing he might have embarrassed her, he added with an attempt at jocularity:

"Well, it's fortunate you haven't any children."

"I have one," she replied enigmatically, then picked up the heavy basket and went slowly out of the room. . . .

As a result of these disclosures, and a long conversation with the servant, Mary, which occurred soon after Mrs. Frazer had left him, Rendell gained an accurate knowledge of No. 77 and its lodgers.

Briefly summarised, he learned that the house contained a fixed and a floating population and that, roughly, the fixed were Mrs. Frazer's allies, and the floating were the Captain's. The term, fixed, was a relative one, however, as it was conferred on anyone who had been in the house for three months and had no immediate intention of departing. But this stable element was in the minority—and whether or not the palmist and clairvoyante was to be numbered among its members was a problem which would have extended a subtler brain than Rendell's.

But one thing was definite. Respectability had only two representatives. One was a withered old lady, who spoke to no one and lived with a cat in a small room on the second floor. The other was a faded and angular Civil Servant of about fifty, who was nicknamed Clockwork Charlie, owing to the regularity of his daily departures and returns.

Another member of the fixed population was a woman gossip writer employed by a pictorial daily paper, who went to bed one night in seven, and lived exclusively on tinned food. She was as thin as a fountain-pen, but had sharply-cut remarkable features and fiercely intelligent grey eyes. It was whispered that she was of a good family, and that her journalistic activities were the spoils of a battle for independence which she had waged and won in the study of a mellow parsonage in the west of England. Probably this was a fact, for she possessed one of those upper-class voices which charm and madden simultaneously. You heard it long after she had ceased to speak. It was incisive, authoritative, cultured, and triumphant over all competitors. It was heard frequently, for she had a telephone in her room. When she was not in, the bell rang out, hour after hour. When she was in, the voice rang out, hour after hour. She went everywhere, interviewed everyone who came into the news, "covered" every social function—and got thinner and thinner, and more and more vital, as a result of this whirlwind existence. She was killing herself, and no one dared tell her so. Somehow, she compelled admiration and affection. That she belonged wholly to her job was evidenced by the fact that she cried if her "copy" was altered.

The room opposite hers was occupied by a young man of about twenty-three. He was remarkably handsome in a dashing rather desperate way, but had two peculiarities not wholly desirable in a lodging-house. One was that he was unable to remain motionless for a moment: the other was that he could not endure a second's silence. He shaved to the strains of "Hold Me—Never Let Me Go," emitted by an unusually powerful gramophone. It, or the wireless, performed whenever he was in his room. So you always knew.

He had a host of men and women friends—mostly long and thin, and with very definite voices. Rakish cars, laden with a selection of them, often drew up outside No. 77 and hooted—and continued to hoot—till he appeared. He returned usually at three in the morning. If alone, he leaped up the stairs whistling. If with others, the cavalcade would ascend, frequently pausing for one, or other, or all, to emit certain very definite statements in very definite voices. On reaching his room, when alone, the gramophone would immediately begin to function—a cushion having been placed upon it, since the young man held the theory that this device made the instrument wholly inaudible to others, while permitting him to hear it in all its accustomed power.

In due course, Rendell was interested to ascertain that this young man was regarded by his fellow lodgers as a student.

The student was on the friendliest terms with the lady jour-nalist. Frequently, while he was dressing for dinner and she was opening tins—banging them on the floor to expedite the opera-tion—they would shout the liveliest comments to one another, peppering their remarks with the most intimate details concerning the lives of well-known persons—in a manner that was instructive and stimulating to less well-informed people.

The floating population was drab by comparison with these vivid personalities, but, if it lacked colour, it possessed mystery. Its members consisted of men who were either nondescript or sinister-looking, and whose activities could not be imagined. Their stay was short and their departure usually abrupt. They never paid their rent when it was due, never paid it in full, and rarely paid it at all. They were always in their rooms—or never in them. They seldom received letters, but had interminable conversations on the telephone at the back of the hall, to which one could listen for half an hour without deriving any clear conception as to their purport. This floating population was either extremely active, or lacked occupation—and one or two of its members only went out by night.

Rendell obtained this graphic account of the lodgers from the servant, Mary, whose faculty for observation impressed him by its breadth and penetration. Subsequent experience only confirmed the facts as narrated by her. Nevertheless, two minor problems, and a major one, presented themselves to Rendell. Why did the withered old lady with the cat, and the faded angular Civil Servant, live in such surroundings? These were the minor problems, but Mary solved them instantly by explaining that the old lady could hear nothing, and that the Civil Servant loved noise. "He'd be lonely without it," she added disparagingly.

The major problem was Ivor Trent's presence in such a house—but Rendell did not mention this to Mary. He gave her five shil-lings, however, thereby obtaining the first claim on her services.

Soon after his conversation with her, Rendell went to luncheon, returning at about three o'clock. He encountered Captain Frazer in the hall, who made it clear in a number of staccato sentences that in future he would deal with inquirers about Trent. He implied that his object in so doing was to spare Rendell the irritation of continual interruptions, but the latter was not deceived. Frazer's curiosity had been quickened by the discovery that Marsden did not know that Trent had had rooms in the house for years, and the Captain was now determined to ascertain whether all Trent's friends were equally ignorant. Their brief conversation revealed to Rendell that Frazer had always disliked Trent and was jealous of him, and that therefore any circumstances unfavourable to him gave Frazer an underground satisfaction.

But the number of callers diminished rapidly. Every post brought a pile of letters for Trent, but callers at No. 77 became less and less, greatly to Frazer's annoyance.

In fact that afternoon only Marsden appeared. He arrived at about five o'clock, brushed Frazer aside, and made his way to Rendell's room in a state of considerable excitement.

After the briefest of greetings, and with no reference to the manner in which he had contradicted Rendell's statements the evening before—statements which Marsden's subsequent inquiries had established as facts—he shot a number of questions at Rendell with great volubility.

"Well, what do you think about all this? Is he better? Have you talked to any of the people who have called to inquire? Has he asked to see me? I've been thinking about this all day and can make nothing of it. I resent his deceiving me. I tell you that—flat! There's a mystery behind all this, and I doubt if it's a pleasant one."

"And I'll tell you something else too," Marsden raced on, as Rendell remained silent, "I dined with Vera Thornton last night. She's known Trent about three years and saw a lot of him till just recently. Well, she knew nothing about his being here. But that's not the point. Trent never told me how well he knew her, although I met her once at his flat."

"Why the devil should he?" Rendell asked mildly.

"Because I'm an old friend of his. That's why. You seem to forget that he and I have been friends for years."

"I've not forgotten," Rendell said slowly, "that you told me last Sunday that you didn't know much about him."

"Damn what I said last Sunday. The night before I'd had a talk with that Denis Wrayburn, and he'd muddled me. Incidentally, I loathe and detest Wrayburn more than anyone I've ever met."

"Is that why you described me to him, told him my movements, and then let him go to look for me?"

"Yes, it was—if you want to know."

"I did want to know, that's why I asked the question."

"Wanted to see what you'd make of him," Marsden said quickly. "Did he find you?"

"He did, and we dined together."

"Well, and what did you make of him? Had he a theory about Trent being here? He's a theory about most things."

"He wasn't in the least interested."

Marsden gave an indignant shout.

"He wouldn't be! He's an inhuman icy little egotist! God! I can't stand him! Sometimes he impresses you when you're with him, but—later—you find that everything he said was pretentious rubbish. Vera loathes him. You did too, I'll bet."

Rendell hesitated.

"I'd find it difficult to say just what I do think of him," he said at last. "But he's not a negligible person."

"Oh well, never mind him! Look here—I may as well tell you everything—though this is between ourselves, mind! I like Vera. I like her a lot after our talk last night. But I've made a discovery about her."

"And what's that?" Rendell asked, as Marsden suddenly became silent.

"She's afraid of something. I'm certain of it. And I believe it's something to do with Trent. Of course I may be wrong, but she seemed odd. And—and——"

Again Marsden broke off, but almost immediately he went on:

"Well—this *really* is between ourselves, mind!—she wanted to come back here at ten o'clock to see if Trent was quieter. That struck me as damned peculiar. Why, we didn't leave this place till after seven! Also, from something she said I gathered that she didn't think Trent had many women friends—lot of acquaintances, of course, but not many women friends. And she seemed damned anxious to know just what sort of a person *you* were."

"Did you enlighten her?"

"I told her that you were a well-known consulting mining engineer, who'd been all over the place, and made a good deal of money. And I explained that, till last Sunday, I hadn't seen you for years. But what the hell did she want to know about you for?"

"All very mysterious, Marsden, I agree."

"Anyway, she's very intelligent. She knows several languages and has a job in the foreign department of a bank. Did you know? And she reads a lot. She knew my work quite well. She really *is* very intelligent—attractive too. I'm seeing her again tomorrow. In fact, I mean to see her pretty often."

A long silence, then Marsden suddenly exclaimed:

"Look here, Rendell! I'd like to ask you a straight question."

"Go right ahead."

"*Do* you know Trent?"

"No."

"Never seen him?"

"No."

Marsden hesitated, then risked it.

"And your story as to why you came here is a true one and omits nothing?"

"Yes."

"Well, all I can say is that the whole damned thing from first to last is the most extraordinary business I've ever run into."

He rose, collected his crutches, then announced with great emphasis:

"But one thing is certain. I'm going to get to the bottom of all this. I'm going to find out why Trent's been here for years and told none of his friends. I've made up my mind about that. I'm going to find out."

Rendell rose and got Marsden's overcoat.

"Well, I don't want to discourage you," he said slowly, "but I've a feeling that you won't find it an easy job. Still, I wish you luck. I'll be seeing you before long, I expect."

XI

W{HEN} Marsden had gone, Rendell looked round the room, surprised to find himself alone. Soon, however, he found he was restless and irritable, and in a manner hitherto unknown.

Sentences from the many conversations he had had since his arrival at No. 77, nearly forty-eight hours ago, shot across his memory. Then, one after another, he seemed to see Rosalie Vivian, Vera Thornton, and Denis Wrayburn. He felt that each was a character from a different drama, in each of which he was destined to become involved. Yet, from another angle, the whole situation was fantastic. These people were strangers to him. He had met them owing to a sudden interest in Ivor Trent—a man he did not know and had not seen—a man who was lying ill upstairs in this impossible house.

But it was useless to speculate about him. It would be comparable to an attempt to assemble a jig-saw puzzle, of which many of the sections were missing.

He stood motionless, staring into the fire, amazed by the extent to which his curiosity had been captured by Trent. He felt that now—at this actual moment—he must take some action that might produce additional data concerning him. Otherwise, he would spend the evening in a mental cul-de-sac. He must find someone who knew Trent. His conversation with the servant had revealed that none of the present lodgers had met him. There was nothing to be learned therefore from them.

He drew the curtain apart and looked out. The sky glimmered with the light of a hidden moon. The pavements were wet but the rain had ceased. Rendell decided to go and have a drink somewhere before dinner.

Then he remembered the barmaid who had called to ask about Trent. Rummy! Yes, that was what she was called, and she served in the long bar of the Cosmopolitan. He would go there and see what happened.

He left the house, walked quickly towards the King's Road, half regretting that the decision to visit Rummy necessitated going to the West End. Already he had become subject to the illusion, which Chelsea creates, that its unique atmosphere removes it from the common categories of town, country, or suburb. Physically, London may be near, but—psychically—it is far removed. It is true that the foundations of this illusion tremble once the King's Road is encountered. The unending roar of that long narrow thorough-fare disturbs the calm certainties of even the ripest Chelsea residents. Rendell, however, preserved a remnant of illusion by taking a taxi on reaching the King's Road, telling the driver to go to the Cosmopolitan.

On arrival, he glanced through the glass door before entering. Rummy was on duty, and Rendell believed that, had he known nothing of her, he would have detected her superiority to her surroundings. The other barmaids were typical—Rummy was individual. The contour and expression of the face, the line of the figure, every movement, indefinably asserted the possession of some quality which had triumphantly survived its environment.

He went to the bar and seated himself on a high stool. Rummy went to take his order.

"Well, you don't remember me?"

She looked up at him quickly.

"Yes I do. You're the gentleman I saw at Potiphar Street yesterday. Nice of you to come so soon." She smiled, then added: "Didn't think you'd come yet a bit—even if you came at all."

A man a few yards to Rendell's right rapped the counter and Rummy went to attend to him.

"How much, m'dear?"

"What! You going, uncle? Short visit to-night. Let's see. One and nine."

"I'm not very well, m'dear. It's me knees."

Rendell glanced at him. He was stout, heavily built, with a bulky head and projecting teeth.

"It's me knees," he repeated. "Otherwise—all right. There you are, m'dear."

He went out slowly, leaning heavily on his stick.

"That's uncle," Rummy explained, "been here every day, so

they say, since his wife died twenty-five years ago. But never mind about him. How's Mr. Trent?"

"Somewhat better, I'm told."

"That's something, anyway. Funny his being taken queer like that."

"Very," Rendell agreed. "I'll have a glass of sherry. What are you going to have?"

"I'll have a packet of cigarettes, if you don't mind."

She got his drink, then, as a number of men entered the bar, she was busy for some minutes.

Rendell amused himself by watching the expressions of the men she was serving. Most of them looked at her with varying degrees of appetite. One calculated her points with the cynical appraisement of long experience: another adopted a confidential air implying intimacy: a third inquired loudly as to her activities the night before, guffawing answers to his own questions: a fourth leered at her, believing he was smiling: while the fifth stared at her breasts with an expression of leaden apathy. All were over fifty. There were not more than three young men in the crowded bar.

Having served their drinks, Rummy returned to Rendell.

"Yes, funny being taken queer like that," she began, picking up their conversation where they had dropped it. "Did give me a shock when I saw that paragraph. Couldn't believe it. Quite upset me, it did."

"Did you know where he lived, Rummy?"

"No. I didn't know anything about him—really. Just knew his name and that he wrote books. That's all. Sometimes he wouldn't come in for months together."

While she spoke, she wiped the counter, or emptied an ash-tray, or rinsed a glass in a hidden receptacle, or polished it till it was ready for use. But she performed these activities automatically, giving Rendell her essential attention. Also, while she talked, she glanced round mechanically, noting arrivals and departures, distributing salutations—and frequently darted away to execute an order or to receive payment.

"Yours is a hell of a life, Rummy!" Rendell exclaimed when she returned after her sixth trip to a customer.

"Oh well, it's a job. You last about twelve years in a bar, you know—if you're lucky."

"And then?"

"Well, if you're in a place like this, and you want to stay on, you become a dispensing barmaid."

"A *what!*"

"Dispensing barmaid. You know—you're not in a public bar like this, you're in a bar behind, and serve the waiters who come with orders from the café."

"That must be pretty uproarious, I imagine. What do they pay you?"

"Twenty-six shillings a week. But there's tips, of course."

"There would need to be. And what time do you start?"

Rummy laughed gaily.

"Well, I never! You're just like Mr. Trent. He always wanted to know everything about my job. Ask questions, and listen for hours —sometimes he would."

"Well, and what time *do* you start?"

"Nine thirty. You see, all these racks here have to be scrubbed each morning. We do two hours charing first thing. Look at my hands! And then there's requisitions and stock to check, and one thing and another."

"Tell me this—do you have all the drinks you're stood?"

"Oh no—couldn't! We keep one under the counter and produce it for the customer to see. Then, later, we take the money. Some of them give us money. Sometimes we say we'd rather have cigarettes—like I did to you."

Again she laughed.

Rendell gazed at her in silence. Here she was, in this bar— young, attractive, virginal—for hours every day, surrounded by smoke, laughter, coarse jokes. A human target!

"What are you thinking about?" she asked.

"I was thinking that it's a hell of a world, Rummy."

"Well, really, I shall begin to think you *are* Mr. Trent in a minute! He used to say it was a hell of a world. And the questions he used to ask me! You've no idea."

"Didn't talk about himself much, then?"

"Oh no! He's not like the others. He's strong, so he doesn't have to tell you all his troubles, like most of them. I never guessed he was so well known. The paper said *eminent*."

"Ever read any of his books?"

"Yes, I read one. He knows everything, if you ask me."

Rendell got off the stool and held out his hand.

"I must go, but I'll come again."

They shook hands.

"I've enjoyed our talk," he added.

"So have I. Do come again. It makes such a difference having a chat with someone—well, you know—like you—sometimes. If it's only for a few minutes. You've no idea what a difference it makes. You get miserable sometimes—feel you'd do anything—then someone comes in, not like the usual lot, and you feel all right again."

"I'll come in before long."

"Will you? I'd be glad if you would. Good night."

"Good night, Rummy."

He bought a paper as he left the bar, then went to dine at an obscure restaurant where he was unlikely to find anyone he knew.

During dinner he went over his conversation with Rummy, seeking to identify himself imaginatively with her existence. Was that what had interested Trent? And was he a writer because he possessed this faculty for identifying himself with the thoughts and emotions of others to an exceptional degree? Anyhow, one thing was definite: there was no mystery in Rummy's relations with Trent.

Rendell dined quickly, then glanced at the paper while he smoked a cigarette over his black coffee. But, although the news from every quarter was sensational, it failed to hold his interest. He felt he was waiting for the end of an interval in an exciting play. But the fact that he could be so absorbed in the destinies of a number of people, unknown three days ago, clearly revealed the extent of his own loneliness.

"I knew I was pretty down to it," he said to himself, "when I asked Marsden to dine with me last Sunday, but I didn't know how bad it was."

He rose, paid the bill, then drove back to Chelsea. When he

opened the front door, a man was descending the stairs. Rendell glanced at him, then said instinctively:

"You won't mind my asking, but are you the doctor?"

"I am. I've just left Trent."

"I wonder if you'd mind giving me a minute. I shan't keep you long."

"That's all right."

"Good! Thanks. Come in here—and what about a drink? Whisky and soda?"

"That's an idea. Thanks."

The doctor glanced round the room mechanically. He was about thirty-five and was obviously tired. He sank into a chair, then watched Rendell's movements as if glad to give his attention to the trivial.

"That about right?" Rendell asked, handing him a drink.

"Drop more soda. Thanks. Not sorry to have a drink. Pretty stiff day—and I was called out in the night."

"Well, it's a damned shame to keep you, but it won't be for long. I don't know Trent, but I've a letter and a message for him—both pretty important, I gather. So I want to know what you think of him."

"Nothing organically wrong. I should say he's been in a highly nervous condition for some months—and has had some kind of a shock."

"You wouldn't let him see anyone?"

"He wouldn't, if I said he could. Any more than he'll open that pile of letters he's got up there. Anyhow, he's too excited to see people."

"He's chosen a lively house to be ill in."

The doctor smiled.

"I ought to have had him out of it on Sunday night. Afterwards, he refused to go, and I thought it best to humour him. Ever seen his rooms? Oh well, they are all right. He's really got a little flat up there—and an attractive one. There's a door at the bottom of the staircase. It's quite cut off from the rest of the house. In fact, with its double doors and windows, it's remarkably quiet."

There was a silence, then Rendell asked:

"Has he a night nurse?"

"No, only a day one. She'll go soon. Mrs. Frazer's going to take Trent on. She'll get extra help to allow her to do so. Incidentally, that is Trent's idea, not mine."

Then, after a long pause, the doctor added:

"Of course it's a queer case. No doubt about that. I see plenty of neurotic cases—God knows!—nowadays. But he's a bit new to me. Don't repeat this, but—when you're with him—you feel that he's longing for you to go."

"To *go*," Rendell echoed with considerable emphasis.

"Yes. He wants to be alone. The nurse irritates him—I irritate him. He doesn't mind Mrs. Frazer. He's used to her, I suppose. If I called another doctor in to-night, I'd bet a lot that he would say Trent was well."

"Do you mean that?"

"I do indeed. Of course, he'd see he was nervous, excited, irritable—but he'd think a few days' rest would put that right."

"Yes, but after all," Rendell protested, "the man collapsed in the hall on Sunday night—and you don't do that for nothing."

"I agree—but a highly-strung man like Trent can do it without it meaning a vast amount. I attend a number of artists, and I know what tricks their nerves can play them. Anyhow, if you've a letter and a message for him, send them up. He'll ignore them, but you'll have no further responsibility."

He finished his drink, rose, then added :

"Still, I'm glad I was called in. Not sorry to have met Trent. I read one of his books—I forget the title—but it interested me. A patient of mine told me to read it—a barrister. Every read any?"

"I read one—read it three times."

"Really? Odd you should be in this house."

"Yes, isn't it? But I mustn't keep you. I'll send up the letter and the message."

"Best thing you can do. Well, I'll get on. Good night."

"Good night—and many thanks."

Rendell went to the front door to see him off, then returned to his room.

He lit a cigarette and began to pace slowly up and down.

PART III

LABYRINTH

I

VERA THORNTON wandered restlessly round the sitting-room of her flat in Bloomsbury, glancing at the clock every other minute. Then, with an impatient gesture, she sat in a low chair by the fire and closed her eyes. Several minutes passed, but she did not move.

The room was square, well furnished, in a manner that made no concession to modern ideas—with the exception that the walls were almost bare—but its chief characteristic was an absence of personality. Its atmosphere proclaimed that it was occupied, but not lived in, and this fact was significant, as the flat had been hers for two years. Furniture, colour scheme, intimate possessions, lacked individuality. They were mute observers, not collaborators, and so they remained anonymous.

She continued to sit motionless, leaning towards the fire, but the immobility of her attitude indicated conflict rather than repose. The body was taut, the features tense, and the closed eyes suggested concentration, not peace. An observer of any penetration would have imagined that she had disciplined herself to remain physically inert while inwardly raging with impatience.

She started violently when the telephone bell rang.

She let it ring for some moments, however, while she went to a mirror, arranged her hair, and assumed a social expression as if a visitor were about to be announced.

At last she picked up the receiver.

"Yes."

"It's Peter—Peter Marsden."

"Well?"

"Well—as you were so insistent—I went to Number 77——"

"You're not ringing up from there?" she interrupted quickly.

"No—this is a public box. I've just left. There's no great news about Trent. He's not delirious now and——"

She made a muffled exclamation.

"What?"

"Nothing," she replied. "Go on."

"I had a long talk with Captain Frazer. He took me down to his study. You've no idea what an odd room——"

"Yes, yes! Well?"

"How impatient you are! Well, the gallant Captain has one or two theories, not too favourable to Trent and——"

"What do you mean? What did he say?"

"Oh, he suggested that Trent had those rooms not to work in but to facilitate his amorous affairs."

Her hands tightened convulsively, but she made no sound.

"Frazer backs his theory," Marsden went on, "by saying that it's the only explanation of his friends' ignorance concerning those rooms. The Captain is very communicative, particularly if you lend him half a crown. But, all the same, I fancy he knows more than he says."

"Why? What do you mean?"

"How intense you are! I only mean that he gives you a look implying he could say more if he chose. After all, his wife was looking after Trent when he was delirious and so——"

"Did Frazer mention me?"

"Wait a minute—I must think. Oh yes, he quoted you as being one of those who knew Trent and yet was ignorant that he had those rooms. And he added that you ought to have known."

"What did he mean by that?"

"My dear girl, I don't know. Probably that you'd known Trent some time and that therefore it was odd. But that's enough about Potiphar Street. Look here, I've got to see you again—and soon. I can't get you out of my head, do you know that? Keep thinking about you. . . . Are you there?"

"Yes, yes. I was thinking. We'll meet to-morrow night, if you like. Come here at about seven. Did you see Rendell?"

"No, I did *not* see Rendell!" Marsden exclaimed irritably. "I never cared much about him and—the last few days—I like him less than ever. What the devil is he doing at Potiphar Street, anyway?"

"But he's reliable, isn't he? I mean, you'd trust him, wouldn't you?"

"Oh yes, of course! If Rendell said he'd keep his mouth shut, he'd keep it shut. I admit that—but it doesn't make me like him."

"Still, you're certain of it?"

"Yes, quite certain. You are an odd person. What's Rendell to you? I believe you're a dark horse. Now I must get on. I've work to do. But I'll come at seven to-morrow, and I want to talk to you rather seriously. I liked you a lot, you know, even the first time I saw you at Trent's flat, but you wouldn't look at me then. Till to-morrow."

"Yes, to-morrow. Good-bye."

She replaced the receiver but did not move. Several minutes passed, then, with sudden resolution, she touched the receiver—hesitated—and failed to remove it. But her thoughts evidently proved so disturbing that a moment later she snatched the receiver and rapidly dialled a number.

At last a voice responded to the summons.

"I want to speak to Mr. Rendell."

"I'll see if he's in. What name shall I say?"

"It's a private call."

"Oh, very well. Hold the line."

Vera waited, drumming the table with her fingers. The delay seemed interminable, then she heard:

"Rendell speaking. Who is it?"

"It's—Vera Thornton."

"Hullo! How are you? What can I do for you? Anything?"

"Yes, as it happens, you can. Would—would you mind coming here—now? I'm in my flat in Bloomsbury. It's—well—important, or I wouldn't trouble you. Do you think you could come now?"

"Yes, I'm free enough. You mean *now*, literally?"

"Yes, if you could."

"Right! What's the address?"

She gave it to him, then added:

"It's good of you to come."

"That's all right."

She put down the receiver, then passed the palms of her hands over her forehead and thick black hair. She repeated the movement several times, as if to still tumultuous thoughts. Some moments later she rose wearily and went into the bedroom to change.

Long before she expected it, the sound of the bell pealed through the flat.

"You've been very quick."

"I came in a taxi. Am I too early?"

"No, please come in."

Rendell followed her into the sitting-room, trying to appear at ease with little success.

"Do sit down," she said abruptly, "and—and try one of these cigarettes."

"Thanks. Are you on your own here?"

"Yes. I've been here for two years."

"I see. Very central, of course."

A long silence followed. Any attempt at small talk was ludicrous. Vera stared into the fire and Rendell sat opposite her, glancing more than once at her powerful figure and dark fanatical eyes.

"Can I trust you—really trust you?"

The deep tone of her voice, breaking the long silence, almost startled him:

"Wait!" she exclaimed, just as he was about to reply. "I've only met you once—in that awful house. You'll think me mad, but—but I've *got* to confide in someone. I believe I can trust you. That's why I asked you to come here to-night."

Her submissive tone, and the absence of that defensive armour she had worn at their first meeting, so surprised Rendell that he hesitated before replying.

"Anything you tell me will go no further," he said simply. "You can rely on that absolutely. But I'd like to know if you've told anyone else what you propose telling me."

"No—no one. And I can't tell you all."

The blood invaded her cheeks so swiftly that in an instant she was scarlet.

Rendell looked away, greatly embarrassed, but almost immediately she went on:

"It's about Ivor and myself. I've got to tell you. You'll see why later."

She passed her hand across her forehead.

"I don't know where to begin. I'll have to start some way back, I suppose. It will be rather long, I'm afraid."

"Say what you want to in your own way. It won't go an inch further."

"I'd better begin with my family. They live in the Midlands. I've two brothers—one twenty-six, the other twenty-five. I'm twenty-four. And I've three sisters younger than I am—the youngest is twenty-one. My father is a business man, rich and—notorious."

"In what way notorious?" Rendell asked as she broke off.

"Oh, for affairs with women—nothing more interesting than that. He doesn't care what anyone thinks, and when he's drunk he will do literally anything. More than once he's brought one of his women to the house."

"That's not too good, I admit. What did your mother think about it?"

"I doubt if my mother has thought about anything for years. I imagine that her wedding night was the real date of her death—whatever the actual one may prove to be. She had six children—one a year—and after that I should think she was only too glad when my father became openly promiscuous."

She spoke with such bitterness that Rendell could only wait for her to continue.

"I won't go into details about my brothers and sisters. I'll only say that they are *his* children—and leave it at that. Anyway, you wouldn't believe me if I told you the facts. My brothers are in my father's business, but they do practically nothing. And my sisters concentrate on getting a good time. My father, as you can imagine, is not in a strong position to restrain them in any way. When they want money, they blackmail him for it—politely and successfully. The house is pandemonium—a good example of meaningless modern existence."

She attempted a laugh as she took a cigarette from the box by her side.

"You've made it very plain to me why you cleared out," Rendell said slowly.

"Why—and how—I cleared out may interest you. When I explain that I was a student, that I worked hard, won scholarships, and so on, you will be able to imagine what my life was like in that hell of a house. But you won't be able to imagine what it was like when I found myself a prisoner in it with nothing to do. That happened when I was twenty."

"No, that couldn't have been easy. What did you do?"

"Read Ivor Trent's books."

She looked at him oddly, then went on:

"I read his books. I read them again and again. He seemed like a god to me. I knew whole pages by heart. He became my idol, something to worship in the midst of noise, mental squalor, and filth. He represented everything I admired—everything that gave life meaning. He was my ideal—made flesh. That may sound cheap, sentimental, hysterical. But not to those who have had to find a dream, or just die inch by inch."

Her tone suggested all this was so familiar that it had become monotonous.

"And how long did that last?" Rendell asked after a long silence.

"About a year. Then two things happened. The first was that I came into a few hundreds which an aunt had left me, but which I did not get till I was twenty-one. The second was that I went mad."

Rendell's astonishment produced a peal of laughter from Vera which was too near hysteria to reassure him.

"Yes, I went mad," she repeated. "But, first, I must tell you that I had written to Ivor and he had answered my letter. Well, when I came into that money I packed a bag, said nothing to my family, and came to London."

"To Trent?"

"Yes, but he had no idea I was arriving. It was the act of a fanatic. I *was* a fanatic. What a pity you do not know his elegant flat near Cork Street! Still, try to imagine the scene. Ivor at home, and alone. A ring at the bell. A young woman, with bag, facing her ideal—believing he would be her destiny. Why don't you laugh?"

"I don't think it very funny," Rendell replied. "Did he?"

"He was—interested. I can't think of a better word. He soon realised my situation, my emotions—everything! It was impressive how quickly he identified himself with my state. Also, he was very remarkable in appearance. So I was completely done for."

"But what on earth did he *do*?"

"Gave me tea—which was very orthodox of him, as tea forms a part of every English crisis. Then he rang up a man and put him off. And then—well—he cross-examined me so subtly that I believed I was telling him things spontaneously. We dined together and then he sent me to bed—early."

Again she laughed, finding it a little difficult to stop, and then leaned back in her chair pretending to be amused by Rendell's expression.

"Do you mean you slept in his flat?"

"Yes, in the spare room. Most decorous! And we had breakfast together, and he survived that searching ordeal—and remained my idol."

"Well, go on!" Rendell exclaimed impatiently as she remained silent, "you can't stop there."

"No—neither did he. But that comes later. He seemed rather glad I had turned up from nowhere. He'd just finished a book— perhaps that was why. Finally, he got me a room near his flat. I lived there, feeling I dwelt on the frontier of heaven."

"But didn't you write to your family?"

"Oh yes, I sent a line—with no address—saying I was in London and that I was never coming back."

"And you've never been back?"

"Never!" she exclaimed angrily. "I write twice a year to my mother, and she replies telling me what sort of weather they've been having. My break with them was final. I did achieve that."

"And then?"

But she did not answer. She rose and began to wander about the room. When she spoke, her sentences were disjointed. Rendell could not see her face.

"Well, eventually, he discovered—exactly—how I regarded him. That took some time. I mean, for him fully to realise. Then— well—he cured me. No, don't ask any questions! I—I can't tell you everything. I told you I couldn't. He showed me that he wasn't—well—precisely what I had imagined him to be. He came down from the pedestal very successfully—and he made me watch his descent."

Then, after a brief silence, she suddenly shouted:

"You needn't think I became his mistress—because I didn't!"

"But——"

"You don't believe that, of course?"

"I believe you," Rendell managed to say. "I can't see what you'd gain by lying to me."

There was a long silence. When she spoke, her voice was so low that he only just heard her.

"He humiliated me—in every way he could imagine. He showed me very clearly that he was not my Christmas-card conception of him. And—now—I hate him."

"You don't—you love him."

"Yes, I love him."

Her voice was so low that Rendell hardly heard the words.

The silence that followed seemed endless. The atmosphere was heavy with conflicting emotions.

At last she said in a harsh, metallic voice:

"Let's make this short. All this is a preface. Eventually, when he was bored, he got me a job. I was well educated. I knew several languages. He knows plenty of influential people—and he got me a job in the foreign department of a bank."

"How long ago was that?"

"Two years."

"But you've seen him since then, haven't you?" Rendell asked, mystified.

"Yes, when he sent for me. But I've not seen him for months."

She returned to her chair and faced him.

"Now, listen! I've trusted you as if you were God. No one knows what I've told you. But I had to tell you because I'm terrified."

"Terrified!"

"Yes, he's been delirious. No, wait, wait! *Delirious*. God knows what he may have said. Listen! Mrs. Frazer was with him—and I'm afraid of her husband. He knows something. Yes—he—does! I can tell by the way he looks at me. He might blackmail me. I can't sleep, I tell you!"

"But I assure you," Rendell burst out, "there's nothing to fear from Captain Frazer. His wife knows him too well to tell him anything. That's definite."

"How do you know? How *can* you know?"

"I've had a long talk with her, and with Frazer, and with the servant. I know the situation in that house. No one would tell Frazer anything—or pay any attention to what he said. If he made up anything, I'd guarantee to make him take it back—and keep his mouth shut in future. That I can promise you—definitely."

"Yes, but—Peter Marsden! He's friendly with Frazer. He might hear something and—well——"

"Well?" Rendell echoed, as she did not continue.

"I think Marsden cares about me. You see, there's only one thing I can do—marry, and get away from London, and forget everything. It's my only chance. Don't imagine I could love Peter Marsden. All that's over. It's broken—and thrown away. I just want an existence now. That's all. I've had enough of asking a lot. I only want a little."

Then, after a brief pause, she asked:

"You're certain I'm—*safe*?"

"Quite certain. And if you want anything done at Number Seventy-seven, I will do it. I don't make promises lightly. But I do make that one. You can go to bed and sleep to-night."

She leaned forward and put her hand on his knee.

"You must have loved someone once to have understood and helped me like this. I shall never forget it. I'm strong, as a rule. I'm not an hysterical person. But Ivor was stronger—he's terribly strong."

"You're tired," Rendell said, rising, "so I shall go—and you must go to bed early. I expect we shall meet again before long."

He held out his hand, which she took in both of hers.

"No, don't come out," he went on. "You stay here. Good night."

"Good night."

He left her, and a moment later the front door closed behind him.

Vera buried her head in her hands and began to cry convulsively.

II

AT two o'clock on the following Saturday, Denis Wrayburn walked slowly down Potiphar Street on his way to No. 77. As it was warm, he had removed his hat, thereby permitting the errant breeze to do what it would with his long black hair. This fact, and his narrow bearded face, occasioned the mirth of an errand-boy, who emitted a series of caustic comments, followed by a number of hilarious whistles. Wrayburn, however, remained unaware of these attentions and continued to walk towards his destination—slowly enough to justify the assumption that he wished the proceeding to occupy the maximum amount of time.

When he reached the front door, his actions showed that he had experienced the usual difficulty in obtaining a response to a knock. It was also evident that he had evolved a technique to deal with it, for he grasped the knocker firmly and continued to deliver a series of resounding blows until the door was opened.

On this occasion Marsden performed that function.

"Hullo, it's you!" he exclaimed, without enthusiasm. "What the devil did you knock like that for?"

"To ensure speedy admittance," Wrayburn replied, investing each word with significance, greatly to Marsden's irritation.

"You don't care who has to open it, I suppose?"

"Not in the smallest degree."

He passed Marsden and entered Rendell's room—where he discovered Vera Thornton.

"Only you," was his greeting to her. Then he moved the chair Marsden had vacated nearer the fire, and sat down just as its late occupant returned.

"Well, of all the——"

But Wrayburn interrupted:

"Is Rendell expecting you two?"

"No, he isn't. Why?"

The silence to this query continued until eventually Marsden realised that it constituted Wrayburn's refutation of his claim to the chair. He glanced at Vera, who made a gesture expressive of her contempt for Wrayburn—which the latter intercepted.

"How are you progressing with your enquiries as to what Trent said when he was delirious?" Wrayburn asked her, with icy detachment.

Having thus gained complete psychological ascendancy over his companions, Wrayburn proceeded to ignore their presence.

But Marsden, who had obtained some sensational news, began to discuss it with Vera—hoping that Wrayburn's curiosity would prompt him to ask questions which he would refuse to answer.

"Yes, the nurse has gone," he said to Vera. "That's definite. And there's been the devil of a row between Mrs. Frazer and her husband. She's packing him off to her sister in Ramsgate. He's furious—but he'll go because of the money she's giving him. There's no end of changes."

But at this point he was interrupted by the sudden entrance of Frazer, who burst into the room in a state of considerable excitement.

"I'm leaving this hole," he announced, "and for good! Everything is to be turned upside down for Trent. My wife is going to nurse him, if you please. Extra help in the house—to enable her to do it. You know that, I take it? But *I'm* not saying all I've found out—not by a long way. I'm putting two and two together—things I've remembered, and things I've *heard*."

He paused, glanced at Vera, who became crimson, and was about to race on when Wrayburn extended a long thin arm towards him and demanded:

"Shut that door. There's a draught."

Frazer kicked the door to noisily, then went on:

"Nice thing, though, that I don't know who's in my own house. I find that artist's model has been here since Monday. I thought she'd turn up. *She* knows more than she'll say about our distinguished invalid——"

He got no further, for the door opened and Mrs. Frazer appeared, followed by the artist's model.

"I'm not having this," Mrs. Frazer announced.

"You're not having *what*, my good lady?" Frazer enquired from the eminence of his dignity.

"You coming into Mr. Rendell's room and talking about things you know nothing about."

"Know nothing about!" Frazer shouted. "No decent person would have a room in this house——"

"Hold your tongue! You're making a fool of yourself."

"I've let you make a fool of me. Come on! Let's see whether you'll lie to these people as you lie to me. Why do none of Trent's friends know he's had rooms here for years? Why don't they?—why don't they?"

"That's his business, not yours. You'd have been in the gutter if it hadn't been for him."

"You hear that?" Frazer demanded, turning to the others. "Very well. All right. You're witnesses. Now I know what to do."

"You'll go away, that's what you'll do," his wife said in the same steady tone.

"You want me out of the way, my lady. I know too much. I know more than you think—more than *any* of you think. And I shall hear what goes on while I'm away. *That's* all arranged. I'm off—and I'm leaving London in less than an hour."

He flung himself out of the room, banging the door behind him.

Vera rose quickly.

"Why, where are you going?" Marsden asked.

"There's something I want to ask Captain Frazer."

She hurried out of the room before Marsden could reply.

Frazer was half-way up the stairs. He turned on hearing the door open, then came down slowly.

At their first meeting he had detected that Vera was frightened and had instinctively intensified her fears by making enigmatic statements to her or to Marsden, knowing that the latter would repeat them.

"Come down to my study," he said in a confidential whisper. "We can talk there. The basement stairs are rather dark. Allow me."

He took her arm, guided her down the stairs and into his room.

Then, instead of releasing her, he took her other arm in a firm grip, turning her so that she faced him.

"Now, what is it? No secrets between us, I take it. No need to go into details perhaps——"

Her eyes flashed apprehensively, greatly to his satisfaction. He had long sought a victim on whom to inflict the spite accumulated by his daily humiliations. Of what she was frightened he had no conception. But as the merest hint concerning details clearly terrified her, his ignorance was unimportant.

He pressed her arms more tightly, but she made no protest.

"Don't tremble. You can trust me. Lucky for you that you have to deal with an officer and a gentleman. I understand—I understand! You're very handsome, and our friend Trent is too distinguished a person to be quite normal."

He spoke entirely at random, but the effect on her was such that he put his arm round her, thinking she might collapse.

Possibilities—amorous and financial—raced through his mind. A sense of power thrilled him. He could put her on the rack at will.

"Hold on, or we shall have *you* delirious, and that won't do."

Her cheeks flamed and she looked away.

"Now, it's all right," he went on. "I'm going away, but I'm going to give you my address. I shall write to you, of course."

He went to the table and wrote his address on a slip of paper.

"Here's the address. And yours is?"

She told him, and he noted it carefully.

"You may have to come down to see me, Vera. That could be managed, I take it."

"It wouldn't be easy." Her voice was a whisper.

"Of course, you've a job. Perhaps at the weekend?"

"Yes, but——"

"No one would know. You do everything I tell you—and it will be all right. I've had some expenses owing to all this, but you can send me a few pounds later on to cover that. Yes!"

He hesitated, but her attitude was so submissive that he went to her and put his arms round her.

"You're all right, I take it?"

"Yes, I'm all right."

He lowered his clasp and pressed her to him. She yielded herself so abjectly that victory intoxicated him and he kissed her on the lips.

Meanwhile, in Rendell's room, Mrs. Frazer stated a number of facts, clearly and concisely.

The nurse had gone. She was going to attend to Trent, and a friend would take her place in the house. Her husband was going away. She implied that Trent wished these arrangements, and was paying the extra expenses involved. He continued to be very excited, slept most of the day, and the doctor still visited him. He could see no one, and all his letters remained unopened.

Also Mrs. Frazer was making other changes. Miss Ratcham, the lady journalist, was not well and was going to her people in Devonshire for some weeks. Incidentally, she was furious with Frazer for not giving her the paragraph about Trent—and was also furious with the latter owing to her failure to interview him.

Mr. Archibald Fortesque, the handsome student in the room opposite Miss Ratcham's, had been summoned home to account for his extravagance and laziness—and Mrs. Frazer did not propose to have him back, in view of the number of complaints she had received concerning him.

Also, and finally, she had given notice to all undesirable tenants, every one of whom her husband had admitted when she was absent.

She ended by saying:

"I'd rather be empty than have such people. And the lady who calls herself a palmist is also leaving. I'm telling you all this because you are friends of Mr. Trent's—and because you may know of respectable people who want rooms."

Marsden instantly announced his intention of taking Mr. Archibald Fortesque's apartment, when that restless and musical gentleman vacated it. Also he thought he could find some lodgers for Mrs. Frazer.

It was at this point that Vera and the Captain returned—the former very flushed and the latter very truculent.

"Now, my lady, I'm off. And I'm not coming back. That's clear, I take it. So good-bye, Mrs. Basement, and——"

"Oh, shut up, Frazer!" Marsden exclaimed angrily. "We're talking about important things. We've all had quite enough of you."

The Captain drew himself to his full height, then looked down on Marsden with an air of triumph which astonished him.

"You said, I believe, that *you* had had enough of *me*. You are a wit, my good man, a wit!"

Marsden replied angrily, and Frazer became insulting. Then, when everyone in the room was shouting—except Wrayburn— the door opened and Rendell appeared.

"Hullo! A committee meeting!" he exclaimed. "I thought I'd come into the wrong room."

Mrs. Frazer's attempts at apologies were drowned by the Captain and Marsden, who continued to insult each other, while Vera—desperate—vainly tried to restore harmony.

This went on for some minutes, then Frazer, fearing to compromise his victory over Vera, diverted his anger to his wife and began a stormy tirade as to his wrongs and the shortcomings of No. 77.

Interruptions were frequent till eventually—when all were talking simultaneously—the servant opened the door and announced:

"A lady to see Mr. Rendell."

A dramatic silence descended.

Then Rosalie Vivian came into the room.

III

SHE stopped on the threshold and looked round, greatly bewildered. Rendell, who was vaguely aware that her extreme pallor was not the only change in her, crossed the room swiftly and held out his hand.

"I'm so glad you've come. I was expecting you."

The commonplace words recalled the others to the necessities of the situation. Mrs. Frazer went out of the room, murmuring apologies, followed by the model, who had contributed little to the discussion. Captain Frazer, who was impressed by Rosalie's appearance, drew himself to his full height, shook hands with Rendell, saying that he was leaving town immediately. Then, with a glance at Vera, he marched out—Marsden and Vera following him.

Only Denis Wrayburn remained, who now rose, gave an almost imperceptible bow to Rosalie, then said to Rendell:

"I came only to say that I find that *Sunday* after dinner will suit me better than Monday. You have the address? That's all right, then. Sunday—early. That's to-morrow, you understand."

He looked at his watch, gave a peculiar kind of shiver, then went swiftly out of the room.

"Who are all these people? Why are they all here?"

"There's been a bit of a disturbance," Rendell replied, "and——"

"Are they friends of Ivor's?"

"Yes, most of them."

She looked up at him quickly.

"That very dark woman—why was she trembling?"

"Was she trembling? I didn't notice. I'd only just arrived."

"What is her name?"

"Vera Thornton."

"And the woman with the red-gold hair—who is she?"

"She's a model, I believe. I've never seen her before."

Rosalie pressed the palms of her hands against her eyes as if to protect herself from all external impressions.

"I can't stay," she went on quickly. "I came because—because— wait! Yes! You said you'd be in every afternoon at three for a week. I cannot come here again for some days. Will you be in all next week at three? Could you do that?"

"Yes, of course. I'm so sorry all those people were here when you came."

He paused, glanced at her, then exclaimed:

"But you're in mourning!"

"My husband is dead."

He stared at her.

"Which day was I here?" she asked.

"Tuesday."

"He died on Tuesday. Last Saturday he was taken ill suddenly with influenza. He became worse every hour. He died on Tuesday—while I was here."

"While you were here!"

"Yes—here."

Rendell was about to speak, but she silenced him with a quick movement. When she spoke again her voice was a whisper.

"He was buried yesterday. . . . Gone! There's his room, his clothes, his golf-clubs, my photograph on his writing-table—all waiting. But he's gone. Shall I tell you something? Yes. I will tell you. When he was alive, I lived with him—I understood him. But, now he's dead, he's someone else. Do you know that? *Someone else.* He was commonplace, kind, indulgent, rather stupid—and always the same. And now he is—terrible! He's become a part of every silence."

"Now, listen to me," Rendell said abruptly, in the manner of one about to make an authoritative statement, though he scarcely knew what he would say next. "You've had a dreadful shock. You loved him and——"

He got no further. She shook her head so decisively that he broke off.

"No. I did *not* love him."

She raised her head and looked at him, her eyes brimming with tears.

"Ah, if you knew the relief of saying that—at last! I have never dared to say that to anyone, not even to myself. I have crushed that knowledge down—down into a dungeon. I dared not admit it. I told myself that I *did* love him. I repeated it—to prove it. I repeated it, hoping it would become true."

She gazed at him with such suffering in her eyes that Rendell looked away. But she seized his arm with sudden nervous intensity.

"Tell me this—do the dead know the *secrets* of the living? Do they discover what we never dared to tell them? And if they know, do they care? Do the dead *suffer*? Tell me that."

"I do not know," Rendell replied. "How should I know?"

She looked up at him with unseeing eyes, then said slowly:

"I do not think the dead suffer. They discover our secrets, but they do not care. Perhaps, to them, life here seems very distant and infinitely small—a game of children in a nursery. They only smile at the secret which frightens us. And, anyhow, they would forgive, don't you think? Surely the dead would forgive the living?"

"I don't know what to say to you," Rendell replied. "You've a vivid imagination. Well, all I can tell you is that I do not think I'm a coward—physically. I've been in danger more than once. But my imagination frightens me—and I've little enough of it. But, look here, we've got to be practical. You're not alone, are you? You're with friends?"

She studied him for some moments with a meditative expression.

"What a nice person you are," she said at last. "So nice—and so stupid. Why should I come to you, a stranger, if I had friends? You see how stupid you are? I am alone. I have left his flat. It's all just as it was, but it is locked up. The eight-day clock is still ticking in the sitting-room. I can hear it. *Tick . . . tick . . . tick.* I shall never go there again, and I shall sell everything, or give it away. I've a suite in a private hotel in Knightsbridge."

"But——" Rendell began, but she waved him into silence.

"His friends think I've gone to the country. Only his lawyer knows where I am. There's business to be done, you see. He's left me everything, do you know that? But I don't want it—I have enough money without his. But I can't stay any longer. I must go."

"And you will come one day next week?"

"Yes, next week."

She looked round the room, as if to convince herself of its actuality, then went slowly out, followed by Rendell.

They walked to the street in silence. A large car was waiting. She got in and drove away without saying another word.

As he returned to the house, Rendell discovered that she had not asked how Trent was.

IV

Wrayburn had so stressed the necessity for early arrival on the Sunday that Rendell dined at seven o'clock and reached 4, Waldegrave Road, Fulham, soon after eight.

The house was the gloomiest of a gloomy row. It was tall, menacing, and few of the windows were illuminated. Opposite it, instead of houses, was an abnormally high wall—enclosing some institution—which overshadowed the pedestrian and created the atmosphere of a barracks or a prison.

Rendell pushed open a rusty gate, groped along a cobbled path, and mounted narrow steep steps. Then he pulled the bell, thereby awakening a melancholy peal in a crypt-like basement.

The door was opened by a breathless woman, resembling a barrel, who asked what he wanted.

"I have come to see Mr. Wrayburn."

"Have you now! Well I never! Come in."

Rendell went in. The hall was dimly lit, but, nevertheless, he gained a clearer view of the woman who was regarding him with heaving curiosity. She had a round puffy face, mottled with red patches, and black eyes like boot-buttons. Distrust had branded her features. Possibly she was unconsciously aware of the fact, for she always assumed a jovial expression.

"Come to think of it, I don't know if he's in."

This remark, like those which had preceded it, was uttered in the tone of one making a joke.

"Best way to find out is to go up and see. Seeing's believing, so they say. I'll show you his room."

Rendell followed her, convinced that this offer proceeded from curiosity rather than courtesy. They mounted slowly to the top of the house. A proceeding which occupied some time, and one which developed a complicated wheeze in the landlady.

She groped to a door and opened it. Darkness.

"There! He ain't in! What did I tell you?"

She switched on the light and Rendell went into the room.

Its appearance surprised him, for it contradicted the expectations created by the exterior of the house, and those collected on the long ascent to the top of it.

It was a large oblong room with pale green distempered walls, which were entirely bare. The uneven boards were stained black. There was no carpet, but several rugs of varying sizes formed a geometrical design on the floor. In a corner was a divan bed. Near the window stood a writing-desk and within arm's length was a row of dictionaries, ranged on a shelf fastened to the wall. A card index-cabinet, numerous bookcases, a typewriting-table, and a compactom were arranged with mathematical exactitude. Order predominated—every effect was calculated. There was nothing to offend, and nothing to distract—nothing to charm, and nothing to repel. Logic had frozen everything into a final unity.

"Didn't expect to see a room like this, I'll warrant. No more don't I, as you might say. All his doing—not mine. Did everything himself, he did. Stained them boards, distempered them walls, brings his own furniture! And all as cool as you like. Say-nothing sort, he is. Does for himself, too. Yes, believe it or not, *I* never come in here. Makes his own bed! I said to him once, I said: 'Some woman's missed a treasure in you—what a husband you'd make.' Lor, he did give me a look."

She laughed noisily, then went on:

"Sure he's expectin' you? Precious few come to see him."

Rendell said nothing, hoping she'd go.

"You're looking at that gas-fire—and well you might! Ever see such a big one in all your born days? Well, I daresay *he* wants it. A colder-looking feller I never did see. Fair gives me the shivers to look at him. But that there gas-fire! I have to laugh whenever I see it. It's what they call an Oxo size in the shops."

A slight movement at the open door made them both turn. Wrayburn stood in the entrance surveying them with passionless enmity.

The landlady crossed to him, talking noisily, but two swift movements of his hand towards the stairs were too contemptuous to be ignored. Her chatter died and she went out, looking over her shoulder at him with an expression of frightened astonishment.

While she descended the stairs laboriously, Wrayburn stood in the doorway listening. When all was still, he said to Rendell:

"Now that the hoofs of that *animal* can no longer be heard, we can sit down. You're not in a hurry, are you? You're *not*! That's all right then."

He pressed his hand to his forehead and stood motionless with closed eyes.

"I say!" Rendell exclaimed. "You're not feeling ill, are you?"

"The vibrations of that quadruped are disruptive," Wrayburn replied slowly. "Also, it's cold. You think it's cold, don't you?"

"Yes," Rendell lied, finding the evening a pleasantly warm one. "But tell me this," he went on. "Are you sure you're not over-working?"

"I am *not* working. I finished a bout with the world a few weeks ago. A bout with the world is my term for a job, you understand. I've saved some money. When it's gone, I shall re-enter the arena—probably."

The pause before the last word, and its emphasis, isolated it in much the same manner as a spot-light gives prominence to one figure in a crowd.

Rendell glanced at his companion, not knowing what to say. Wrayburn had stretched himself limply in the arm-chair opposite him, but the tightly-clenched hands testified to some act of inner compulsion—some rallying of the will.

Two or three minutes passed in silence.

Suddenly Wrayburn leaned towards the fire and rubbed his hands. The light had returned to his eyes. He then consulted his watch and announced:

"Eight minutes past eight. That means we've the *whole* evening. That's satisfactory, very satisfactory."

"Time seems to interest you very much," Rendell remarked. "I've noticed it before."

Wrayburn flushed swiftly, making a convulsive movement with his whole body.

"Time, my good man, is something that has to be organised—like bouts with the world, money, landladies, and other horrors. But before we go on to something else," he added, with lightning rapidity, "I want to make one or two statements about Ivor Trent. Just one minute, though."

Wrayburn removed his shoes, put on slippers, then offered Rendell a cigarette.

Now, this last action surprised the latter, for he knew that Wrayburn never smoked, and disliked others doing so in his presence. Also Rendell noted that the cigarette offered was a specimen of the brand he preferred.

"Thanks very much, Wrayburn. You notice everything—even the kind I smoke. Really good of you."

"And now," Wrayburn began, with that flick of the hand which signified the dismissal of a subject, "I want to warn you not to form opinions of Trent on those preposterous friends of his you are meeting."

"Why on earth not?" Rendell demanded.

"Because they represent his time-killing activities."

"Time-killing activities!" Rendell echoed.

"Do you mind," Wrayburn replied, separating each word, "*not* repeating a sentence of mine? I find it peculiarly exasperating. You *don't* mind? You're sure? Excellent! You must understand that Trent amuses himself when he is not writing. And he does that because he refuses to achieve his destiny. Wait! I'll explain that."

Wrayburn rose, leaned against the mantelpiece, so as to derive the heat of the fire at its maximum intensity. Then, by way of preface to what he had to say concerning Trent, he gave Rendell a brief summary of the state of the world—as he saw it.

Rendell had never listened to anything in the least like it. He had reason to know, from his own experience, that conditions everywhere were chaotic, but Wrayburn's lightest assumption went infinitely deeper than that.

He announced as a platitude his belief that the structure of society had collapsed. He stated that dictators, economic theories, and militant nationalistic movements were only the convulsions of a civilisation on its death-bed. He asserted that all talk about "recovery" was the chatter of fools or charlatans. And he ended with the statement that, when the Stock Exchange was regarded as the national pulse, the end was not near—it had come.

"Good God!" Rendell exclaimed, "you do see the writing on the wall."

Wrayburn writhed. Any hackneyed quotation caused him physical suffering.

"The writing on the wall, my good Rendell, ceased long ago. Writer's cramp was the reason." Then, after a brief pause, he added: "Surely all I've said is commonplace enough, isn't it? Do say, of course. But, if not, it's rather tedious. I mean, really, it is so obvious—so drearily obvious."

He looked at Rendell with puzzled curiosity.

"You read the papers, reports of public speeches, and so on, don't you?" he asked at last.

"Yes, I do," Rendell replied.

"Then surely you've detected the death rattle? Anyhow, anyhow," he exclaimed, moving both arms in a swift horizontal gesture, "assume it, my good man, assume it! I'm only asking you to accept the fact of disintegration—which is yelling for acceptance everywhere."

"Still," Rendell objected, "there are some signs of recovery."

"You think the nations are slowly climbing back to the pinnacle of 1914, do you? Possibly you are right. There is a minor boom in armaments at the moment."

Rendell put his cigarette out and lit another. The fact that Wrayburn held such opinions interested him more than the opinions themselves. His detachment from the fate of all things human was so absolute that he might have been a spirit from Jupiter, sent to the earth to survey its conditions, who would return in due course and render his report. For, to Rendell, Wrayburn seemed a consciousness, not a man—a consciousness which watched human destiny, untroubled by any feeling for humanity.

He glanced at the slender body, the narrow head, and the dank little beard.

"He's a dead man, bar his brain," was Rendell's final conclusion.

"But what's all this to do with Trent?" he asked impatiently, hoping to narrow Wrayburn to the personal.

"Just one minute, if you don't mind," he replied in a tone which would have been unendurable in anyone else. "You're so extraordinarily ignorant that certain additional preliminaries are necessary."

Wrayburn then proceeded to give an account of the activities of different groups of people to-day who, finding themselves confronted by disintegration, are seeking to create some values to give life substance.

He described briefly every type of modern Movement:—every Group, every Cult—sacred, profane, economic, artistic, political—till Rendell's brain reeled. He revealed their aims, theories, beliefs, dogmas, aspirations with such definite knowledge that it was evident he had been associated with each—either as adherent or investigator. To Rendell many of these Movements seemed fantastic, but Wrayburn convinced him that each and all existed—and that each passionately believed that it held a panacea for all ills of the human spirit.

He ended by saying:

"Nothing new in all this, of course. It must have been very much the same in Alexandria in the year 200."

"What I can't make out about you," Rendell said explosively, "is that you seem to be outside everything—I'd rather you believed in Russian Communism than nothing."

"Russian Communism, my good man, is only Peter the Great's experiment carried to its logical confusion."

Then, a moment later, Wrayburn added:

"Just one minute. Then I'll come to Trent."

Wrayburn got a kettle, which he filled and put on a gas-ring, then cups and various utensils. Rendell took this opportunity to move a good yard further away from the enormous gas-fire, which had long since roasted him. Then, having unbuttoned his waistcoat, he watched Wrayburn fascinated.

Intent on his activities, he proceeded with punctilious care. He studied each cup, every spoon, jugs, and so on till convinced of their cleanliness. They were then arranged in logical sequence. At a precise moment, cups, teapot and jugs were warmed. Ingredients were exactly measured. He might have been a priest performing a rite.

Finally, China tea was prepared for himself—and a cup of black coffee handed to Rendell with the statement:

"I know you find this poison innocuous, so I give it to you with equanimity."

Rendell was astonished. First the cigarettes—and now the black coffee! There could be only one explanation. This was Wrayburn's method of stating that he welcomed him and wanted him to come again.

This discovery revealed the extent and degree of Wrayburn's

isolation. Rendell lacked vanity, and therefore realised that it could only be his physical presence that Wrayburn needed. Mentally, they spoke different languages. That was definite. What Wrayburn regarded as truisms were nightmares to Rendell. To listen to him was to watch the solid shrink to the spectral—the sane dissolve into the mad—and the living stiffen into the petrified. Yet this wisp of humanity, this mental waif, this unique being wanted him— Rendell!—to sit in his room and to listen to him!

"He wants a *human* gas-fire as well as the other one," was Rendell's private analysis of the situation.

But, aloud, he said:

"Devilish good of you to remember I like black coffee. It's first-class, too. Better not spoil me, or I shall be here too often."

"It's all right then, is it? Really? Excellent! You'd better have the cigarettes near you."

Wrayburn curled up in his chair and looked round approvingly.

"I like this—just this! Everything *shut out*. Yes, very pleasant— eminently satisfactory!"

He looked at his watch.

"Nine-twenty-two. You said you weren't in a hurry. That's all right then."

There was silence for some minutes. Wrayburn seemed to be exploring the rare sensation of satisfaction in much the same manner as a frozen tramp—suddenly finding himself before a fire— surrenders to the investigating warmth.

"Coming to Trent," Rendell said at last, but was instantly interrupted.

"I *was* coming to him. The essential quality in him can be stated in a sentence. Potentially, he is the New Man."

"The *what*?"

"The New Man," Wrayburn repeated coldly. "Even to you it must be a commonplace that the only deliverance for humanity lies in a new order of consciousness. Everybody knows that nowadays. The *old* consciousness and all its works is toppling to ruin. Nothing can be done with *that*. It will just go—and it is going."

Wrayburn paused, but as Rendell said nothing, he went on:

"The only salvation lies in the coming of the New Men. Four-dimensional men, if that phrase helps you. Potentially, Trent is one of them."

"But—well—damn it!" Rendell exploded. "I'm quite out of my depth, of course, but—well—what will these New Men be like?"

"They will think and feel from a new centre. They will have new motives, new aims. They will be priests of a new vision. They will possess a *cosmic* consciousness. But, frankly, Rendell, I wouldn't try to understand, if I were you. I'd just accept the idea. You'll find it simpler."

"That's undoubtedly true," Rendell agreed. "So tell me what you meant when you said earlier on that Trent's friends represent only his time-killing activities."

"So they do—so does his writing, on another level. Trent is strong. He has Being. But he evades his spiritual destiny by amusing himself with that hulking Vera—who is as repressed as a bomb—and dear Peter Marsden, to whom he once gave two ideas. Our Peter rattles them about in his empty skull like two sixpenny-bits in a money-box."

Rendell laughed, somewhat against his will.

"You've heard him rattle them, haven't you?" Wrayburn inquired judicially. "He rattles them, and then looks at you as if to say: 'Hear what I've got.'"

"You couldn't say what they are, I suppose?"

"Definitely! One is something about the *spiritual structure* of a book. He's always rattling that one. The other one is Trent's belief that man contains in himself the potentiality of a new being. Our Peter doesn't rattle that one so often. He's not certain that he knows what it means. Also, I gave him an idea once. I told him that Trent's books were only a by-product of an intense interior activity."

Rendell was too startled to reply. He remembered that Marsden had used these three phrases when he had dined with him—exactly a week ago.

His thoughts ran on till eventually he asked:

"What about Rosalie Vivian?"

"She's a point better," Wrayburn conceded grudgingly. "At any rate, she *feels* what is going on in the world, although she knows none of the facts. She's rather like a seismograph. She vibrates when there's an earthquake, although she does not know what an earthquake is. That's why she's a psychic invalid."

"But is she a—psychic invalid?"

Wrayburn leaned forward and peered at Rendell. His expression suggested that he had had immense experience of idiots, but was now confronted by an unknown type.

"Can't you *see* that?" he asked at last. "Can't you see she lives in a psychic thunderstorm?"

"She's certainly very nervy."

"Nervy!" Wrayburn's tone made the word ridiculous. After a long pause he went on: "Yes, Rosalie is a point better. And so is Elsa."

"Who is Elsa?"

"That model with the hair. But Trent ought not to loiter with any of them. It's an evasion of his destiny."

"And you're not interested in the fact that he never told you he had rooms in No. 77?"

"Not in the smallest degree," Wrayburn replied contemptuously. "I'm not interested in where people's bodies are. I'm interested in their potentialities."

Neither spoke for some moments, then Rendell reverted to an earlier phase of their conversation.

"Do you regard yourself as one of the New Men, as you call them?"

"No, my good man, I do *not*. I am a wholly negative person. I cannot make any organic contact with humans. One reason is that I regard small talk as the babble of articulate apes. I am like a bubble. I can only maintain my shape by remaining in the void. Trent is different. He has Being. He might be a link between the Old Order and the New—if any link is possible."

Wrayburn gave the flick of his hand to indicate that this subject was dismissed.

He rose and began to wander about the room, giving Rendell excerpts from experiences encountered in his bouts with the world. He had a dossier relating to every job he had had which contained an exact account of his duties, the amount of his salary, and descriptions of the people with whom he had had to associate. The last were very penetrating character studies. Wrayburn called them "psychological evaluations." Rendell spent some time reading them, impressed by their insight, repelled by their inhumanity.

"Good Lord, Wrayburn," he exclaimed, "you analyse these people as if you belonged to a different species."

"I do. If I were a dictator, I would exterminate them. Never mind about a managed currency. What we need is a managed *pestilence*. Whole hordes of people ought to be obliterated. Nothing can be achieved owing to their deadly inertia. They rivet themselves to the skeleton of tradition. Also, they breed with fearful fecundity. They spawn and cumber the earth with their replicas. And I fancy that dear Peter and the bulging Vera will shortly enter holy wedlock and perpetuate their insignificance in a herd of dense-faced brats. Devouring bodies, my good Rendell, *devouring bodies*."

Rendell decided to make a frontal attack.

"I'm not sure I'm not a devouring body myself. Anyway, I'd like to know this: why does it interest you to see me?"

Wrayburn flushed, then said quickly:

"One reason is that you are a disturbed person. When you were *happy*, you must have been totally uninteresting. But now you're disturbed you'll have to make some move. Probably you'll marry again—but it will be a dangerous sort of affair this time. Or you'll do something quite stupid. Possibly become a Fascist."

Rendell laughed.

"Well, if I become a Fascist, I promise to come and drink black coffee here in my black shirt."

"When Fascism comes to England, my good man, its adherents will not wear black shirts. Incidentally," Wrayburn went on quickly, "it's interesting that men have ceased to be men and have become *shirts*. Red shirts, black shirts, brown shirts, blue shirts— but men no longer. That's interesting. An age is known by its symbols."

"But why not black shirts for English Fascists?" Rendell demanded.

"Because England creates its own emblems—it does not import them. My private theory is that English Fascists will wear *boiled shirts*. In fact, I'm certain they will. The Boiled Shirts! A Middle-

Class Militant Movement to Crush Bolshevism. Imagine that, my good Rendell. A chance for the bourgeois to die in evening dress. The Boiled Shirt would be a real national symbol. It would signify Middle Class Social Snobbery, the Public School Spirit, Playing the Game, and all the rest of it. Labour members would rush to join. It will be an inspiring spectacle—the Back Bones of England in Boiled Shirts."

"That's very amusing, Wrayburn, and now——"

"Before you *go*," Wrayburn cut in, startling Rendell by this anticipation of what he had been about to say, "you may have wondered why I gave no sign of recognition when Rosalie Vivian came into your room yesterday."

"I did think it odd, because I knew you had met her."

"I guessed she did not want the others to know that she had come to inquire about Trent."

"But—but——" Rendell began, greatly perplexed.

"It was also obvious that she had called to inquire before—and had made herself known to you. Otherwise the servant would not have announced her as a lady to see *you*."

"You're uncannily quick about some things, Wrayburn."

"People who live on a tight-rope have to be quick, as you call it. You can explain to her, if you like, though I am completely indifferent as to that."

Rendell rose.

"You're going now?"

"Yes," Rendell replied, "I think I ought to get along."

Wrayburn hesitated, then asked in a tone of measured precision:

"Do you think you might walk some of the way to Potiphar Street?"

"Well, I hadn't thought of it. But I've no objection. I'd rather like some air."

"Then I think I'll come, too."

"Of course. Why not?"

They put on their overcoats, then went down the gloomy stairs in silence. Directly they reached the street, however, Wrayburn began a long and intricate account of how he was postponing his next bout with the world until the last possible moment.

He walked with Rendell till they were within a short distance of Potiphar Street. Then he said good night and left him.

Rendell had gone perhaps fifty yards when he felt a hand on his arm. As he had not heard anyone behind him, he started violently, then came to a standstill.

It was Wrayburn.

"I only wanted to know whether you've been bored. You haven't? You're certain? That's all right then—that's all right."

V

It was Rendell's custom to glance at the envelopes of his letters during breakfast, but not to open them till it was over. Then he would light a cigarette and give them all his attention.

On the morning following his visit to Wrayburn he received more letters than usual. He turned them over, guessing their contents, as most of them had been forwarded either from the club or his office. But there was an exception, and it baffled him.

He studied it minutely, but this scrutiny only convinced him that the handwriting was unknown. Had he seen it before, he would not have forgotten it—of that he was certain. It was a sensitive, nervous hand—the epitome of a personality.

He stood the letter against the sugar-basin, then propped *The Times* in front of him, intending to read it while he breakfasted. But, more than once, his attention reverted to the envelope till, finally, he left the leading article unfinished and speculated concerning his unknown correspondent. Arriving at no conclusion, he finished the meal abruptly, lit a cigarette, and opened the letter.

It was from Rosalie Vivian.

He found it necessary to read it twice in order to master its brief contents, for the satisfaction created by hearing from her so dominated the first reading that it dulled his understanding.

At last he put the letter down. She wanted to see him, but could not come again to Potiphar Street. Hence she asked him to go to her hotel in Knightsbridge that afternoon. If he did not telephone, she would expect him.

The inner satisfaction created by this request not only surprised Rendell, it also made him realise how persistently Rosalie had haunted his thoughts since their first meeting. Simultaneously, he discovered that the prospect of seeing her had transformed the day. The tentative arrangements he had made shrivelled to insignificance. Also, for the first time for nearly a year, he gave a thought to his clothes.

Nevertheless, these reactions disturbed him. It was true that Rosalie stimulated him, that even the thought of her quickened his imagination, but it was also true that he was slightly afraid of her. She was like a magnificent creature in a cage. He admired her, pitied her—but the thought of sharing her captivity alarmed him.

He began to pace up and down the room, surprised by the nature and intensity of his thoughts. Then, suddenly, he remembered a sentence Wrayburn had said to him the night before.

"Probably you'll marry again—but it will be a dangerous sort of affair this time."

Rendell came to a standstill, then stabbed his cigarette to death in an ash-tray.

"I'll have to take a pull on myself," he announced angrily. "I'm losing balance. Damn it, I'll become as queer as the people I'm meeting if I'm not careful."

He arrived at Rosalie's hotel soon after three-thirty. He had some difficulty in finding it, as it was off the main thoroughfare and had rather a narrow entrance. He passed through a courtyard, then paused—aware of the presence of the unfamiliar. The quiet of seclusion surrounded him.

"Clever of her to find this," he said to himself, "I'd never heard of it."

Directly he gave his name at the bureau, a page was summoned, and he was conducted to a lift, which deposited him on the third floor. Then he went down a broad, thickly-carpeted corridor till the page stopped at a door and knocked.

She rose to greet him as he entered a small round-shaped room, the intimate atmosphere of which surprised him. The means by which she had imposed her individuality on it escaped his masculine intelligence. He was aware only of the result. The curtains were drawn, but concealed lighting softly illuminated the room.

"I have shut out the day, I hope you don't mind," then, noticing his interest, she added: "You like the room?"

"You might have been here for years."

He sat down, then made a number of commonplace remarks, to which she did not reply. Rendell, too, was only dimly aware of their purport, for his essential attention was occupied wholly with her appearance.

Till now, he had seen her only in outdoor clothes, and the absence of hat, fur coat, and gloves seemed to intensify the disturbing element in her beauty. Also, for the first time, Rendell became aware of her figure. It was lithe, perfectly proportioned, and sensitive to a degree so removed from his experience that only an extravagant comparison seemed appropriate. It suggested an instrument fashioned to transmit an unknown music. Her black clothes emphasised the pallor and frailty of her features. But, in repose, no less than in animation, an aura of intensity invested her. The unexpected seemed imminent in her presence.

Rendell's commonplace chatter flickered out, and he felt—and looked—embarrassed.

"There ought to be more people like you," she said slowly in her rich deep voice.

"Why? What do you mean?"

"It was imaginative of you to talk about the weather—to say the hotel was quiet—that it was clever of me to find it. It was your way of telling me that, if I wished, this meeting could be formal—unlike those at Potiphar Street."

"Well, perhaps," he stammered, "I really don't know."

"Although you must know perfectly well," she went on, as if he had not spoken, "that I asked you to come here because I wanted to tell you everything. Didn't you know that?" she added, after a pause, as Rendell said nothing.

"Well, I suppose it did occur to me."

"I have to tell you everything—or not see you again. I either trust people entirely, or not at all."

A long silence ensued. To be alone with her in this intimacy lulled Rendell in an odd interior kind of way. He felt he had entered her world, and that each moment yielded one of its secrets.

She sat cross-legged, her hands clasped round her right knee, her head thrown back. When she spoke it was as if she were continuing a reverie aloud.

She told him of her childhood in an old house surrounded by a great rambling garden, circled by trees, twenty miles from London. She was an only child, and her parents had spoiled her. From the age of twelve she had been educated by governesses, as her parents did not approve of the schools in the vicinity—and refused even to contemplate sending her away.

Swiftly, vividly, she evoked the spirit of the old house with its tree-ringed garden. The world of her childhood emerged—not as a memory, but as something still existent. She seemed to walk back to it, becoming, on the way, the child who had inhabited it. Then, with a few sentences, her parents came to life. Rendell saw the invalid father, who went for a drive each morning at eleven, each afternoon at three, when the weather was fine, and who spent the rest of his time reading Gibbon, or studying the financial columns of the newspapers. A kind, rich, too-indulgent man, who clung to a rigidly-defined code, not permitting a thought to stray beyond its orthodox limits. Rosalie revealed him as he had appeared to her when she was fourteen: a bent, wizened man, in an old smoking-jacket, puffing his pipe, and shuffling round his large untidy study—cursing the Germans and the air-raids, and endlessly proclaiming the Decline and Fall of the British Empire.

Then, with a sentence or two, Rosalie conjured up her mother. A fraily-built, beautiful woman, whose Trinity consisted of her husband, her daughter, and her home. She moved about the house like the spirit of tranquillity, dowering each room with a dreamy radiance.

"I was fifteen when the war ended, and during the next few years I discovered—most unfortunately—that I was a talented person."

"Why unfortunately?"

She gazed at him with blue, frightened eyes for some moments— then laughed.

"I had a gift for drawing, and a gift for acting. I was told that I ought to have my voice trained, and that I ought to study dancing. I was excited, several careers seemed to be beckoning me. Money was poured out in an endless stream for lessons. Every morning the car took me to London. For a year I studied drawing. Then I gave that up and spent a year at a dramatic academy. They said I was most promising. But I gave that up, too. Then for some time I went from one voice-producer to another. But, eventually, I decided I was destined to be a dancer. That lasted some time. And then, suddenly, I gave *that* up—and stayed at home and began to study Spanish."

"But why didn't you stick to anything?"

She looked at him enigmatically.

"Because I discovered that each meant work—and I hadn't the will. Work—endless work—month after month, year after year! And the greater one's gift, the greater the necessity for work. I was done for, directly I had reached the limit of what I could do natu-rally. I was a dilettante, a gifted amateur. And I was surrounded by students who *had* to achieve something. A car did not bring and fetch *them*."

"Well, and then?" Rendell asked, as she remained silent, staring at the fire as if she had forgotten his presence.

"I stayed at home and read. I was about twenty-one then. I read all sorts of books. I had no method—I just read anything that came my way. I drugged myself with reading. I didn't want to go out into the world—it reminded me of my failure. I lived for three years in a kind of trance. Then—Paul Vivian turned up."

She leaned back and closed her eyes. Over a minute passed before she continued.

"My father met him through some business or other. He was years older than I was—nearly forty. He began to come to the house frequently—so kind, so solid, so reliable! But, somehow, you could not believe he had ever been a child. But my people became very fond of him. And then—he fell in love with me."

She rose slowly, then stood looking down—the firelight kin-dling her features and dark curly hair.

"He fell in love with me," she repeated. "Soon, he asked me

to marry him. I refused. Then he asked again—and again—and again! Still I refused. He wasn't fiery, he was—patient. So were my parents. They wanted me to marry him. They were a little worried about me. They thought I was a trifle *wayward*. That was their word. And here was Safety First—proposing regularly each month."

She knelt down swiftly and peered into the fire.

"I can see a face!" she exclaimed, with the sudden gaiety of a child. "I'll show you. No! It's gone!"

She remained crouched before the fire. It was some moments before she went on.

"So there I was with the three of them. And the three of them were willing the same thing. I could feel their united will closing round me like a contracting iron ring. I began to feel depleted. I spent whole days lying on a sofa. Twice a week Paul came to dinner. Every day he sent flowers. And mother began to say: 'Don't you think, darling, you'd be happier if you *settled down*?'"

She leaned her head back and laughed—a joyous, rippling laugh.

"And I said to her: 'I don't love him.' And she said: 'That sometimes comes afterwards.' And I asked: 'After *what*?' But she didn't answer."

Again she laughed.

"And then, at last, weary of it all—and not knowing what to do with my life—I said I'd marry him. I told him I didn't love him, but that didn't seem to worry him. It would have terrified me. Everyone was radiant. Paul dined with us nearly every night. At the week-ends he took me out in his large car—and told me what a glorious and thrilling thing common sense was."

After a pause, she said softly: "My God!"

Instantly, however, she raced him:

"And then we bought clothes—such lovely clothes!—and then the wedding. The bride, a little pale and trembling, perhaps, but then—well, you understand—she would be quite different—*afterwards*. And then, the departure for the honeymoon. Tears. Fluttering good-byes. 'You *will* be good to her, Paul?' A manly hand-shake. And then an invalid old man and a frail woman craning out of the window to see the last of the receding car."

Then, after an imperceptible pause, she turned to Rendell and asked:

"Would you like some tea?"

"Tea!" he almost shouted.

"Yes, why not? People drink tea in the afternoons. Some take milk, some sugar, some neither—and some take one or the other. Some have China tea, some Indian, some Russian—but tea they all have. It's one of those things that are definitely done."

"I could not drink tea to save my life," Rendell announced emphatically.

"Very well. We'll have sherry later. Smoke a cigarette, and let me know when you would like the next instalment of the serial."

"What an incalculable being you are!" he exclaimed involuntarily.

"Well, don't worry too much—there won't be any more like me soon. But that's an idea of Ivor's, and he comes—later."

Neither spoke for some moments. Rendell gazed at her crouching in the firelight. She looked like a child who somehow possessed a woman's body.

"Now we continue the serial."

She pretended to pick up an imaginary book, opened it, then spoke as if she were reading aloud.

"The bridal pair, still thrilling with the raptures of first and passionate love, in due course returned to the mother country. Glamorous visions of golden Italy still quivered within them, but life—alas!—is not one long romance. So they settled down in the large commodious London flat—and each day Paul went to his prosperous business in the City. But what of little Rosalie? Ah! what of her?"

"Don't," said Rendell suddenly.

"Don't *what*?" she demanded.

"Don't tell it like that."

"Sorry! Do you want to know what it was really like?"

"Yes."

"It was hell. For a few months I hoped I'd have a child. I didn't want one particularly, but it was my last chance. Do you understand that? No! You won't understand that. Anyway, it didn't happen. I had a nervous breakdown instead. Consternation! The family summoned! The great panacea of *afterwards* had failed. Physicians arrived. Injections were pumped into me. One young doctor said I needed 'an outlet.' He was sacked immediately. Two eminent greybeards then approached. One said nothing, and the other agreed with him. Loaded with guineas, they heavily vanished. Then, having refused to have all my teeth out, and having refused to have my appendix removed, I was sent to a nursing home on the East Coast—in the winter. Do you know the East Coast well? No? Then you should go there—in the winter. The air is—really—very remarkable."

"Still, I got better slowly," she went on. "Paul only came at weekends. And I met a woman there I liked: grey-haired, very lined, with eyes that were saying good-bye to life. I sobbed my story out to her one night. 'Tell me, what can I *do*?' I kept saying. She took me in her arms and kissed me. That was all. Then she went away. So I spoke to another woman. And she said: 'Learn to love your husband—it's your only chance.'"

"Well—and then?" Rendell asked, as she remained silent.

"What? Oh yes! I came back to London and began to try to love Paul. Have you ever tried to love anyone?"

"No. I imagine it's not easy."

"There are several methods—and I tried them all. One was to keep repeating all Paul's virtues. He was so kind, so indulgent, so solid, so dependable, so punctual! That list became my rosary. But, somehow, this method wasn't a scintillating success, so I tried another. I kept telling myself how fortunate I was. I had a home, food, cars, lovely clothes, jewels, servants. I kept telling myself that I was free because I had such a large cage. Then I began to wander about the streets, staring at old women selling matches—or crouching in corners, covered with rags. I tried to become happy by studying the misery of others. But, somehow, it didn't work. Then I stayed in the flat and tried to imagine what it must be like to live in a slum. And I discovered that I *was* living in a slum—of a different kind. Then I became religious, and tried to believe that my marriage was the will of God. But that didn't work either, because I knew it wasn't. It was the united will of my parents and Paul. And then—well, then—I had another nervous collapse. Rather an unpleasant one."

She put her hand to her forehead, a shiver rippling her body.

"I—I felt queer—mentally. It was odd, rather frightening. Sometimes I forgot I was married. Once, when Paul came to see me in the nursing home, I asked who he was. But that wasn't all. I was terrified of that day when I should look back across the flat, monotonous years and be forced to say: 'Yes, that was my life. I have lived like that, and—before long—I shall die. It is nearly over, and it has been—that!'"

She paused for a moment, then went on:

"Also, I began to be afraid of air-raids. When I was fourteen, a bomb had fallen near our house. Still, I got better—slowly. The doctor kept saying that what I needed was *ballast*. I suppose that was why, eventually, Paul took me for a long sea trip."

She leaned back and laughed, stretching her hands toward the fire.

"Don't get impatient," she continued, "the climax approaches. We returned to England, and then, soon—just as my third nervous collapse was approaching—I met Ivor Trent."

"How long had you been married then?"

"About three years. I was twenty-seven. I had read Ivor's books, of course. Some people we had met on the trip asked us to dinner, and he was there. He was in the hall when we arrived. While Paul was taking off his overcoat, we stood motionless, looking at each other."

There was silence, till she said slowly:

"Somehow I've got to make you understand."

Then she described graphically her life with Vivian—its regularity, its monotony. The oppressively solid luxury of the flat: Paul's City friends: the same conversations endlessly repeated in different words: the restaurants they visited: the plays they saw—everything defined, everything organised, everything hardened by habit. Not only did she evoke her life with Vivian, and the atmosphere investing it, but she also made Rendell feel the numbing effect of this repetitive existence.

"That was my life when I met Ivor. And I had had two nervous collapses as a result of it. And I was on the way to a third."

"I shall tell you everything," she said slowly. "The night I met Ivor I felt we were alone, although I hardly spoke to him and scarcely looked at him. He talked a good deal and I—heard my own language again. I was afraid of him. I was afraid of his power over me. When we said good-bye, I dared not look at him. The next afternoon he rang me up."

"He rang me up," she repeated, "and asked me to go to his flat. I obeyed like a slave. He seemed to know everything about me without being told. I went again to his flat—and again—and again. And then he took me as easily as you could take a cigarette from that box."

"But *when* was that—exactly?" Rendell asked involuntarily.

"Three years ago."

He was glad she was not looking at him. The discovery that Trent had made Rosalie his mistress just at the time when Vera Thornton had entered his life, so bewildered Rendell that he dared not speak lest his tone should betray him. So, for a considerable period, Trent had been intimate with these two women—neither of whom was aware of the other's existence.

"When I was with Ivor, I had no regrets, no remorse, nothing! It seemed inevitable that we should be lovers. I went to his flat every other day. If I had not met him I should have lost my reason. I *know* that is true! He saved me—and he saved my marriage. I know that sounds odd, but it's the truth, all the same."

Rendell was about to speak—but she sprang to her feet and stood before him, gesticulating wildly.

"But—Paul! You understand? *Paul!* Had he known about Ivor, his world would have flown to pieces. To live with him, day after day, night after night, knowing that! And he was happier than he had ever been because I was returning to life under his eyes. Was I to tell him that Ivor was the reason—that when Ivor took me in his arms I sobbed like a child because the ice round my heart was melting? Was I to tell him that?"

"Look here," Rendell began, "you mustn't excite yourself——" but she silenced him with a gesture.

"I made Ivor come to the flat. I—I liked the three of us to be together. I can't explain. Paul wasn't surprised by my friendship with Ivor. He knew I'd dabbled with the arts. Above all, he trusted me entirely. That's a dreadful feeling—to be trusted entirely! No woman could stand it indefinitely."

"But what about Trent?" Rendell asked. "How did *he* see it?"

Rosalie hesitated, then said slowly:

"He—well—he thought it was inevitable, and he made *me* feel it was. He's a very powerful personality, you know that. No, of course, you *don't* know that! Well, he is. He controlled me completely. If, when I was alone, a sudden fit of terror or remorse seized me, I telephoned him—or went to him—and he made me calm again."

Rendell said nothing. The knowledge that Vera had also visited Trent during the first year of his liaison with Rosalie—and that he had treated her very differently—made Rendell feel that he was becoming Trent's accomplice.

But, fortunately, Rosalie seemed to have forgotten him. She had sunk into a chair and was now gazing in front of her, seeing the memories she had evoked.

"How long were you lovers?" Rendell asked at last.

"Three years. He had just finished a book when I met him. Listen! Only a few days ago, he suddenly said he was going abroad to work again. I begged him not to go, but it was useless. He seemed not to listen. I was terrified of being left alone with our secret. I *knew* I'd become hysterical and tell Paul. But, almost immediately, Paul became ill. He got worse and worse. Then, on that Monday night, I saw that paragraph in the paper."

She made a movement with her hands as if thrusting aside something she feared to face.

"If I had not met you, when I came to Potiphar Street, I should have gone mad. Do you know that? Ivor was delirious! I was certain he would betray our secret to strangers. I was afraid of blackmail. I was afraid of everything. My God, that Monday night! I never dreamed that Paul was going to *die*. I thought he would discover everything. Ah, you don't know what I went through that night!"

"I'd like to ask you one question," Rendell said, after a silence, "though I suppose it's an odd one."

"Ask me anything. You know everything now."

"When Trent is better, would you marry him—say, in a year?"

"No—not now. I thought I was everything to him, but I found I wasn't."

"Because he wouldn't give up going away when you asked him?"

"Yes." Then, suddenly: "Do you despise me?'"

"No."

"Not even if I tell you I am glad Paul is dead?"

"No. We all go through hell, sooner or later, and—afterwards— we don't feel like judging others."

She did not reply. Rendell glanced at her. She was lying back with closed eyes, looking like a child asleep in the firelight. He did not know which disturbed him more deeply—her pathos or her beauty.

"I'd better go," he said gently. "You're tired."

"No, no! Please don't go. You—you must have some sherry. I'll get it."

"No, really!" Rendell exclaimed. "I don't want any. You are exhausted and need a rest, and so I'd better go."

They had both risen. Suddenly she put her hand on his arm.

"Stay here and dine with me. I shall be alone otherwise. And I'm afraid of being alone. I've a maid with me—but she's out to-night. Do stay. Please stay."

The appeal in her eyes embarrassed Rendell, and he looked away.

"Very well, but——"

"You will! You'll dine with me! And you'll tell me about yourself. And why you are in that horrible house. And—and everything!"

"Yes, on one——"

"Ah, you are kind! I was afraid of to-night—afraid of sitting alone by that fire, hearing voices and seeing things! But now I shall be all right. Then, perhaps, I shall sleep to-night."

"I'm staying on one condition," Rendell announced firmly, "and that is that you have a rest now. I'm going to pull that sofa nearer the fire and you're going to have an hour's sleep."

"Very well. And you'll sit there and smoke. Wait!"

She ran into the bedroom, returning almost immediately with an eiderdown.

"Look!"

"Good! Now, down you go!"

She obeyed him and he covered her with the eiderdown.

"Now go to sleep at once. Not another word!"

"What a nice person you are!"

"To sleep at once," Rendell repeated, switching off the lights.

He sat down in an arm-chair with an air of finality.

Ten minutes later the sound of regular breathing haunted the room.

VI

RENDELL'S visit to Rosalie created an intimacy which transformed his days so swiftly that the process was effected before he was aware of it.

During the next month they met almost daily, and most of these meetings were of long duration. Frequently they would spend the whole day together, the result being that he obtained a deeper knowledge of her than a greater number of briefer meetings, over a longer period, would have afforded.

Soon he half believed that several different women inhabited her body in turn—one yielding possession to the next with bewildering rapidity.

The range of her emotions; the lightning transitions from mood to mood; her sudden exaltation; her swift relapse to inertia, all fostered the belief that although, physically, she was one woman—psychically, she was a dozen.

He would leave her, apparently tranquil as a child, intent on some problem relating to clothes. He would return and discover an hysterical being, lashed by memories and fears. As any attempt at consolation precipitated a new crisis, he learned to say nothing—and to wait. And he learned this from her maid, whose devotion to Rosalie beggared every example of loyalty known to Rendell. She loved and served her with the self-immolation of a saint.

"How on earth do you stand this!" Rendell exclaimed on one occasion when his patience had collapsed.

"She makes you forget it all with a word or a look," the girl replied, with the conviction of experience.

Again and again, Rendell had reason to remember Wrayburn's statement that Rosalie was a "psychic invalid," but as this diagnosis ignored her fascination, it gradually lost its significance. She quickened Rendell's imagination, thereby making the world more beautiful and more mysterious. He began to feel life as she felt it. And he learned that although she had no mental consistency, she possessed an emotional logic which revealed itself only to sympathy. He began to respect this, although her actions often dismayed or embarrassed him.

Impulse ruled her. Lacking it, she lapsed into inertia. Prompted by it, she would act instantly and with a total disregard of the conventions. At its bidding, she would rise and leave a restaurant, speak to a stranger, or do some deed which demanded considerable moral courage. Her sensibility to atmosphere—her penetration into the characters of people, with no data other than their appearance—fascinated and bewildered Rendell till he could not decide whether he had been blind before meeting her, or whether he, too, was becoming a psychic invalid as a result of her influence.

Her demands, therefore, were many and varied, but he yielded to all of them. She was experiencing freedom for the first time and was determined to indulge its privileges. This determination expressed itself in a number of ways, one being that she wanted to explore a London she had only glimpsed from the security of Vivian's car. She had known only the thoroughfares, she now made Rendell take her into the by-ways. It was her reaction to her husband's orthodoxy. The sheltered life had been a cage—a warm, spacious, luxurious one—but a cage none the less. Also, this penetration into an unknown London set a gap between her and her memories. It created the illusion that a long period of time separated her from them. As nothing recalled the past, it receded.

Often, however, Rendell found her impulsive acts embarrassing. One night, when they were walking down Bond Street, she suddenly became interested in a street walker, who was hanging about with a dog on a lead.

"Why does that woman have a dog?" she demanded.

"I don't know, Rosalie, just a whim, I expect."

"Perhaps she loves the dog—perhaps it's the only thing she does love. I'm going to ask her."

She turned and went up to the woman, Rendell having no alternative but to follow, which he did very reluctantly.

"Why do you have that dog with you?"

"I'll soon tell you that," the woman replied. "You see, it's like this. If a policeman sees me speak to a man, he thinks twice about doing any thing if I have a dog with me."

"But why—why?" Rosalie demanded.

"Well, if he takes me up for soliciting, he has to take *me* to Vine Street—and *the dog* to Battersea. So he thinks twice."

She laughed noisily.

Rosalie stared at her, then thrust a note in her hand and walked away quickly.

But, almost immediately, she stopped.

"You're laughing!" she exclaimed indignantly.

"I was," Rendell admitted. "I was amused by the inventive genius of the underworld."

"It's horrible! This whole town is horrible! We're all dead people—just dead people walking about. There's nothing in front of us. You ought to be able to feel the Future. Do you know that? You ought to be able to stretch your hands out and *feel* it. But if you do stretch them out, there's nothing—nothing! We're ghosts in a fog, looking for life."

"You can't see things like that, Rosalie."

"Looking for life," she repeated.

But these excursions into an unknown London were intermittent. Sometimes, for days together, she refused to leave her hotel. She would sit silent, hour after hour, thereby giving Rendell ample opportunity to review the situation.

His first discovery was the extent to which his association with Rosalie had banished Trent to the background of his mind. But it was the change in her attitude to him which chiefly interested Rendell. She seldom referred to him and, if questioned, only repeated that his refusal to remain in London—just before her husband's death—had convinced her that their relations were not what she had imagined. Even Rendell's revelations that Trent had had rooms in Potiphar Street for years, and that he had lied about going abroad, did not greatly disturb her. She was of those who trust absolutely or not at all. Trent's refusal to stay in London had half-undermined her faith in him. Rendell's revelations completed that process.

But although she seldom referred directly to Trent, she would sometimes ask questions which related indirectly to him.

"That day I came to your room and found it full of people," she once said suddenly. "There was a woman there. She was very agitated. What did you say her name was?"

"Vera Thornton," Rendell replied.

"Vera Thornton," she repeated.

Rendell waited but, as she remained silent, he began to speculate concerning her affair with Trent.

The more he reconstructed this drama, the more Trent's part in it amazed him. To make a neurotic woman his mistress—a woman who had had two nervous collapses and was on the threshold of a third—to maintain that relationship for three years, visiting her flat and meeting her husband—was an enterprise so outside the boundaries of Rendell's imagination that the attempt to bring it within them only revealed the impossibility of any understanding of Trent. Leaving aside all other considerations, why had Trent added risk to risk till they piled mountain-high round him? And what type of power must he possess to have been able to control Rosalie during those three years? Only one thing was certain—his belief in that power must have been absolute, otherwise he would not have dared to leave her, intending to stay away for a year.

And, during a great part of this period, Trent had been in involved relations with Vera Thornton.

It was at this point in his speculations that Rendell finally surrendered all hope of elucidating the mystery of a man capable of such complexities.

What touched him more nearly, however, was his own relations with Rosalie. His daily association with her affected him in a number of ways, none of which reassured him. He was becoming more sensitive, more alive and alert to aspects of people and places of which formerly he had been unaware. Her influence probed all that was dormant in him. He found himself confronted with everything he believed was behind him. Old impulses challenged him. Established certainties became less solid. A strange light slowly invaded his world, altering perspectives, and transforming past and present. He felt life more vitally, responded to it more organically, and so discovered riches even in the commonplace. But, also, he began to experience an irritability which flamed into being with an intensity wholly disproportionate to its cause. More and more frequently he found himself reacting to trifles in a manner which dismayed him.

But Rendell did not realise Rosalie's power over him till it was established. His defences crumbled before he knew he was besieged. Rosalie's fascination differed from that of many women in that it was most potent in her absence. When Rendell was with her, he was aware of her weakness. It was when he was alone that he discovered his fetters.

Hence, although the desire for her companionship increased progressively, it was shadowed by a deepening uneasiness. Consequently, while wanting it to continue, he hoped that it would end.

"You can't stay in this hotel much longer, can you?" he asked, one night when they were dining together. "What about your people?"

"I can't make plans."

"But you'll have to, Rosalie!"

"I can't! I'm stunned—and I want to remain stunned. My mother keeps writing to ask when I'm going to join her in Italy. I told you, didn't I? that my father died a year ago, and since then mother practically lives in Italy with her sister. She spends nothing and keeps sending me money. But I can't go to her yet."

"But why not?"

"It will make the past real again. When I am with you, it does not exist—because you had no part in it. But, with her, I shall remember. I shall see faces and hear voices. Then I shall be ill again. Don't you understand yet that I'm *afraid*?"

Rendell said nothing and a moment later she added:

"I shall have to go—soon. And then—explanations, lies, hypocrisy! Two women talking across an abyss!"

She was silent for the rest of the evening and Rendell regretted having questioned her.

But, a week later, she announced the date of her departure with characteristic suddenness, and in somewhat dramatic circumstances.

It was a Thursday. Rendell was to dine with Rosalie at eight o'clock. He had had a business appointment which had occupied most of the afternoon and returned to Potiphar Street to dress soon after six-thirty.

To his surprise, he found a letter, addressed in Rosalie's writing, in a prominent position on the mantelpiece.

He tore it open and read:

> Come—directly you get this. Don't dress. Come. Now!
>
> R.

Ten minutes later he entered her sitting-room, but instantly came to a standstill and looked round in astonishment. The room was a chaos of trunks and clothes.

She waved her maid to the bedroom, then crossed swiftly to him.

"Wait! Don't speak! I've seen her!"

"Seen *whom*?" Rendell demanded.

"That woman—Vera Thornton."

"You've seen——"

"Yes, yes, *yes*! I've just told you so."

"But where?"

"At Potiphar Street. Listen. Do listen! Suddenly—this afternoon—I knew I'd have to go to Italy. I cabled, saying I was leaving to-morrow. Then, I couldn't be alone. I wanted to see you. I thought you might be back earlier than you expected. So I—are you listening?"

"Of course, I'm listening!"

"So I got a taxi and went to Potiphar Street. I was just going to knock, when the door opened and—there she was. I told her I wanted to speak to her. I made her come into your room."

"Well?"

"I made her sit down. She's ill—did you know? She's been unable to work for some days. Then I told her about myself and Ivor."

"You mean you told her——"

"Everything! She looked like a ghost. At first she didn't believe me. Then she told me that while Ivor and I were lovers, *she* had been visiting his flat regularly. And then I didn't believe her."

She paused, then raced on.

"But she was afraid of me. Wasn't that odd? I said to her: 'You were his lover too?' And she blushed and said she wasn't, and that she hated him. I thought she was going to faint. She stared at me as if she had never seen anyone like me."

"I'll bet a lot she hasn't," Rendell cut in, but Rosalie went on as if he had not spoken.

"Then, suddenly, she seemed to regret having told me she'd been to Ivor's flat. She made me promise not to tell anyone. And then she began to cry. She sobbed—and I knelt and put my arms round her."

"There's no one in the least like you anywhere."

"And I told her I was going away to-morrow. And that I would never tell anyone about her and Ivor. I don't count you. And I also told her I should never see Ivor again."

"You mean that?"

"Yes—never! That woman wasn't lying. She *had* been to his flat regularly. She's hopelessly in love with him—and she's terrified of something. Help her, if you can, won't you?"

"Yes. Did she mention me?"

"No. But help her—do help her. She's not far from a collapse. I know the signs. Tell me, why did Ivor lie to me?"

"Did he—in so many words?"

She stared at him with blue bewildered eyes.

"Why, what do you mean?"

"Did he say you were the only woman?"

"No, but——"

"You assumed it. And so did Vera Thornton. And there may be others." Rendell paused, then added: "You're right not to see him again."

"Never! But, whatever he is, I shall be grateful to him—always. He saved me. Nothing alters that."

"How did you leave Vera?"

"I told her I would help her, if I could, and that you would have my address. Then I left her. But, in the hall, I ran into that woman with the lovely hair. You said she was a model, didn't you?"

"Yes; Elsa. Did you speak to her?"

"No, it was all rather odd. Directly I saw her I stopped. We stood and gazed at each other. I felt I'd known her always. She smiled, then opened the front door for me. And I took her hand and said good bye."

"But——"

"Later, later! I'm terribly busy."

She knelt down and began to rummage in a trunk, then called her maid, and an endless conversation began concerning what she should wear on the journey. No sooner was a decision reached than it was ridiculed and the discussion renewed. Half-filled trunks were ransacked, drawers and wardrobes pillaged, till the room resembled a shop that had been struck by lightning.

Rendell stayed till nearly ten o'clock. He returned the next morning at eleven—when Rosalie informed him that she would not be able to go as she had no stockings. He was about to refer to the dozens of pairs he had seen the night before, but a sign from the maid silenced him. He agreed that the journey to Italy must be postponed. The three of them then remained seated on trunks, listening to the ticking clock, till Rosalie suddenly became helpless with laughter. Finally, she leapt up, kissed the maid, said she was a darling, and announced that she would go to Italy. After which, she swung round to Rendell and asked if there would be time to buy a Dachshund puppy she had seen the day before in a Bond Street window. He replied that the presence of a small dog might complicate the journey. But, as this new difficulty was regarded as an overwhelming reason for not going to Italy, Rendell promised to inspect the Dachshund the next day and purchase it—if he found its attractions irresistible.

They then discovered that Rosalie had not bought the tickets.

So Rendell, having ascertained that Milan was their destination, went out and returned in due course with the tickets.

The question of passports then precipitated a new crisis. The maid said Rosalie had them. Rosalie replied that she had never seen them—and that only criminals required them. She then asked Rendell to go and buy some. Half an hour later they were found at the bottom of the only trunk packed by Rosalie.

The whole of the hotel staff were then tipped—not on the basis of services rendered, but according to whether or not Rosalie regarded them as nice people.

Then, having dissuaded her from buying a new hat—and having given her some French, Swiss, and Italian money—Rendell began to regard her departure as a possibility.

They left the hotel soon after one o'clock: Rosalie and Rendell in the car, the maid following in a luggage-laden taxi.

He said little during the drive to Victoria. She was going—and he did not know whether they would meet again. Although they had met almost daily for a month, she had never referred to the future. For Rendell, however, it was a fundamental issue. He knew that if their companionship were renewed, he would become wholly dependent on it. He would ask her to marry him. He knew he would do this, although his logical faculty regarded such a pro-ceeding as worse than folly.

But, if they did not meet after to-day, sanity would prevail—and he would escape.

He glanced at her. She was leaning forward, gazing at the thronged street with an expression that was half curiosity and half bewilderment. It seemed to him that she had no part or place in the world, that her physical presence in it represented a cruel caprice on the part of destiny. She was an outcast, endlessly seek-ing the realm from which she had been banished. And so, to her, the normal was the unreal; the extraordinary the familiar.

On reaching Victoria, Rendell was fully occupied till ten min-utes before the train left. Then he joined Rosalie on the platform, leaving the maid to attend to the arrangement of the light luggage in the carriage.

Rosalie took his arm and they walked up and down the plat-

form. She disassociated herself so entirely from the bustle surrounding her that she created an illusion of solitude.

Up and down they went, while she talked quietly on a number of
subjects in no way connected with the journey. Rendell forgot time,
place, circumstances. The sound of her voice, the pressure of her
hand on his arm, the rhythm of her movement hypnotised him.

Porters began to bang doors.

"You'll have to get in, Rosalie."

They returned to the carriage and Rendell held out his hand.

"You'll come—in a month?" she asked, as if referring to a long-
established arrangement.

"In a month!" he exclaimed.

"Yes, to bring me back."

"And then?" he heard himself ask.

"Oh, then we'll just go on as we have done. You'll take me to
places and show me things."

He did not reply. Her hand remained in his.

"You'll come—in a month?" she repeated.

A whistle blew.

"Yes, I'll come—and bring you back. Jump in! Quick!"

She got in a second before the train started.

As it began to move, she leaned from the window and beckoned
him. He had to run to keep up with her.

"Don't forget to go and look at that puppy."

She waved her hand and vanished.

Rendell stood motionless till the train had disappeared.

At last he turned and walked slowly towards the barrier—a sentence of Wrayburn's circling in his mind.

"Probably you'll marry again—but it will be a dangerous sort of
affair this time."

VII

ONE result of Rosalie's departure was Rendell's rediscovery of
Time.

During the last month, time had been an ally: now it re-emerged as an adversary. The hours no longer flitted past like dancers. Each seemed a cripple in a never-ending queue.

Rendell's next discovery was the changes which had occurred at Potiphar Street. It is true that these had been effected some weeks ago, but as he had done little more than sleep in his room during the last month, he had remained unaware of them. Now he realised their extent and effects.

Captain Frazer was still at Ramsgate and no indication was obtainable as to the probable date of his return. Most of the undesirable lodgers had also departed. Mrs. Frazer continued to devote the whole of her time to Trent, her former duties being executed by Elsa, who, nevertheless, remained invisible—a feat which intrigued Rendell and one which continued to intrigue him. But, above all, Marsden was now a lodger. This fact had not affected Rendell during Rosalie's regime, but, with her departure, it became increasingly prominent owing to Marsden's importunity.

At first Rendell resented the casual manner in which Marsden assumed that his company would be welcome, but this resentment was short-lived, for Marsden was perplexed—and this perplexity began to interest Rendell.

In the first place, Marsden's curiosity concerning Trent no longer existed. He seemed to have forgotten that Trent was still in his rooms at the top of the house. Marsden was obsessed by Vera, and to such a degree that to confide in Rendell was a psychological necessity.

The first night Rendell spent in his room, Marsden appeared soon after nine o'clock.

"So you *are* in—at last! What the devil have you been up to lately? I've been here well over a fortnight now, and haven't caught a glimpse of you. I began to think you must have gone."

"No, not yet—but I'm going in a month."

Marsden lowered himself into a chair, then put his crutches on the floor.

There was a silence, then he announced abruptly:

"I'm worried."

"What about?"

"Vera."

Rendell moved uneasily, then began to fill a pipe. To discuss Vera with Marsden was a disturbing prospect—in view of his inside information concerning her. There are circumstances in which even to listen is hypocritical.

"To begin with," Marsden went on, "I don't mind telling you I'm in love with her."

He shot an angry glance at Rendell, evidently fearing that the latter might regard this information as amusing. Marsden was morbidly sensitive concerning his physical disabilities.

Eventually he continued:

"I mean, really in love with her. I want to marry her."

"Have you told her so?"

Marsden writhed with irritability.

"No, I have not! It's not so simple as all that, my dear Rendell. You see——"

He broke off abruptly. When he went on, it was evident that he was not saying what he had originally intended.

"I mean—damn it all! you can't ask a woman to marry you when you can see she's ill and worried. But what bothers me is this—what the hell's the matter with her."

"Have you asked her?"

"Of course I've asked her! She says it's only nerves. And that before long she thinks she's going away for a week-end to get some air. It's all damned unsatisfactory. But thank the Lord for one thing —she doesn't care tuppence about Trent. Never mentions him. At one time I thought she cared quite a bit for him. But I was wrong. I fancy they were little more than acquaintances. In fact, I'm almost certain they were. After all, I only met her once at Trent's flat."

At this point Rendell discovered that his pipe wasn't drawing properly. He knocked it out, cleaned it, and refilled it slowly. But Marsden was not expecting any comment from him. He was evidently considering whether or not to tell Rendell something, for he kept glancing at him, then at the fire, thereby revealing a state of considerable indecision.

"Look here, Rendell," he burst out at last, "there's something I've got to explain. I've meant to tell you before. It's this. That foggy Sunday we dined together, you remember?"

"Of course I remember. The place was empty and we talked about Trent while we dined."

"Yes—well—it's not easy to explain. You see, it's like this. I hadn't seen you for some years and——"

"And you'd every reason to think it would be years before you saw me again," Rendell cut in.

"Well, I don't know. Still, perhaps you're right. Yes, I think you *are* right. Well, what I mean is, I believe I talked as if I owed Trent quite a lot."

"You certainly did."

Marsden twisted uneasily on his chair.

"I—I was romanticising. That's the point I want to make. I believe I told you some schoolboy incident about a bully. And—and one or two other things. Well, I exaggerated. I want you to know that."

Rendell said nothing. Marsden's manner irritated him even more than his remarks. He was convinced that Marsden had told the truth when they had dined together—and that now he regretted it. Why this should be so Rendell could not imagine, but it was very clear that the necessity for this conversation—whatever that necessity might be—was a whip to Marsden's vanity.

"Why are you telling me all this, Marsden? What does it matter to you what I think about your relations with Trent?"

Marsden started a sentence, then abandoned it. He began another—and broke off. After which he fidgeted with his tie till Rendell's patience exploded.

"Oh, for God's sake say what you've got to say—or let's cut the whole thing out!"

He almost shouted the words.

Marsden stared at him in astonishment, but there was a respectful note in his voice when he said:

"I say! You've altered. You used to be a collected person. What *have* you been doing lately?"

Rendell put his pipe down, then got up and took a cigarette from a box on the mantelpiece.

"I don't want you to tell me anything, Marsden. But, if *you* want to, then say it—or leave it alone. So I ask again: what does it matter what I think about you and Trent?"

"It does matter," Marsden replied emphatically. Then, after a pause, he exclaimed angrily: "Do you think I want all that nonsense I told you repeated to Vera?"

"Oh, so that's it?"

"Yes—*that's* it! I don't want her to think I'd be a nobody if I hadn't met Trent."

"You can count on me not to say anything to her."

"Then you've not told her what I said that Sunday?" Marsden asked eagerly.

"Not a word of it."

"Good! That's all right. And you don't think she'll want to discuss Trent with me?"

"But you said she didn't."

"I know, but I mean in the future. Supposing we married, I don't want to be cross-examined about Trent."

"I'm sure she won't want to be either. You can put the whole subject out of your head."

Marsden settled himself more comfortably.

"Good! I shall wait till she's a bit better and then I'll ask her to marry me. But I tell you again—there's something odd about her. I was at her place the other night and—when the postman came—she went as white as a sheet. I'm damned if I know what's wrong."

This was the first of several conversations, none of which enhanced Rendell's opinion of Marsden. What did interest him, however, was the news concerning Vera, for Rendell could not imagine what could have produced this new frenzy of fear. She had seemed satisfied that her secret was safe when he had left her that night at her flat. What had happened since? Did she regret her confession to him? Possibly. Anyway she was avoiding him. That was certain.

But, apart from Vera and Marsden, there was Denis Wrayburn—a deeper problem than either and one which touched Rendell's conscience.

He had only seen Wrayburn two or three times during the last month and, on each occasion, Rendell had made the meeting a brief one. It was easy to explain this neglect by enumerating the demands made by Rosalie, but this explanation would have been more convincing if Rendell had felt that he wanted to see Wray-burn now he was free. But he did not. He saw little of him, despite a deepening premonition that he was necessary to Wrayburn, in some mysterious way.

In the first place, the house in Waldegrave Road depressed him. There it stood, the gloomiest in the gloomy row, in a narrow badly-lit street which seemed eternally shrouded in mist. The high wall opposite the dreary houses made oppression more oppressive. To walk down Waldegrave Road was to experience the monstrous sensation that one was the only mourner at one's own funeral.

Wrayburn's room, too, began to affect Rendell unpleasantly. The mathematical precision dominating every detail created a non-human atmosphere. Rendell felt that the room was inhabited by a brain, not a man. And although he attempted to dismiss this new sensibility as an effect of Rosalie's influence, he became more and more subject to it. Soon, every visit to Waldegrave Road represented a definite act of his will. And every visit created a deeper dislike of the road, the house, and Wrayburn's room.

But the chief fact was that Wrayburn himself interested him less and less. This discovery shocked Rendell, for their first conversations had been stimulating. Subsequent ones, however, lacked substance. To sit listening to theories, criticism, and abstract ideas made Rendell feel he was suspended in a void haunted by a voice. Every thing familiar disappeared. Wrayburn was the eternal onlooker. He stood, remote and removed from the arena—watching, assessing, defining. He was not alive, he was a commentary on life. He haunted the human scene, notebook in hand. He saw everything—and felt nothing.

Often, Rendell ceased to listen. The pedantic voice went on, but Rendell would begin to think about Rosalie. Sometimes he seemed to see her beauty hovering behind the chair in which the inert Wrayburn sprawled. Then he would marvel that one world could house two beings so dissimilar.

The first meeting after Rosalie's departure bored Rendell. This fact emerged like a mountain from a sea of mist. But, to Rendell's dismay, he somehow knew that Wrayburn had expected and feared the advent of this boredom. And, knowing this, Rendell realised that the experience was not a new one for Wrayburn. It had happened again and again. He had had hosts of acquaintances—but to-day he was alone. Rendell knew, although he was never told, that he was Wrayburn's only visitor. And this knowledge disturbed him, for it imposed a responsibility for which he felt totally inadequate.

But it did more than this. During the last year Rendell had imagined that he had experienced loneliness. A glance at Wrayburn convinced him that he was a stranger to it. Rendell had only felt lonely. Wrayburn *was* loneliness. It enclosed him like a coffin of ice.

So although Rendell visited him two or three times after Rosalie's departure, it was at the prompting of pity. But Wrayburn was not deceived. He had known that Rendell was bored long before the latter had realised it. Wrayburn was familiar with recurring decimals.

But he said nothing. He withdrew into himself as if making a final demand on inner reserves.

Then, one night, Rendell received a postcard. It was the first communication he had had from Wrayburn. It consisted of a line, written in a thin spidery hand.

Come, to-morrow at eight—for five minutes.

D. W.

Precisely at eight o'clock Rendell reached 4, Waldegrave Road and pulled the bell, then stood listening to its sepulchral summons in the dark depths of the basement.

In due course, the barrel-shaped landlady appeared. She was breathless, as usual, but somehow her round puffy face with its red patches seemed especially repellent.

Rendell attempted to hurry by her, but she planted herself resolutely in the narrow hall, thereby barring the way very effectually.

"Oh, it's you, is it? Well, you can tell young Touch-Me-Not that he can't kid me. *See?* I know he's ill—and won't say so. Shivering up there like a rat, he is, although that gas fire of his is going fit to roast an ox."

She scowled malignantly at Rendell.

"Take the trouble, I did, to go up all them stairs yesterday to see what had happened to him. Door locked, if you please! 'It's only me,' I calls out. But no reply from Hoity-Toity. 'It's me—Mrs. Munnings!' I fair shouted. I did straight. And what do you think he says? 'Go away.'"

Her little eyes flashed with anger.

"'Go away!' There's a gentleman for you! 'I'll go,' I says, 'but don't say I didn't come, when you get worse.' I was put about, I can tell you. I know his sort. Snake in the grass, if you ask me."

Rendell escaped and hurried to Wrayburn's room, the door of which had been unlocked at eight o'clock precisely.

Wrayburn was in bed. He did not speak, or give any sign of greeting when Rendell entered the room, the atmosphere of which was that of an oven. Rendell glanced at him, at first casually, then apprehensively. Illness had accentuated the narrowness of the face to an alarming degree. He lay motionless, staring through Rendell with cold implacable eyes, while the latter fully realised what a stick of a man Wrayburn was. The bedclothes did not reveal the contour of a body. The head on the pillow was the only evidence that the bed was occupied.

"What's wrong with you?" Rendell began, but he got no further.

"Just one moment."

Wrayburn raised himself, slowly and with difficulty, then produced a notebook from under his pillow, which he handed to Rendell.

"I want you to get the things listed there—and to bring them here to-morrow morning at ten o'clock."

The list related chiefly to food, with precise details of the shops at which it was to be procured and the price to be paid.

"I'll do that, of course, but——"

"I shall then be independent of that *animal* downstairs. Tell her if she comes to this room again, I shall instantly give her a week's notice."

He leaned back on the pillow and closed his eyes.

"But look here—I can't leave you like——"

"Please go now. Lock the door after you, then push the key under it."

The tone was so final that Rendell obeyed. He glanced again at Wrayburn. He seemed like a man whose will was turned wholly inward.

Rendell went out, locked the door, pushed the key under it, then went downstairs. He gave Mrs. Munnings Wrayburn's message, ignored her angry comments, and left the house. The next morning he returned at ten o'clock with the stores Wrayburn required. He accepted them in silence, then waved Rendell out of the room.

Several days passed, during which Rendell's anxiety increased till he was about to go to Waldegrave Road, if only to ascertain whether Mrs. Munnings knew how Wrayburn was. But, knowing that Wrayburn would deeply resent any interference, he decided to wait another day before making any inquiries.

At nine-thirty that night, however, when Rendell was alone in his room, writing to Rosalie, the door opened and Wrayburn appeared.

Rendell was so intent on his letter that he remained unaware of Wrayburn's presence till he looked up and saw him standing in the doorway.

It might have been the shock of thus discovering him, or something spectral in his appearance, but a sudden chill invaded Rendell as he sat looking up at him.

He rose slowly and took a step towards him.

"Hullo! Are you——"

"Could you oblige me with a bottle of whisky?"

Wrayburn spoke with icy precision.

"Yes, of course, I'll get it."

Rendell turned, not sorry to escape from Wrayburn's steely scrutiny. The request amazed him, for Wrayburn never touched alcohol. Presumably he wanted the whisky for medicinal purposes.

Rendell shot a glance at him unobserved. Wrayburn was no better—that was certain. Only his will was maintaining him.

"There you are," Rendell said, handing him a bottle. "Anything else? Or are you all right now?"

"I'm all right—now."

Rendell turned and bent down, intending to lock the cabinet from which he had taken the bottle. He had always locked it when Captain Frazer had been in the house and continued to do so from habit.

Hearing no movement behind him, he assumed that Wrayburn had gone, so he took the opportunity to arrange the bottles in the cabinet before locking it.

Nearly a minute passed.

"Good-bye, Rendell."

He started violently. He had been certain that Wrayburn had gone. He rose quickly and turned round.

But the room was empty.

"Well, I'm damned! I suppose he's all right. Anyway, you can't ask him anything."

He returned to the table and tried to continue his letter, but it was useless. Wrayburn haunted him. He kept looking up to see if he had returned.

At last he abandoned the letter, and began to pace the room, reviewing his relations with Wrayburn from their first conversation in that restaurant to their extraordinary meeting to-night.

Finally, he went to bed. But he slept abominably, owing to a succession of bad dreams—in every one of which someone called to him in a language he did not understand.

VIII

THE next morning Rendell left the house soon after breakfast and was out the whole of the day.

He returned at six o'clock to find Marsden in his room—a pale gesticulating Marsden, who brandished a newspaper frantically.

"Wrayburn!"

"Well, what's wrong?"

Marsden thrust the paper at him.

"Look! . . . There!"

Rendell took the paper mechanically, but continued to gaze at Marsden incredulously.

"For God's sake, read it, Rendell!"

TRAGEDY AT FULHAM

MAN FOUND DEAD IN GAS-FILLED ROOM

The print became a blur and the paper fell from his hand.

"Wrayburn?"

Rendell did not recognise his own voice.

"Yes, yes! Read it!"

Rendell picked up the paper.

He read slowly—frequently finding it difficult to understand the simplest words.

He learned that at twelve o'clock that morning a Mr. Scott—who was a lodger in 4, Waldegrave Road, Fulham—thought he detected a faint smell of gas on the top floor. He knocked several times on the door of a room occupied by a Mr. Denis Wrayburn, but could obtain no reply. Becoming alarmed, he went downstairs and informed the landlady, Mrs. Munnings. She went with him to the top floor and he knocked again more violently, but with the same result.

Then, with great difficulty, Scott broke the door in. The room was full of gas. Wrayburn was lying fully dressed on the bed—dead. He had been dead for some hours.

Scott immediately telephoned the police, who arrived a few minutes later. Soon after their departure a reporter appeared, to whom Scott gave a graphic account of his discovery.

On a little table by the bed were three pound notes, and a bottle of whisky—half empty. But what amazed Scott were the elaborate precautions taken by Wrayburn to ensure that no gas should escape from the room. Windows, door, fireplace, were covered with thick close-fitting felt. Even the cracks in the boards were plugged with wadding. "It must have taken him hours," was Scott's final statement.

Rendell folded the paper carefully and put it on the table. Then he picked up his hat.

"Why—what—where are you going? Rendell!"

Marsden shouted the last word, for Rendell had turned and was going out of the room.

A moment later the front door closed behind him.

He began to walk rapidly, unaware of direction. The rain which had been threatening all day was now falling heavily, but he did not notice it. On and on he strode, conscious only of a necessity for speed. . . .

That gas fire . . . that huge gas fire . . . the bottle of whisky—half empty. . . . He had plugged the cracks in the floor with wadding. . . . The cold grey eyes, intent on their task. The long slender fingers—

Wrayburn!

Long-forgotten incidents flashed upward from his memory, like sparks. That first visit to Wrayburn's room—the cigarettes, the black coffee. Wrayburn had walked back with him that night. Yes, nearly to Potiphar Street. Then they had parted. And—a few moments later—he had felt a hand on his arm. "I only wanted to know whether you've been bored. You haven't? That's all right then—that's all right."

(The rain was blinding him. He couldn't see where he was going.)

Lying fully dressed on that bed. Dead for some hours. That's what the paper said. . . .

When was it he had come for the whisky? Last night? Yes, last night.

"Could you oblige me with a bottle of whisky?"

"Yes, of course, I'll get it."

. . . . *How* many days had passed since he had taken those things to Waldegrave Road at ten o'clock that morning? Four days? Five days? *Five* days! He had been alone in that room for five days—his body an arena where Will had wrestled with Illness. And yet, *had* he been ill—physically? Or had his Will had Loneliness for adversary?

Courage! Wrayburn's courage! To pit himself alone against a world—to make no concessions—to take his stand on himself. What a Will had been sheathed in the fragile scabbard of that body!

. . . . The way he used to flush suddenly . . . the quick flick of his hand to dismiss a subject . . . the slender body . . . the narrow head . . . the dank little beard.

Wrayburn!

There was something rare about him; something beautiful, with a non-human beauty; something unique.

Thrown away on a rubbish heap! A spirit to whom the world was a wilderness. A spirit, seeking its kindred and finding them not. A spirit doomed to come to earth—perhaps to expiate the dark acts of its pride. The Stranger—the Solitary—the Alone.

Wrayburn!

That gas fire—the rugs arranged on the floor in a geometrical pattern—the way he studied each cup to make certain of its absolute cleanliness—the row of dictionaries on that shelf—the divan bed. . . .

And he had become bored by him. He had visited him less and less frequently. Only to listen had been asked of him—but he had refused even to listen. The last human being had deserted Wrayburn. Each day his money grew less. (Three pounds on the little table by the bed!) Every hour the necessity for another "bout with the world" came nearer. For five days he lay on that bed and watched it come nearer—nearer.

And then—his last bout with the world. . . .

The rain must be heavier than ever. He had run into something. It was a tree. He was on the Embankment. His clothes were drenched.

That night at the restaurant! Wrayburn had given his hat and coat to the waiter, telling him precisely how they were to be dried.

His clothes—Wrayburn's clothes.

"Wouldn't you *guess*, from their general neatness and all that, that this rig-out is the *only one* I possess? Wouldn't you—wouldn't you?"

That is what he had said.

Were his clothes still in that room at the top of the house?

Mrs. Munnings!

Wrayburn—Mrs. Munnings. . . .

But, of course, all this would pass. This storm of emotion and memory would not last. He would forget. Days would become weeks, weeks—months. He would go to Italy. (Rosalie! Yes, yes, of course—Rosalie!)

And yet, perhaps, sometimes—suddenly—he would remember a night of rain on the Embankment.

Rain, rain, endless rain—drenching him, blinding him!

Wrayburn!

DURING the next few days Rendell became the chief actor in the last two scenes of Wrayburn's tragedy—the inquest and the funeral.

He gave evidence at the former, but was not required to identify the body, as Mrs. Munnings performed that duty with an exuberance which amounted to gusto.

After which, she steeped herself in the grim squalor of the inquest with the liveliest satisfaction.

Nevertheless, unwittingly, she rendered a service, for her evidence revealed a rock-like certainty that insanity was the cause of Wrayburn's suicide. In fact, she hotly contested the suggestion that his insanity was of a temporary nature. She dogmatically asserted that Wrayburn had been mad the first day she ever set eyes upon him—nearly a year ago.

"The morning he took the room, I said to Mrs. Marks—'You mark my words,' I said to her, 'there's a screw missing somewhere.' And she says to me: 'Then don't you take him, but—there!—no good talking to you. Always helping others, you are.' But I says to her——"

Mrs. Munnings, being restrained by the coroner at this point, concluded her evidence by giving her account of the five days preceding Wrayburn's suicide.

Frequently her voice sank to a whisper in order to italicise her more dramatic statements.

"I told him he was ill. But—no!—he must know best. Door always locked—and never a sound. No doctor, and him getting what meals he had. Yes! believe it or not, that's what he did. I'd creep up all them stairs and listen. Lor! I could hear my own heart beating. I could straight. Then I'd put my ear to the keyhole. Nothing! One evening I called out: 'You all right, Mr. Wrayburn?' Not a sound! I stood there all gooseflesh."

A brief pause.

"Up I went again the next morning. Don't you think I neglected him! Not me! I always feel sort of motherly to me lodgers. Silly,

I daresay, but I do—it's me nature. So up I went next morning—and there was an envelope pushed under the door. Lor! I thought, here's a change! And what do you think it was? *A week's notice."*

Mrs. Munnings looked at the jury—her little black eyes extended to their maximum capacity.

"A week's notice! It stabbed me to the heart. God forbid that I should say a word against the departed—no, not me! Vengeance is mine, saith the Lord. And then, the next night, I think it was, anyway it was *the* night, I happened to be in the hall about nine o'clock, I should say. And I heard someone coming downstairs."

A long pregnant pause.

"It was *him*. Lor! I thought it was a ghost. Step by step, he come down them stairs. I can see him now. He looked that queer I thought he was walking in his sleep. I did straight. 'Don't tell me you're going out a dirty night like this,' I says to him. Scared I was, and I don't mind owning it. He passed me—as near as that—and never a word. Opens the front door and out he goes."

Mrs. Munnings nodded her head repeatedly and significantly.

"Well, I went down to wash up some things, and then I go up and into a room off the hall—and stay there, in the dark, with the door ajar. And then before so very long I hear a latch key. There I stood in that dark room, holding the door open an inch or two. *He* never knew I was in that room, watching him. I see him go up the stairs slowly—carrying a bottle of whisky. Lor! I said to myself, here's a change. Up he goes, but he stops once and leans against the banisters. Then he goes on, and I never see him——"

Mrs. Munnings collapsed, and received the ministrations of Mrs. Marks.

Rendell was the last to give evidence.

He explained that he had known Wrayburn only a few weeks; that he was a highly-strung sensitive man of considerable intellectual capacity; and one who held the most pessimistic views concerning world conditions. Wrayburn was a thinker and a student. He had no friends—apparently no relatives—and no money. He had gained a precarious living in a number of jobs—all of a temporary nature. He was ill—and the necessity for obtaining employment preyed on his mind. He was very independent and would have refused any offer of financial help. Also, and above all, he was terribly lonely. It was impossible to over-emphasise that fact.

"I blame myself bitterly," Rendell concluded, "for not seeing him more often. I knew he was lonely, but I failed him. As I said earlier, Wrayburn apparently had no relatives, but I shall, of course, make myself responsible for the funeral."

Suicide While of Unsound Mind.

This verdict did not satisfy Mrs. Munnings. It was too familiar to be dramatic. She had expected something sensational. She did not know the meaning of *Felo-de-se*, but she liked the sound of it. Also, her sense of reverence was outraged by the knowledge that Wrayburn would receive Christian burial. Mrs. Munnings didn't like that at all—and she was confident that God wouldn't like it either.

Still, she recovered. And the chief cause of that recovery was Rendell.

Till now, Mrs. Munnings had regarded him as a nobody. The fact that he was Wrayburn's friend had convinced her of his social insignificance. But the proceedings in the Coroner's Court transformed this opinion. He was going to pay for the funeral! Clearly, therefore, he had money to waste. A pauper's funeral was quite good enough for Wrayburn. Also, the coroner had treated him with respect. Yes, there was something impressive about him—although he was living in a Chelsea lodging-house.

Mrs. Munnings became cringingly obliging to Rendell. Then, as that was not an outstanding success, she adopted a confidential motherly manner, referring to Wrayburn on one occasion as "our poor boy." But, as Rendell remained unresponsive to these solicitations, Mrs. Munnings consulted Mrs. Marks. The latter, however, had not been idle. She had made certain underground inquiries at No. 77, and was therefore in a position to report that Rendell was a proper gent who had money to burn.

Mrs. Munnings' next move was to hint—in the pleasantest manner possible—that Rendell might find Waldegrave Road more comfortable than Potiphar Street. She even suggested that, as Wrayburn's room was now vacant, he might care to take it—for old times' sake.

These attentions infuriated Rendell, but he was forced to conceal the fact, for he was determined that Mrs. Munnings should not attend the funeral. As that lady anticipated that function with ghoulish cravings, diplomacy was essential. And friendly relations are conducive to successful diplomacy.

"About the funeral, Mrs. Munnings."

"Lor, Mr. Rendell! You've taken the very words out of my mouth."

"You could help me quite a lot, if you would."

"Anything to oblige *you*, Mr. Rendell."

"It's like this. I've put an announcement in the papers, of course. Among other things, it says: 'Flowers to 4, Waldegrave Road,' and——"

"Flowers! There won't be no flowers! Why, the pore feller hadn't a relative and——"

"We don't *know* that," Rendell cut in. "He may have some in the North. So I think it would be better if you and Mrs. Marks stayed at home—in case of unexpected arrivals. It would be a great relief to me if you did."

"Well, I've said it before and I say it again—anything to oblige *you*, Mr. Rendell."

But her tone lacked conviction, for disappointment paralysed her. Rendell's request created civil war in Mrs. Munnings. Determination to please him conflicted with her desire to attend the funeral. But her greed was greater than her morbidity and so it triumphed. It was, in fact, so much greater that she accepted Rendell's flimsy fiction, concerning the possible arrival of relatives, in a wholly uncritical spirit.

That night Rendell went to Marsden's room and briefly reported his success. He ended by saying:

"So there will only be the two of us at the funeral to-morrow. We leave here at twelve."

"But—I'm not coming!"

"You're not!"

"No. Funerals depress me."

"Really?"

"Oh yes, frightfully. But, I say," Marsden went on quickly, "did you actually put an announcement in the papers, mentioning flowers, and all that?"

"Yes, of course. Wrayburn's known hosts of people in his day. Surely to God someone will turn up—or send a wreath—or do something!"

"I doubt it," Marsden replied judicially, "people are pretty callous nowadays. Personally, I'm not sending a wreath, but then—of course—we didn't hit it off. That's the fact—and there's no point in being sentimental."

"None whatever."

Rendell left it at that, and went down to his own room.

So, at twelve the next day, a hearse—with one wreath on the coffin—and a car, with one occupant, left Chelsea.

It was a blank anonymous day, grey with frost, but Rendell scarcely noticed it. He was in that state in which nothing seems so fantastic as facts. He was attending the funeral of a man called Denis Wrayburn. He was paying for it. He was the solitary mourner. A few weeks ago he had not known of Wrayburn's existence. He had met him because of Ivor Trent—a man he did not know, and had not seen. Those were the facts, but they seemed like fictions. Rendell felt he was watching himself.

Then, incontinently, he remembered a remark of Rosalie's concerning Wrayburn. He had asked her what she made of him and, after a silence, she had said:

"Have you ever seen a photograph of a polar landscape?"

"Yes—why?"

"I saw one once—and it reminded me of Wrayburn."

That was pretty good, in its way. Terror—isolation—beauty. Yes, he knew what she meant. . . .

It would take some time to get to the Crematorium. It was odd how he had instinctively decided on cremation. They had asked him about an urn and a plaque. He had not replied—and the man had said:

"Some people decide to have the ashes scattered in the garden."

And, again, he had known instinctively that this was appropriate. Then nothing would bear witness to Wrayburn's sojourn on earth. Somehow that seemed right to Rendell. . . .

He looked out of the window. A man had taken his hat off and now stood staring at the hearse with apathetic interest. He had a round red face, with fish-like eyes, and a heavy corpulent body. Nevertheless Rendell felt grateful to him. He had become Wrayburn's mourner for ten seconds.

At last the car drew up at the Crematorium. Rendell went to the chapel, confident he would find someone who had known Wrayburn. But it was empty.

A few minutes later the brief service began. Rendell occupied the pew for the chief mourners, but he heard and saw nothing. He was alone. That fact dominated him. No one else had come, or sent a flower.

At a given point in the service, the coffin slowly moved from its resting place and disappeared through a narrow aperture. Rendell watched it vanish, feeling that a fantastic dream had reached its climax.

The service ended—and the parson shook hands with him. Then an official appeared and asked.

"Would you care to see the garden, sir?"

"Thank you. Yes, I should."

They walked in silence till they reached a long colonnade, facing a garden.

"It doesn't look its best to-day, sir, I'm afraid, but it's a beautiful garden."

"I am glad to have seen it. Thank you so much."

And now? Well, now, of course, he would drive back to Chelsea. It was over. There was nothing more to be done here.

He went to the car and said to the driver:

"Take me to 4, Waldegrave Road, Fulham, will you?"

After all, he would *have* to see Mrs. Munnings once more.

Meanwhile, Mrs. Munnings was awaiting him in a state of prostration, the day having proved an unfortunate one for her.

In the first place, she and Mrs. Marks had made certain preparations for the refreshment of Wrayburn's relatives. Tea had been laid in Mrs. Munnings' room, and a large cake—coated with magenta-coloured icing—stood proudly in the centre of the table.

But time had passed and no one had arrived. This in itself

was irritating enough, for Mrs. Munnings had rehearsed a long speech—dealing with her devotion to the departed—and was anxious to deliver it. Mrs. Marks, too, eagerly anticipated this event—having heard the speech three times, and not wishing the experience to be repeated indefinitely.

But the non-arrival of relatives was not the cause of Mrs. Munnings' prostration. In fact, she had forgotten it. It was a scratch—and Mrs. Munnings had just received a blow.

She had been out most of the morning with Mrs. Marks, and certain of her lodgers—who were most anxious to see her—had remained ignorant of her return till nearly one o'clock. Then three of them burst in on Mrs. Munnings and Mrs. Marks and announced that they must speak to the former on a matter of urgent importance.

Two were elderly women, the third being an old man with a jovial expression, who drank a bit, but always paid his rent regularly. They represented Mrs. Munnings' oldest and most reliable lodgers. Also, and above all, each of them was afraid of her.

But now they trooped into her room—very excited, very scared, and all talking simultaneously. It was some time therefore before Mrs. Munnings could elicit a coherent statement, but, first by shouting them down and then by cross-examining each in turn, she managed to learn the facts.

Briefly summarised, these were to the effect that, since the night of Wrayburn's suicide, they had slept very badly. At first they had thought this was only nerves, but—last night and the night before—each of them had heard sounds in Wrayburn's room. Yes they had! Mrs. Munnings could say what she liked, but they *had*. Sounds of hammering—then a curious sound as if someone was on hands and knees plugging the cracks in the floor. And that wasn't all! Last night Miss Wilkins—the elder of the two women—had heard someone in the passage outside her room. She got up and opened the door—and there was a Figure on the stairs with a bottle of whisky in its hand. Oh yes there was! She saw it with her own eyes, and seeing was believing, so she had always been told. And Miss Wilkins wasn't staying any longer in a haunted house. No, she wasn't—not likely! And neither were the others. They were all frightened to death—and they were all going now. They had packed and were leaving immediately. And here was a week's rent. And if Mrs. Munnings took their advice she'd get rid of the house just as soon as she could.

They then trooped out of the room, leaving the house a few minutes later—all three having crowded with their belongings into one taxi.

For nearly a minute Mrs. Munnings stood like a waxwork staring at Mrs. Marks, then collapsed into a chair as if she had been pole-axed.

Mrs. Marks glanced at her, realised it would be some time before she became articulate, and therefore decided to continue a complicated piece of knitting which she kept for emergencies. But, as she worked, she sniffed more and more frequently. Her opinion of Mrs. Munnings had fallen to zero. Fancy her believing that nonsense about the house being haunted! Haunted me foot! Those three lodgers had wanted to give notice for years, but hadn't had the pluck. Wrayburn's suicide had given them their chance—and they had taken it. And Mrs. M. had believed them! Fancy her being that soft! She—Mrs. Marks—would have shown 'em! Haunted, indeed! She'd have given 'em haunted.

Mrs. Munnings prostrate: Mrs. Marks knitting. This was the tableau presented when Rendell entered the room.

"No one turned up then," he said briskly, seeing nothing but the magenta-coloured cake in the centre of the table.

Mrs. Munnings rose slowly—in a manner suggesting the birth of a mountain.

Mrs. Marks put down her knitting.

A menacing silence descended.

"Well, there it is, can't be helped," Rendell went on. "You've been to some expense, I see. Perhaps that will cover it."

He put a pound note on the table.

"Cover it!" Mrs. Munnings gave a shrill laugh, then turned to Mrs. Marks. "Here am I—ruined!—and he gives me a pound note and says perhaps that'll cover it."

Mrs. Marks sniffed, then said she was sure that the gentleman meant no harm.

"Ruined!" Rendell exclaimed. "Who's ruined?"

"Me three best lodgers gone! *Gorn!* There's their week's rent lying on that table! And all because of him—the little rat!"

"But why——"

"'Cos they say the house is haunted! That's why! Didn't I know it—didn't I say to you, Mrs. Marks, didn't I say he done it just to spite me? The little rat—the little *rat!*"

Her voice rose to a falsetto scream of rage.

"And me sitting here waiting for his relatives! The little bastard was likely to have relatives! He knew this would happen. He's ruined me! He's *ruined* me!"

She trembled so violently with anger and self-pity that Mrs. Marks was impelled to inform her that it didn't do no good to carry on like that.

"Quarter day comin', and me three best lodgers gone! And all the rest will go! Yes, they will—every one of 'em! I'll be empty! Everyone will say: 'Don't you go to No. 4—it's haunted.' I'll be begging on the streets! Me—Sarah Munnings! Yes, I shall, I tell you! *And he knew it.* The little rat knew it! It's his revenge!"

Fury so possessed her that Rendell thought she was going to have a fit. The patches on her puffy face had turned purple; the little eyes were black points of hatred; the barrel-shaped body shook convulsively.

Rendell, feeling genuinely sorry for her, was about to suggest some monetary compensation, but Mrs. Munnings—noting the change in him—abandoned hysteria a little too abruptly and made a frontal attack.

"It's no good your standing there staring! It's gospel truth I've told you, as Mrs. Marks knows. The least that you can do, seeing as how you had a hand in all this, is to take rooms here yourself. And take 'em at once. And pay a good rent for 'em."

"Quite out of the question," Rendell replied curtly. "I'm going to Italy soon."

Italy! Soon!

Mrs. Munnings' last hope collapsed.

"And what's to happen to *me?*"

"I don't know."

He turned and began to walk towards the door.

"You can't leave me here—ruined! You can't do it."

She ran after the retiring Rendell and seized his arm.

"His furniture! The little rat's furniture! *That's* mine, anyhow. And I'm going to sell it. See?"

"Oh sell it—and be damned to you!" Rendell shouted, then went out, banging the door behind him.

X

THE next evening Marsden went to Rendell's room at about seven o'clock and, finding it empty, proceeded to make himself as comfortable as possible. Noticing that the cabinet in which Rendell kept his whisky was unlocked, he mixed a drink—took a cigarette from a box on the mantelpiece—then lit the fire. After which he lowered himself carefully into an arm-chair, put his crutches on the floor, and surrendered himself to comfort.

He closed his eyes and drifted imperceptibly into a day-dream. Gradually the actual Marsden receded. The man he would like to be slowly emerged. This dream-Marsden became clearer and clearer till the man in the arm-chair identified himself wholly with him.

This dream-Marsden was rather an impressive person, being tall, slender, handsome—and a first-class athlete. He had played Rugby for England and was now a famous golfer. Fortune had been prodigal to him on every level. He was rich, well-born, a member of half a dozen good clubs, and a prominent figure in smart society. Women went mad about him.

This dream-Marsden had a house in town, a place in the country, and went abroad frequently to the right places with the right people. He had a Rolls-Royce and a Bentley. Also, Vera was his wife. He had married her because it was obvious that her life depended on him. He was her idol. He derived his subtlest pleasure from stretching her on the rack of jealousy. Naturally, he wasn't faithful to her. That was scarcely likely when half the loveliest women in London were crazy about him. And, of course, he made no attempt to conceal his infidelities from Vera. On the contrary, he paraded them in order to torture her. When jealousy made her desperate, and she began to abuse him, he would threaten to leave her. Having thus brought her literally to her knees, he would forgive her. Then he would go away for another week-end in order to assert his freedom. She had forgotten that she had ever known Ivor Trent. She——

But at this point Marsden's day-dream ended abruptly, for Rendell came into the room.

This sudden return to the actual irritated Marsden. The contrast between his imaginings and the facts was too wide to be bridged in a second. A swift transition from the dream-Marsden to Marsden the cripple was very unpleasant. It martyred his vanity.

He looked up at Rendell with a smile resembling a scowl.

"Hullo! I wanted to see you last evening, but thought I'd better not, as you'd been to the funeral. Did it go off all right?"

"Yes, it—went off all right."

"Good! No one else there, I suppose?"

"No one."

"Any wreaths?"

"No."

"I thought not. Well, that's that! Now, look here, I've not come to chat. It's pretty important really. I want your help."

Rendell got a drink then sat down opposite Marsden. He felt tired and depressed, consequently the prospect of a conversation with Marsden was not inviting.

"What is it you want? I'm not feeling too good and——"

"It's about Vera. I've got to settle things with her one way or the other. I can't go on like this, and neither can she. She's worse than ever."

"I daresay, but I don't see what all this is to do with me. You say you want to marry her. Well, why don't you ask her? That will settle things one way or the other."

Marsden fidgeted, then said jerkily:

"Yes—of course. But—well—you see—I'll put it like this. I haven't a lot to offer. In one way, I mean. That is, I'm not rich. I've a little private money, but—we'd have to live in my cottage in the country."

"Well?"

"And—and that means, of course, that she'd have to give up her job."

Again, Marsden hesitated. Manner, tone, gesture, plainly revealed how he resented the necessity for stating facts.

"And, of course," he went on, "I'm not all I might be—physically."

He gave a shrill little laugh, then added:

"Well, you don't say anything."

"I'm waiting to hear what you want me to do," Rendell replied.

"I see. Well, briefly, it's this. I want you to sound Vera. I—I want you to tell her the facts and see if she'll marry me. Mind you," he went on quickly, "I think she will. I want to marry her immediately. I've got a special licence and——"

"You want *me* to ask her if she'll marry you!"

"Yes, I do. And I want you to go to her place to-night. She expects *me* at eight-thirty, but I want you to go instead. Then you can tell me to-morrow what she says. I'll be here about this time."

Rendell did not reply for some moments. If he refused, he would not see Vera before he left for Italy. Perhaps it would be better to go. Rosalie had asked him to help her if he could.

"Very well. You said eight-thirty?"

"Yes."

Rendell finished his drink, then rose.

"I'll have to go, Marsden. I'll get a sandwich or something on the way."

"Good! And I'll see you—here—about this time to-morrow."

"Yes, all right."

Rendell put on his overcoat and left Marsden without another word.

He reached Vera's flat just before eight-thirty, pressed the bell, and waited. Over a minute elapsed, then he rang again.

A few moments later a light was switched on in the hall and the door opened.

"You!"

She stared at him incredulously.

"Yes—Rendell."

He tried to speak in his normal tone, but her appearance alarmed him. Her face was swollen and deep lines circled her eyes.

She invited him to enter with a movement of her hand and he followed her into the sitting-room.

He noticed a half-filled suitcase on the table and was about to ask if she were going away, when she turned to him and demanded:

"Why have you come?"

"It was Marsden's idea."

"What does he want?"

"He wants me to put certain facts up to you—and then to ask you a question. If your answer is 'yes,' he will come here himself to-morrow night."

"I shan't be here to-morrow night. I'm going away for the week-end."

Rendell glanced at her. She flushed crimson and said angrily:

"I suppose I can go away for the week-end if I want to, can't I?"

"Of course, but you don't sound as if you *do* want to."

Her anger flickered out and her mouth began to tremble. Then she sank into a chair and buried her face in her hands.

"Now, this won't——"

"Oh, go away! For God's sake go away! I can't stand this for another minute!"

"That's all very well, but——"

She sprang up and faced him. "I'm going to spend the week-end with Captain Frazer!"

"*Captain Frazer!* What on earth are you talking about?"

"Listen! You must listen! You remember that day at your room —the day he left for Ramsgate?"

"Yes, well?"

"I discovered—that day—that he knew about me and Ivor. Yes he *does*! I went down to that room of his and found out that he knew. He frightened me and I promised anything. Then he wrote to me——"

"You damned little fool!"

"I tell you he *knows*! He wrote asking for money. I sent it to him. Then he wrote again—and again. And then—then he said I'd got to go and spend a week-end with him, or——. I said I couldn't get away. I said I was ill. But, now, I've *got* to go. And I'm going to-morrow."

"You *damned* little fool!"

"But I tell you——"

"And I tell you," Rendell cut in, "that Frazer knows nothing—nothing whatever. He saw you were frightened about something—and traded on it. Show me his letters."

"But, but——"

"Get me his letters. We'll soon settle this nonsense. I only want to see how far he had the nerve to go."

She went to the bedroom, returning almost immediately with a small pile of letters.

Rendell read them carefully.

"I'll keep these two," he said at last, handing her the others.

"But what are you going to do? You mustn't tell him I've shown these to you. I'm afraid of him. I daren't quarrel with him."

"Don't talk nonsense, but listen to me. I shall go to Rams-gate——"

"You!"

"To-morrow and bring back a statement, written and signed by Frazer, saying that he knows nothing against you and that he is most grateful for the money you've lent him. Also, that he'll repay it as soon as he can. You'll have that statement to-morrow night."

"He won't give it to you."

"Yes, he will. I understand Frazer pretty well. He'll do what I want."

"You really believe that?"

"I promise it. And I suppose this is why you've been avoiding me. You've plenty of brains, Vera, but—emotionally—you're a bit of a fool."

She sank into a chair and began to cry.

"But I suppose you were so frightened you didn't know what you were doing. Was that it?"

"Yes."

He went over to her and took her hands in his.

"Come on. I'm going to put you into a more comfortable chair."

He raised her gently, then led her to an arm-chair near the fire.

"Now, have a cigarette."

"Why are you so good to me? I was nearly mad to-night."

"Then why didn't you send for me?"

She did not reply, and he went on.

"Well, it doesn't matter. Tell me—have you had anything to eat?"

She shook her head.

"Then I'll go out and get something."

"No—really!—I couldn't eat anything."

There was a long silence. Eventually Rendell asked:

"Do you feel up to discussing Marsden?"

"Yes, I suppose so. What does he want?"

"He wants you to marry him."

"Then why did he send you to ask me?"

"Because he feels a bit awkward about it," Rendell replied. "And for these reasons. He hasn't much money. You'd have to live in his cottage in the country. You'd also have to give up your job. And—he's a cripple."

"And I don't love him," Vera added.

"No, but he doesn't know that."

"Oh well, you can tell him I'll marry him."

Her tone was so casual, and yet contained such weariness, that Rendell did not reply immediately.

"You're as indifferent as all that?" he asked at last.

"Yes. You were right when you said I was a fool emotionally. I'll be safer behind bars. So I'd better marry Peter, and the sooner the better."

"Well, you can marry him at once, if you want to. He's got a special licence and——"

"Do you like him?" she asked suddenly.

Rendell hesitated.

"Do you *like* him?" she demanded irritably.

"No."

"I knew you didn't, but I wanted to make you say it. He's weak, mean, and vain. Did you think I didn't know that? But I'm not going to marry him if he's going to cross-examine me about Ivor."

"He won't want to."

"How do you know? Are you certain?"

"Quite certain," Rendell replied. "He's afraid that *you* will want to cross-examine *him* about Trent. You needn't worry about that, but——"

He broke off.

"Well, but—*what?*" she demanded.

"I was going to say that, frankly, to live with Marsden in a cottage isn't going to be too easy."

"I know that. But there might be a child."

She rose and began to wander about the room. Some minutes passed, then she paused near him and asked:

"You know I met Rosalie Vivian?"

"Yes. Why did you mention her?"

"Oh, I don't know. She's very lovely."

Then, after a pause, she added:

"You think she's lovely, don't you?"

"Yes."

"I'd give anything to have her beauty. It's power, and I worship power as only the weak can worship it. Will you see her again?"

"I'm joining her in Italy soon."

She turned quickly to him.

"You're—you're joining her in Italy?"

"Yes, why?"

"Oh nothing! Then, you're very fond of her?"

"Yes."

She began to wander about the room again.

At last Rendell said he thought he had better go. He rose and she came over to him.

"You're *certain* about Captain Frazer?"

"Quite certain. I will bring you that statement to-morrow."

"No, seal it, and drop it through the letter-box. I—I can't see you again after to-night."

"Very well. And I'll tell Marsden."

She went to the hall with him, waited while he put on his overcoat, then took his hands impulsively.

"You've saved me. You know that?"

"Oh well——"

"Yes, you have. And, somehow, I don't mind what you know about me. I could tell you everything."

She leaned down, kissed his hand, then ran back into the sitting-room, leaving the door open.

Rendell hesitated, then went out and down into the street.

XI

Two days later Rendell was alone.

As he had anticipated, the interview with Frazer was brief and conclusive. A hint that he had blackmailed Vera—a suggestion as to possible consequences—so frightened the Captain that he wrote a statement at Rendell's dictation and signed it. The only difficulty was to convince him that, having done so, he had nothing to fear.

Rendell was back in London by six o'clock, and went straight to his room, where he found Marsden waiting for him. The latter, however, left directly he learned that Vera's answer was favourable.

Rendell did not see him again. Marsden gave up his room the following day and went to the country—without saying good-bye, and without leaving a message.

At first this lack of courtesy puzzled Rendell, but eventually it made him appreciate the subtle demands of Marsden's vanity.

It had been necessary to state his position before asking Vera to marry him, but this he had been unable to do in person. To stand revealed on the background of the facts was too humiliating. He wanted to dominate Vera, not to plead with her. He wanted her to regard him as he would like to have been, not as he was. But to tell the truth about himself was not the only indignity which menaced him. A darker shadow gloomed across his imagination—she might refuse him. Marsden winced at the possibility of hearing himself rejected.

Hence he had made Rendell his ambassador. And he bitterly regretted the fact directly he learned that Vera had accepted him. For—now—he instantly assumed that she loved him desperately, and that, therefore, there had been no necessity either to state the facts or to employ an advocate. He had humiliated himself unnecessarily, and he regarded Rendell as the cause of that humiliation. He was determined, therefore, not to see him again. Hence his hurried departure from Potiphar Street.

So Rendell was alone, and this solitude gradually revealed past and present in clearer perspective.

In the first place, he discovered that he had been at No. 77 for nearly seven weeks. Also, that his experiences there grouped themselves roughly into four distinct periods. The first concerned his arrival; the mystery of Trent's presence in this extraordinary house; and adventures with visitors. This first period had occupied just over a week. The second was the month he had spent with Rosalie. Wrayburn's tragedy was the third. And the fourth related to his dealings with Marsden and Vera.

Nearly seven weeks!

And all this had happened to him because of Ivor Trent! Trent— whom he had almost forgotten! Yet all this time he had been in those rooms at the top of the house. No one had seen him, no word had come from him. He had remained as invisible and as mute as destiny.

Why should this stranger have altered the map of his world?

The question found no answer, but others jostled on its heels. If he had known what had awaited him at No. 77 would he have come? Was it madness even to consider marrying Rosalie? Had his mental balance been destroyed as a result of suddenly finding himself in the vortex of Trent's relations with others?

But as these questions, too, remained unanswered, Rendell now tried to assess his own responsibility for what had happened to him.

In one mood, it seemed that two impulses had altered his life. The first had been his letter to Marsden, which had resulted in their dining together on that fog-shrouded Sunday in order to discuss Trent. The second was his sudden determination—that night in the club—to go to No. 77 and inquire about him.

But, in another mood, these impulses seemed secondary, for a prior event had occasioned them. That event was the reading of one of Trent's books. He had read it in Germany, when he was alone and lonely, and it was because he had discovered a deep knowledge of loneliness in the novel that he had become interested in its author.

Often, however, these guesses as to the origin of his experiences at Potiphar Street seemed childish. They had happened. That was the fact. How and why they had happened was a mystery as deep as life itself.

But Rendell was not concerned only with the past during this period of solitude. The present situation in the house intrigued him, chiefly because he heard nothing of Trent. He knew that Mrs. Frazer had been his nurse for some weeks but, even so, it was curious that he never saw her. Rendell realised that this was less extraordinary than it appeared, as he had practically only slept in his room during the last few weeks. But, now that he was in most of the day, there was no sign of her.

As to the lodgers, the majority were recent arrivals, and it was doubtful whether they knew that Trent was in the house. The servant, Mary, had left. There remained only Elsa, the model, who had taken over Mrs. Frazer's duties, but it seemed to Rendell that she avoided him. He encountered her only on rare occasions and then she passed him with only a formal greeting.

One morning when he was pacing the room a sudden thought brought him to a standstill. Soon, he was leaving for Italy. He would bring Rosalie back to London for a time, then, possibly, they would marry—and live abroad. If that happened, he would probably never meet Trent, never unravel the mystery of his relations with others, never discover why he came in secret to Potiphar Street to work. He would remain in his present ignorance. He would never even see the man who had altered the whole of his life.

"It *can't* end like that!" he exclaimed irritably. But as he began to pace the room again, he became more and more convinced that this was how it *would* end.

In the evening he went to the long bar of the Cosmopolitan, hoping to see Rummy. He had been in twice since his first visit, but on this occasion he learned that she had been off duty for some days as she was ill.

Rendell decided he would walk back to Chelsea, and then write to Rosalie. Since her departure she had written two or three times a week and although these letters consisted only of a single sheet, they evoked her image so vividly that Rendell seemed to see her confronting and claiming him.

He reached home at about nine o'clock, then sat by the fire to smoke a cigarette before writing to Rosalie.

The cigarette was half-finished when the door opened slowly.

He looked up and saw Elsa. She stood motionless, watching him intently, her lips slightly parted.

"Thought I'd come to see how you're getting on."

"Very glad you did," Rendell replied as he rose. "Come in and sit down, if you've time. I hoped I'd see you before I went away."

"You're not busy?"

"No, not in the least."

She sank into a chair by the fire. Rendell noticed that she relaxed the whole of her body directly she was seated.

"You sit as if it were a luxury," he said with a smile.

"So it is—if you're used to being terribly tired. I've been a model for years—you knew that? I've often posed for hours when I did not know how to stand."

A silence followed. Rendell did not speak, as he assumed that at any moment she would explain why she had come. Also, a change in her appearance puzzled him, though he could not decide whether she had actually altered, or whether—on former occasions—all his attention had been captured by the beauty of her hair.

She was not looking at him, and he glanced at her repeatedly. She had the eyes and features of a child—but a child who had known privation. It had tautened the face, thereby accentuating cheekbones and chin. But the suffering that had marred her beauty had also individualised it. It was wholly hers, for it epitomised her history.

As the minutes passed Rendell discovered that to be silent with her did not embarrass him. She lay back, outstretched in her chair, with eyes nearly closed. Rendell felt that this physical abandonment expressed her recognition of a kinship between them which had no need of speech. To him, therefore, this silence possessed a unique quality. During it they ceased to be strangers.

Then, suddenly—and inevitably as it seemed to him—he began

to tell her about himself. He spoke quietly, without looking once in her direction. He told her about his profession, what he had done, where he had been. Words presented themselves with unaccustomed readiness. In a few swift sentences he revealed the quality of the life he had lived before his marriage.

"I was that type—roughly. It's a common enough one, of course—certain amount of ability, fair amount of money, keen on adventure. And a real admiration for only one quality—courage. I was free. I took what I wanted, if I could get it. I barged about the world, doing my job, and meeting all sorts of people. I knew quite a lot about men. I had to. I knew nothing about women, because, in those days, they were only a physical necessity. And you don't learn a lot about them that way."

He paused for a moment, then went on:

"Well, eventually, I married. I'd just returned to England after a long absence. She was some years younger than I was, and pretty frail. Half a child, really. God alone knows why she married me! Anyway, her health was bad from the beginning, so it was more like a brother and sister relationship than anything else. In two years she was dead.

"I said just now," he continued, "that courage was really the only quality I admired. Well, during those two years, she showed me a type I knew nothing about. I knew only the kind that goes out to meet danger. She showed me the courage that lies still, and watches—and waits. Well, she died. That was a year ago. And I found that my old way of life was over. Then I discovered that there was such a thing as loneliness."

He then explained how he had come to Potiphar Street, and gave an edited account of his experiences there during the last few weeks. He ended by saying:

"I'm going to Italy soon, but this is what beats me. I suppose it's why I've told you this rigmarole. I don't know. Anyway, it's this. Trent's altered my life—yet I shall probably never meet him, probably never see him."

"What do you want to know about him?" Elsa asked slowly.

"That would take a month. So tell me just this, if you can. Why has he had rooms here for years without telling any of his friends?"

"Because he can only write in those rooms upstairs. He didn't tell his friends for several reasons. One was that he didn't want to be disturbed. But, apart from all that, he belongs here."

"Belongs here!" Rendell echoed.

"Yes. You'll understand everything before long."

"I doubt it! But you seem very definite about Trent. Have you known him long?"

"For ten years."

"You mean, you've known him since he first came here?"

"Yes. The house was full of writers and artists in those days. That was an experiment of Captain Frazer's. I was one of them. Ivor was another. Why do you look so surprised?"

"I don't know. There's something queer about all this. I feel that, underneath, you're excited about something."

"Tell me," she said impetuously, leaning towards him, "have you ever waited for something, longed for something, year after year, till you felt that if it ever happened you just wouldn't be able to bear it?"

"No, I don't think I've ever wanted anything as much as all that."

Rendell rose, took a cigarette and was about to light it, when he suddenly exclaimed.

"You're laughing!"

"I can't help it. I'm terribly happy to-night. Sit down and I'll tell you one or two things."

She was silent for a minute, then went on:

"I was twenty when I came here, ten years ago. I hadn't a farthing. My father was an Austrian, but he died when I was fifteen. Since then I lived with my mother who had an annuity. She died suddenly, when I was twenty. I had no money and knew nothing. Then an artist who admired my figure said he'd pay me to sit for him. So I became an artist's model."

"And that was the position just before you met Trent?"

"Yes. I took a box of a room here. Ivor stayed here for a year, writing *Two Lives and a Destiny*." After a pause she added:

"I knew nothing about men—then. I'd never met anyone in the least like him, in appearance, personality, or anything else. I was crazy about him. It was I who suggested he should write *Two Lives and a Destiny*. It was a great success. Then he took that flat near Cork Street. That was the end of him."

"You mean, you didn't see him again?"

"No, hardly ever."

"But why did he leave you like that?"

"That's a long story. But it wasn't very surprising, do you think? Nearly every artist, when he becomes successful, is irritated by the people he mixed with when he was unknown. Still, there were special reasons in Ivor's case. But that doesn't matter."

"And what happened to you?" Rendell asked as she remained silent.

She rose slowly, then leaned against the mantelpiece and looked down at him with an odd expression.

"What do you suppose happened? I was twenty-one, and an artist's model. Times were bad, and got worse and worse. I starved sometimes—I'd have starved altogether if it hadn't been for Mrs. Frazer. The world just knocked me about, rolled me in and out of the gutter. I got used to watching things happen to me—pretty grim things, some of them."

"And you never even saw Trent?"

"I'd run into him in the street sometimes, but he avoided me. Anyway, I didn't want to meet him."

"All I can say is this," Rendell said slowly, "the more I hear about him, the less I understand him. In fact I gave up trying to make him out long ago. But I would like to know this. How is he now?"

Elsa looked at him enigmatically.

"You'll have to ask Mrs. Frazer."

"But I never see her nowadays."

"You will—soon."

"What makes you think that?"

Elsa laughed.

"You'll see her—soon. I suppose you wonder why I've told you all this."

"Yes, in a way. But I feel you've a reason, though I'm damned if I know what it is."

"Perhaps we'll meet again one day."

"Are you going away then?"

"I only came to help Mrs. Frazer while she was looking after Ivor. I'm not here permanently. I'd better go now. I've a good deal to arrange."

Rendell rose then stood looking at her intently.

"Well?" she asked.

"Rosalie said she felt she had always known you. I know what she meant."

"She said that?"

"Yes."

"I'm glad. She's very lovely."

They stood facing each other for nearly a minute.

"There's something very odd about all this," Rendell said at last.

"About what?"

"You—this conversation—everything!"

Elsa laughed.

"I'll have to go now."

Rendell held out his hand.

"Very well. Good night."

"Good-bye."

He went to the door with her, then began to pace slowly up and down the room.

XII

A SUNDAY, three days later. . . .

Mrs. Frazer glanced upward through the basement window, then—seeing no one—she hurried into the passage and called up the stairs:

"Lily!"

She waited, then called again.

This time a voice from the top of the stairs answered her.

"Didn't you hear me the first time! Is Mr. Rendell back yet?"

"No, Mum."

"Have you been into his room to see?"

"He wasn't there a few minutes ago——"

"See if he is now."

A moment later Lily informed her that Rendell had not returned.

"Well, mind you tell me directly he does. I want to know the moment he comes in."

"Yes, Mum."

"What's the time now?"

"Nearly twelve o'clock, Mum."

With minor variations, this dialogue was repeated every hour till six o'clock—Mrs. Frazer's agitation becoming more apparent with each repetition. Finally, at five o'clock, Lily was ordered to stand sentinel in the hall so that she could report Rendell's return directly that event occurred.

Just before six, Lily hurried to the top of the basement stairs and called into the depths below.

"Mr. Rendell's just come in, Mum!"

Mrs. Frazer ran up the stairs, pushed past Lily, then rushed into Rendell's room without pausing to knock.

"Mr. Rendell!"

"Hullo! Haven't seen you for a long time." Then, after a glance at her, he added: "What's wrong?"

"He's gone!"

"Who's gone?"

"Mr. Trent!"

He turned to her quickly.

"Do you mean he's gone without saying he was going?"

"Yes."

"Well I'm damned!"

"But that's not all. I've never had such a day! She's gone, too—Elsa!"

Rendell stared at her.

"With him, do you mean?"

"I don't *know*. I don't know anything!"

"Tell me what happened—exactly."

"I went up to Mr. Trent at nine this morning. I passed Lily on the stairs and she said you'd gone out very early. Well, I knocked on his door. No reply. I knocked again several times. Then I got scared, so I went in. The bedroom was empty. The door leading to the study was open. I went through. Empty! Then I looked in the bathroom. Not a sign of him! I tell you I was scared. So back I go to the study. And there I found a note. And what do you think it said?"

"Haven't an earthly," Rendell replied.

"It just said he'd gone, thanked me for all I'd done for him—and a cheque for a hundred pounds was enclosed. But that wasn't all. There was a P.S. which said: 'Mr. Rendell can have my rooms for his last week—if that would interest him.'"

"What the devil does that mean?" Rendell demanded.

"I'm sure I don't know. Still, he knew all about you."

"You mean—he knows what you've told him."

"No, I don't, sir. I told him weeks ago you were in the house, and he said that he knew of you, though he'd rather I didn't mention it. Then he went on to say that you had dined with Mr. Marsden on that Sunday he was taken ill."

"Then Marsden must have seen Trent and told him."

"Oh no, sir! Mr. Trent's seen no one."

"But he *must* have!"

"I know he's seen no one. Why, he's not even opened one of the letters that have come for him. He's been alone ever since he came here. And that's eight weeks ago to-day."

Rendell thought intently for a moment, then asked:

"Did Elsa see him?"

"Oh yes, sometimes. During the last week or so, she'd take in his tray when I was busy."

"Then Marsden must have told her that he dined with me on that Sunday—and Elsa must have told Trent. That's the only possible explanation. Well, go on. What did you do after you'd read Trent's note?"

"I went to Elsa's room. It was empty, and all her things had gone. You could have knocked me down with a feather."

"I believe you. But *this* is what I want to know, Mrs. Frazer. When did Trent cease to be seriously ill?"

"Well, sir, if you ask me, he's been perfectly well for weeks."

"What!"

"Ever since I became his nurse. I'm certain of it. And I'm certain of this, too—he's been working."

"How do you know that?"

Mrs. Frazer hesitated.

"I wouldn't have you think I'm the sort that spies on her lodgers, because I'm not. But I got this idea that Mr. Trent was well, and that he was working. So, one night—or early in the morning, rather—I went out into the street. He had not drawn the curtains properly in his study—and I saw a light. That happened more than once. There's a mystery in all this, Mr. Rendell."

"There's a mystery, all right. But tell me this. Did he ask you questions about the people in the house?"

"Yes, he did."

"About me?"

"Yes."

"And did he ask about my visitors? Did he know that Mrs. Vivian, Miss Thornton, and Mr. Wrayburn came to see me?"

"Yes, he asked a lot of questions. And I answered them. The doctor told me to encourage rational conversation. I didn't think there was any harm, and what else could I——"

"And he knew that Mr. Marsden had a room here for some weeks?"

"Yes, sir, he knew that."

"All very interesting," Rendell said slowly. "Now, tell me again, will you? the *exact* wording of that P. S. to his letter."

"That I can do, for I know that letter by heart. I've read it fifty times, I should think. This was the P. S. 'Mr. Rendell can have my rooms for his last week—if that would interest him.'"

"Well, it *does* interest him! And I'll go up now. It's six o'clock. I'm dining late to-night, so I'll spend a couple of hours in Trent's rooms and think things over. Lily can tell anyone who calls for me that I'm out, though I don't expect anyone will call."

"But what do you make of it all, Mr. Rendell?"

"I don't know what to make of it, and if I were you, I would not puzzle my head about it. Why not go and see a friend for a couple of hours and get a change of atmosphere?"

"I think I will. I do, indeed. I've plenty to worry about. I suppose I'll have to get my husband back now."

"I shouldn't hurry about that."

"Oh, I don't mean till you're gone, sir. Here's the key to Mr. Trent's door. The door at the bottom of the stairs, I mean," she added, seeing that Rendell did not understand. "He's got really a flat to himself up there. He spent a lot of money making it quiet and one thing and another. It's completely cut off, as you'll see."

"Right! I'll go up directly you've gone."

She left him, and a few minutes later the front door closed behind her.

He picked up the key, went into the hall, and began to climb the stairs.

<h2 style="text-align:center">XIII</h2>

RENDELL encountered no one on his ascent. Previously he had not penetrated further than the second floor, consequently on reaching the third he paused and looked round. Then he went on to the foot of the stairs leading to the fourth floor—and found himself confronted by a door.

Trent!

He inserted the key, turned it, but the door did not yield. To his surprise, he found that some exertion was necessary in order to open it. He forced it back and discovered that behind the door was another, covered with thick green baize.

"No wonder he didn't hear the noise."

Rendell entered, closing the doors behind him.

Darkness and silence.

He struck a match, then switched on the light. A stairway, flanked by white banisters and covered with thick carpet, was revealed. Rendell stood gazing at it for a moment, then slowly ascended.

On reaching the top he paused again. A broad passage faced him with three shut white doors, one on his right and two on his left. He had the odd sensation that everything was waiting for him.

Eventually he opened the door on his right, thereby discovering a bathroom, but not one which his experience at No. 77 had caused him to anticipate. Even by Rendell's normal standards, it was rather luxurious.

"Does himself pretty well, evidently."

He crossed to the room on the left near the top of the stairs.

It was the bedroom. Rendell glanced round, noting the perfection of its simplicity, then went through the communicating door into the study and switched on the lights.

A whistle of amazement escaped him.

It was a low oblong room, the walls of which were covered with bookcases. Near the window was a writing-desk on which stood a curiously-shaped green idol. Parchment-coloured curtains hanging in deep folds obliterated the outside world. Concealed lighting dimly illuminated the room.

But what had occasioned Rendell's amazement was not the room's contents, but its atmosphere. It was impossible to believe he was in 77, Potiphar Street. He stood motionless, listening to the silence. Somehow this silence was not the mere absence of sound. It was not explained by the material facts of the double windows and the thick pile close-fitting carpet. This silence was alive. Rendell began to believe that the real furniture of a room is the thoughts and emotions of its occupant. This silence disturbed him. It made him feel an interloper, yet, simultaneously, it claimed him.

He looked round. Four large waste-paper-baskets, piled high with unopened letters, were ranged by the wall near the door. On a little table an open book lay face downwards. Under it was a cutting from a newspaper.

So it was here Trent had written his books. *Two Lives and a Destiny* had been written in this room. Here he had lived and worked in secret.

He went to the writing-desk, then stood looking down at it. Nearly five minutes passed. At last he crossed to the fireplace, switched on the electric fire, then stood with his back to it, as if anxious to have the whole room in view.

Gradually he became aware of an intensity in the atmosphere which affected him unpleasantly. It raised his thoughts to a new vibration, quickened his sense of personality—yet, simultaneously, seemed to rob him of it.

"I'm not staying here for my last week, Mr. Trent."

But the sound of his own voice jarred. Then, feeling that he must create contact with the familiar, he went to the window, parted the curtains, and looked out.

Lights gleamed and flashed on the turbulent river. A tram glided over Battersea Bridge. A naked tree writhed under the lash of the wind. But no sound rose to him. He felt like a deaf man looking at the world.

He was about to return to the fire, then, changing his mind, he went again to the writing-desk and stood looking down at it fascinated. Then, scarcely aware of what he was doing, he tried the top drawer on the right.

It yielded, and a pile of manuscript paper was revealed—on which was a sealed envelope, addressed to A. Rendell, Esq.

He picked it up and read his own name a dozen times in order to convince himself of its reality.

So this was why Trent had written that P.S. He wanted him to come to this room—and find this letter!

He slit open the envelope and read:

Dear Mr. Rendell,

I do not know you, but I overheard the conversation you had with Marsden the night I was taken ill.

The letter fell from Rendell's hand.

Overheard his conversation with Marsden that Sunday! . . . Why, the place was empty! . . . There was a hell of a fog and . . .

He picked up the letter and read on.

You dined at the table immediately on the left, if you remember. It is boxed off. I was in the inside seat of the partition next to it, the back of which is surmounted by a rail from which hangs a curtain. I give these details to show that although you could not see me, I was, in fact, literally only a few inches from you.

I was ill or I should not have stayed. As it was, I had no alternative but to overhear. Directly I was well enough to move, I went.

Marsden told you about my first book, Two Lives and a Destiny, *and some of the facts of my life till I was twenty-one. Also, he made certain statements about me. The only ones of any penetration were quotations from Wrayburn. But I do not want to discuss Marsden. It is you who interest me.*

You told him that a book of mine had impressed you because you felt that its author understood loneliness. You insisted on that, in spite of Marsden's stupid protests. That interested me, but, above all, I liked you. I liked a quality that came from you.

Later, I heard how you had come here. You came to inquire about me, then—finding there was a room vacant—you took it and have remained here for weeks.

I know you have met Rosalie, Vera, and—Wrayburn. I know, therefore, that you have heard much of me. I know, too, that soon you are joining Rosalie in Italy.

But there is another, and a deeper, reason why I am writing this to you. You are mysteriously associated with the supreme event of my life— mysteriously, not intimately. You had interested me just before that event occurred—and you were the first person I heard about after I recovered consciousness.

What that event was you will learn—if you read the manuscript on which you found this letter. Do what you like with that manuscript. I am indifferent. I wrote it to save myself—and to make one thing clear. Destroy it, keep it, or send it to my publisher. But I hope that you—a stranger—will read it. That seems right somehow.

I have written this letter at lightning speed. I am leaving here in a few hours. I have not time even to read through what I have written. The manuscript, too, was written at great speed.

I do not believe that you and I will meet. I don't know why I feel that, but I do feel it.

And yet, if you read this manuscript, we shall meet more intimately than if we took each other's hand and looked into each other's eyes.

I am grateful to you.

Sincerely,

Ivor Trent.

Rendell read this letter three times.

Then he took the manuscript and sat down by the fire.

He stared in front of him for some minutes, then started to read.

Part IV

IVOR TRENT'S MANUSCRIPT

A

THEY won't listen! If only they would *listen!* They keep telling me that I collapsed, that I am ill. They argue, talk, give instructions. Yes, all of them! The doctor, the nurse, Mrs. Frazer—endlessly, endlessly!

A thick mist separates me from them. Their voices reach me, but I cannot see them. When I speak, they do not seem to hear. It maddens me. I begin to shout, then hands seize me, force me down on to the bed, and voices—interminable voices—tell me that I must be still, that I must be calm, and that then I shall soon be well.

And I tell them (again and again I tell them) that I was alone in the fog, leaning over the low Embankment wall. The river was invisible: all was drifting desolation. Then I turned and saw—*Him.* A man from the Future faced me. He stood there with the signature of God across his forehead. I gazed at him as the damned gaze at an angel.

But they will not *listen!* They keep promising me that, if only I will be calm, I shall soon be well. They are trying to drag me back to my old life. And I tell them (I keep telling them) that when I saw *Him* my old life ended. At that actual moment when I looked into his eyes, I died—and I was born. Again and again I tell them, but they won't listen—they won't *listen!*

They repeat endlessly that I collapsed when Mrs. Frazer opened the door last Sunday night. Am I to tell them that I fainted because my whole being was rent by Fear and Ecstasy? Am I to tell them that?

I must learn to be silent. I must pretend to agree with them. I must let them think that I want to get well, that I want to become again the man I was. Somehow, I must do this. I must make them believe that I am slowly recovering, then the doctor will come less frequently. The nurse will go. Mrs. Frazer will attend to me. I shall be free. The nights will be mine.

It is useless to tell them of *Him*. They will only think I am mad. But, having seen him, how shall I live in the world? How shall I endure to look back on my old life? I am like one new-born, but one who is nevertheless fettered by the terrible memories of a dead man. And the name of the dead man is Ivor Trent.

People will come up to this dead man. They will say to him: "So glad you're well again. You had a bad time, I'm afraid. Well, don't overdo it. You're highly-strung, you know. You've got to allow for that. Now, take my tip, and go easy for a bit. Have a good time for a few months. Enjoy yourself, and don't think about anything."

Who is to answer them—the dead Ivor Trent or the living?

But now—now, at this actual moment—I must pretend to believe all they say. I will not speak of him again. I will tell them nothing about him. They will only believe that he is a possibility if they, too, have a vision of him. Unless and until that happens, they will deny him. They will say that he is madness.

I will learn to be silent.

"My mystery is for me and for the sons of my house."

B

ALREADY they believe I am better. They no longer use the word "delirious." They say now that I am "very excited." How tediously easy it is to deceive people. . . .

Letters and telegrams keep coming for me. I asked Mrs. Frazer how it is that people have discovered I am here. She was very embarrassed, but eventually I learned that her husband told a journalist I was in the house. I have seen the paragraph in the newspaper. It says that I am in a delirious condition. Everyone will learn that I have had these rooms for years, that all my books have been written here. Captain Frazer will reveal all he knows. That is certain. My secret is mine no longer.

Mrs. Frazer also told me that she has a new lodger. It is Rendell, the man who dined with Marsden last Sunday. She was eager to talk about him. Evidently the doctor has told her to encourage "rational" conversation. She said that Rendell came to inquire about me on Monday night, and suddenly decided to take a room. Why has he come? Why is he so interested in a man he does not know? Perhaps the story he told Marsden last Sunday was lies.

Anyway, what does all this matter to me? I will see no one. I will not open any letters. Let them all make what they can of my secret. Yes, all of them! Not one of them has met me. Each mistook a mask for a face.

I will reveal here the mask—and the face.

Where shall I begin? With the conversation between Marsden and Rendell? Yes, that will do. I will begin there—and work backwards.

Marsden told Rendell how I had delivered him from a bully, and how—years later—I stayed with him in his cottage and "brought him back to life." He added that he believed, on each occasion, I had been concerned only with myself. Rendell did not understand that, so Marsden explained that I had helped him only because I wanted to test the power of my own will. (This idea was Wrayburn's, not Marsden's, but that doesn't matter.)

Well, it is true. In all my relations with others I have been concerned only with myself.

That is what I have to make clear in this manuscript. I have to reveal how I became the mask which people believed was Ivor Trent. I can do this, and I will do it. I have struggled to the summit of the abyss which is myself. I will look down into it and reveal its secrets.

(Was it Richard of St. Victor who defined Humility as self-knowledge? I do not remember, but it is the greatest definition known to me. I found it in an old book which a priest lent me years ago.)

Marsden also told Rendell the story of my first book, *Two Lives and a Destiny*. He explained that it revealed my life till I was twenty-one. That is partly true, but it does not contain what I dared not face—then. And the account it gives of the quarrel with my father is only the ghost of the actual scene.

I will show everything here. Everything!

When I was seven, they told me my mother was dead. The word had no meaning for me. Then they said I should never see her again. I crept away. I wanted to go to her room. I was certain she would be there. Or, if not that, then her dresses would be in the wardrobe. I would look at them, touch them. They would prove that she was still alive, that soon she would come back, that I should see her again and hear her voice.

But the door of her room was locked.

I began to tremble, for I remembered our last meeting.

One night I had wakened to find her kneeling by my bed, her eyes brimming with tears. She was dressed for a journey. In a whisper she begged me not to speak, but to love her always—whatever anyone said. And then she went away.

At the time this had frightened me, but, when I was told she was dead, it terrified me. It had been her farewell.

I said to my father:

"Do people know when they are going to die?"

"No, of course not."

"Mother knew."

"What nonsense is this? What do you mean?"

"She knew," I repeated. "She said good-bye to me. She was dressed for a journey. Is death a long way off? How do you go there?"

Then he was kind to me. He told me to be brave. He said that only courage mattered—and that I must never show my emotions. No matter how deeply I might suffer, I must never reveal it to the world. He said that was the whole secret of life.

Soon after her death, we moved to London. Till then we had lived in Suffolk, but now my father sold the house and its contents. The new London flat contained nothing that had been hers. She was obliterated. He never mentioned her, and he willed that I should never speak of her. I could feel his will freeze the sentence on my lips when suddenly I longed to share a memory of her with him.

In every other way he was kind to me. In Suffolk he had not bothered much about me, but, now, he did everything to capture my affection. We spent whole days together. Soon, I was terribly proud of him. He was distinguished, cultured, and he spoke to people as if their destiny were to obey him. I promised myself that I would be like him when I was a man. Courage was his god—and so it became mine.

And yet, sometimes when I woke in the night, I saw a vision of my mother. She stood before me, radiantly lovely, although she was dressed in rags. Twice I saw her like that. Then, when I was ten, I woke one night suddenly with a great start. She was standing motionless in the middle of the room. A misty light enveloped her, but her features were clear. She stretched out her arms to me. Then she seemed to dissolve till only the misty light remained.

A few days later I noticed that my father was pale and silent. He said he was ill, and that frightened me. I thought he, too, would die. I asked one of the maids what was the matter with him. She said she did not know, but that, a few days ago, a letter had come for him from abroad—and that since then he had been ill.

Nevertheless, he continued to take me for our daily walk in the Park, though he spoke seldom and his eyes had a fixed, steely expression which I had not seen before. Then, perhaps a week after the letter came from abroad, he stopped a bolting horse in the Row. It was an act of stupendous courage, for the animal was thundering along panic-stricken. Everyone regarded him as a hero, and there was a good deal about it in the papers.

Years later I realised that actually he had attempted suicide, but, at the time, I regarded him as a god. Although I was only ten, I tried to emulate him. I willed to fear nothing, and when that proved impossible—as it often did—I hid every sign of cowardice.

I steeled myself against all childish terrors. When I went to school, I tried to behave as if he were watching me. Actually, therefore, it was my father who rescued Marsden from that bully. Marsden now believes that I used the incident as a test for my will. He is right, but he does not know what my triumph cost me. I was ill for days afterwards. Still, I became Marsden's hero—in the same way as my father was mine.

Marsden often spent part of the holidays with us, as his people were in India, and he did not exaggerate when he told Rendell that we thought my father was "God Almighty when we were kids." Every day, every hour, I spent with him widened and deepened his influence over me. He became a unique being, a man raised far above the generality of men. To be like him—that was my creed. And it was a passionate fanatical creed which made each day and every night a living ordeal. To be fearless, distinguished, cultured—to go through the world as if it were one's own—never to be impressed, never to surrender oneself, never to be inadequate to any situation! *To be like him!*

But what quickened the roots of my admiration was his silence concerning my mother. For, now, I believed that this silence represented the triumph of his creed. I believed that he remained silent, although her death had stretched him permanently on the rack. He always spoke contemptuously of women, but—to me—that contempt only revealed his overwhelming love for her. As I grew older, I became convinced that his creed of courage had triumphed over the supreme ordeal of his life. Not even to me would he show the suffering which had turned his world into a wilderness. This belief heightened the pedestal on which I had placed him till he inhabited the clouds. When I prayed, it was not to God—but to him.

I stayed at school till I was eighteen, then, a year later, we went abroad and did not return to England till I was nearly twenty-one.

As the weeks passed, I noticed a change in him. Often when we were together, reading, I would look up to find his eyes fixed on me, his book face downwards on his knee. Also, sometimes he would get up suddenly, hesitate as if he were about to say something, then go abruptly out of the room. I noticed, too, that he was extraordinarily pale, and that he would clasp and unclasp his hands in a quick nervous manner, utterly unlike his normal dignified demeanour.

The night before my twenty-first birthday, he suddenly said in a new disconnected manner:

"It's—well, let me see—it's your birthday to-morrow, isn't it?"

"Yes, to-morrow."

"Ah, I see, I *see*! Well, as a fact—I may as well tell you—you come into a certain amount of money when you're twenty-one."

"A certain amount of *money*! From whom?"

"Well, it's all quite preposterous, of course, but—as a fact—a distant relative died a few years ago and left you some money. Quite unnecessary! I am a rich man. It was an impertinence, really."

"But who was this relative?" I asked, astonished at this information.

"I did not even know her—or scarcely. She lived in Australia. She was—well, as a fact—she was a relative of your—mother's."

I stared at him. He had mentioned her at last! He stood, ashy-white, looking down at me, leaning heavily on a little table by his side.

Then—swiftly, terribly—I *knew* there was some mystery concerning my mother.

I leapt to my feet.

"Where was my mother buried?"

He made a curious whistling noise, exactly like the hiss of escaping steam.

"Where was she buried?" I repeated.

"I do not know."

"You don't—*know*!"

"No—or care."

I went nearer to him.

"So you've lied to me. She died fourteen years ago——"

"Eleven!"

"*Eleven?*"

His arms shot up as if jerked by invisible strings. His face became distorted and his whole body began to writhe.

"Yes—eleven years ago! Eleven! *Eleven!* Died in rags, a pauper! And serve her right, too—the bitch, the harlot, the whore!"

The words fell like a whip across my eyes.

"But it was fourteen years—fourteen!—since she went off with her rat of an Italian lover. For that's what she did. A dago was what she wanted. He knew all the bed tricks——"

A series of foul images followed. He pelted her with obscenities. A frenzy of sexual jealousy surged like lava from the depths of him. He stood swaying from side to side, a twisted, leering, humiliated being—ransacking the dung-heaps of his imagination for filth to hurl at her.

As I watched him, two things happened: one mysterious, the other miraculous.

The first was a consciousness of power which gradually possessed me. The dignity he had so abjectly abandoned became mine. The will-power that had deserted him entered into me. He was revealing the depths of himself. I would reveal nothing. I would live up to his creed. I would remain silent, watching him, till the very excess of his fury reduced him to impotence. And then I would go.

The second—and the miraculous—thing which happened was this. I saw a white mistiness behind him, from which emerged a vision of my mother in all the loveliness that had haunted my childhood. She was more real than the frenzied figure between us. I ceased to see or hear it. I felt we were alone, and that she was revealing why she had left him.

At last gestures and snarls were substituted for words. His passion ceased to be articulate. I waited till silence seemed like a third person in the room, then I turned and went to the door. Just as I opened it, he spoke in a voice that was hardly a whisper.

"Ivor!"

I hurried into the hall, flung on an overcoat and seized a hat.

"*Ivor!*"

I went out, shutting the front door noiselessly behind me.

C

THE next morning I instructed a lawyer to ascertain the amount due to me under the will of my mother's relative. I did not write to my father and he did not know where I was. . . .

I spent whole nights wandering about the streets. My inner world was in ruins. The god I had worshipped had become a gorilla. When I contrasted what I had imagined him to be with what he was, I experienced a terrible interior laughter which frightened me. This fearless, impressive, cultured man, who had kindled the fire of emulation in me, was a mask, a fake, a lie! Just a cheap fraud—a façade with a cesspool behind it. That was what I had worshipped. I had made his creed mine. It was to be my weapon in the world. It had splintered in my hand. I had nothing. I was naked and empty. All I possessed was the deep certainty that to trust another, to believe in another, to admire another was childish romanticism.

Everything seemed to be revealed in a new and a terrible clarity. Where once I had seen faces, I now saw masks. To me—now—courage was inverted fear. Dignity was a pose: culture a sham. The bestial was the real. It was that which was behind everything else. When all else collapsed, it remained. There it stood—writhing and leering and vomiting filth.

Every memory I had of him was tainted. I hated him with a curious cold hatred. He had robbed me of my chance with the world. The lovely had become suspect. He had made a perfume a lie and a stink real. He had fouled my imagination, frozen my emotions, corrupted my thoughts into spies. He had left me with this ghost of a creed—never to believe, through fear of being always deceived. . . .

Somehow the weeks became months—and then came the war.

An immense curiosity gnawed me. Civilisation? We were to fight for civilisation. And what was that? What it seemed? Or was that, too, a façade? Fine words drifted down every wind—Honour, Glory, Patriotism, Honour. Yes, it sounded all right. And youth was going to die for it.

I joined the army in August, 1914.

I was in training for several months, then I had a few days' leave before going to the front. I stayed in an hotel in London. The first night I talked to a priest. He was going the next day, and for some reason I told him my story. He listened in silence till I had finished, then he said:

"Write to your father, tell him you are going to France, and ask if he wants to see you."

"All right," I replied, "if that's what you think."

I wrote the letter, there and then, and posted it.

In the morning the priest came to my room to say good-bye. He gave me a book which I read months later in the trenches. Then he went away, and I never saw him again.

The next day I received my father's answer. It consisted of one word: "No." So I knew he had patched up the façade and hidden himself behind it again.

My last night in London I got drunk, for the first time. And I slept with a prostitute, also for the first time. Then I went to fight for civilisation.

Before I had been in France a month, my father fell dead in the street. But that was only the death of his body. For me, he had died on the night of our quarrel—and half of me had died with him. He had left me everything, but that did not interest me. I had all the money I wanted.

Three years in France, then I was wounded, but I went back just before the Armistice and stayed in the army till 1920. It was something to do.

Then I travelled for some time, trying to find out what was left of me. I discovered there was nothing. I had seen what civilisation was—behind the façade.

Two worlds had ended for me.

I returned to London and picked up with an artist, who told me of an experiment in communal living which was going to be made at 77, Potiphar Street, Chelsea. A Captain Frazer was financing it. The artist suggested I should join it. So I took the rooms at the top of this house.

I suppose that was somewhere in 1922.

D

You, whoever you are, who read this must realise that it is written under great difficulties. I write only at night, but, even so, it is possible that Mrs. Frazer will appear at any minute to ask if I need anything. Also I am given a sleeping-draught, but this has little effect, for I sleep as much as possible during the day. Then they keep bringing me letters, or telling me the names of people who have called to inquire—and how surprised these visitors are to discover that I have had rooms here for years. Rendell has met several of them—my publisher, my agent, Rosalie, Vera. At least, I am almost certain that one of the women was Rosalie. Mrs. Frazer watched her arrival. She happened to be looking out of the study window and saw a taxi draw up. Nearly a minute elapsed before a woman got out, glanced right and left, then seemed about to re-enter the taxi and drive away. But, finally, she approached the house slowly, hesitated again, then almost ran to the top of the steps. I am certain it was Rosalie.

All this disturbs me. It brings ghosts from my old life thronging round me. Also, something queer is happening to me in a deep interior manner. Moments of intense inner excitement flash up in me, raising me to a new level of consciousness. I feel exalted and afraid. A new surging abundant life possesses me, a life which quickens and annihilates. My body seems to become as huge as the earth. I have to touch myself to become aware of my actual shape.

Nevertheless, somehow I must go on with this manuscript. I must show how I became the Ivor Trent whom the people downstairs are clamouring to see.

*   *   *   *   *

It must have been the end of 1922 when I first came to this house. I only came because my artist friend suggested it. Indifference paralysed me. I had no background, no past, no roots. My father had robbed me of everything represented by the words childhood, boyhood, youth. I had no intimate personal life, no memories. Behind me was a void.

But this personal life is not the only one: there is the life of the world surrounding us. Instinctively we believe a number of things concerning it. We hear grand words about it—Justice, Freedom, Honour—and we assume they represent realities. Well, the war revealed that it is a Jungle. The grand words are a façade.

Still, 77 Potiphar Street was interesting. It was full of odd people. Captain Frazer's experiment was a failure from its inception, but it was something to watch, and that was all I wanted—something to watch. Of course, I was tired of it in a month or two, but then I met Elsa.

I met her through going to the studio of the artist who had induced me to come to Potiphar Street. She was sitting to him and was greatly embarrassed by the fact. Later, I learned that it was the first time she had sat to anyone, but, as she was alone and penniless, necessity had made her an artist's model.

I began to go to the studio whenever she was there. At first my presence increased her embarrassment, but soon we became friends. We dined together frequently and, after dinner, we walked up and down the Embankment for hours. Eventually she took a tiny room in No. 77.

Except her appearance, there was nothing remarkable about her, as the word is used, but she was one of those strangely complete beings. Most people come to the world with a soul like an empty suitcase, which they gradually fill—usually with rubbish or worse. She came with her suitcase packed. She was therefore the spectator of her own experience. It foamed on the circumference of her being, it did not penetrate to the centre.

There is tranquillity in joy, and it was hers. To be with her brought peace, as dawn over a silent sea brings peace. She knew little that can be taught, and much that can never be learned. Her beauty was that of a youth whom Nature had capriciously turned into a girl. And her hair was stolen from a god.

To be with her became a necessity. I soon tired of the other lodgers. The artists' jargon, and their incessant quarrels, became very monotonous. The only person besides Elsa who interested me was a young man who believed he was a reincarnation of Nietzsche. He interested me because, after all, that is one way of getting through the world. His monomania was intermittent, however, and when it deserted him he was a highly intelligent rather amusing man. But, after Elsa came to No. 77, I saw much less of him.

Although we spent hours and hours together, I never told her anything about myself. She knew that I did nothing, but she never asked any questions. You could be silent with her, and, often, we were silent. She would lie on the bed in my study and I would stand at the window gazing at the river.

Then one night we became lovers. It just happened. And then, lying in the darkness together, I told her everything about my life. I imagine that took a long time. I know that it was dawn when I had brought my story up to my arrival at Potiphar Street.

I ended by saying something like this:

"That's my life, more or less. And if I have told it as if it were something that is over, it is because it *is* over. I shall go on, of course, but I shall never be able to surrender myself wholly to any experience. I didn't—when you gave yourself to me. Something in me was watching. I know I've a certain type of strength, but it's paralysed. There's nothing for me to do."

Then she said:

"Why don't you write a book?"

"What about?"

"What you've just told me."

"What's the use of that?"

"Well, an artist I sat to last week was telling a friend that if you give expression to thoughts, or emotions, or memories, you become free of them."

"I wonder. Well, if I wrote a book, what should I call it?"

She was silent for a minute, then suggested: "Two Lives and a Third."

"No! Two Lives and a Destiny."

That's how my first novel was conceived. It was written in this room. Often, when I was working, Elsa sat reading, or stood looking out of the window, or rested on the bed. Usually, however, I forgot she was there.

A dæmonic energy surged through me. I was slinging my life at the world. Yet, oddly enough, I ceased to be myself. I discovered that writing is a form of possession. Something drove through me, marshalled the book into parts and chapters, snatched words and phrases out of the air. I ceased to be Ivor Trent. I became as anonymous as a medium in a trance. Although the book was derived wholly from my own experience, that experience ceased to be mine. The events I recorded had not happened to *me*—they were happening to the man in the book. *His* father was not *my* father. I understood his father. I became him. I was each of my characters in turn. And I was all of them simultaneously. I was never Ivor Trent.

This was escape, this was deliverance—to be possessed! To inhabit the psychic realm of thought and emotion! Not to know who one is, or where one is, or what is happening in the actual world! Then, at last, to look at one's watch and so rediscover oneself! To count the pages, and go to bed—not a man, but a crowd!

This is deliverance—the only deliverance I have ever known.

Two Lives and a Destiny took a year to write and revise. I had not read a line of it to Elsa, but, now, I read all of it to her. When I had finished, she said:

"I never imagined it would be like that."

"What do you mean?"

"Not like that. Not as good as that, not nearly as good."

But I discounted her opinion, for I knew she was in love with me. I decided to find out whether anyone would publish it. That would be the book's first test.

So I went to see Nietzsche. I knew one or two of his books had been published.

I found him in his room, lying on a sofa, reading.

"Look here," I burst out, "I've written a novel, and——"

"You've not got it with you?"

"No."

"Right! Sit down and tell me what you want."

"I want to know which publisher to send it to."

"Don't send it to any. Send it to my agent, Voyce. If it's any good, he'll handle it. If it isn't, he'll send it back. But don't tell him I'm living here, because I owe him money. If he should place the book, *then* tell him that I recommended you to go to him. But mind you also say that I'm on a walking tour through the Black Forest."

I sent the book to Voyce. A fortnight later he wrote asking me to see him. A month after, the novel was accepted by Polsons. Four months later it was published.

It was a great and an instantaneous success.

E

THIS cannot be a connected narrative. I am like a man besieged. Letters and telegrams keep arriving; Marsden is demanding to see me; Captain Frazer has discovered that no one knows that I have had rooms here for years. Every hour someone comes to the house to inquire.

It is Wednesday night. The doctor has just gone. He is suspicious about me, that is evident, but—fortunately—I do not look well, as I spent all last night writing. I wrote page after page in feverish haste.

Still, he has agreed that the nurse is to go. She leaves on Friday, and Mrs. Frazer will attend to me. I had a long talk with her after the doctor had gone. I have arranged everything. She is sending her husband to Ramsgate. Also, she is getting rid of the undesirable lodgers. Someone is to be found to take her place in the house. I gave her a hundred pounds and told her to make these changes as quickly as possible.

Above all, I emphasised that Captain Frazer must have gone by Saturday. That is essential. He has discovered my secret, and now he insists on dealing with visitors. I must get rid of him. There is nothing he would not do to make money.

Marsden does not worry me. He called on Rendell yesterday and found Vera with him. Marsden and Vera! They met once at my flat, and I saw he was attracted by her. Wrayburn, too, was here yesterday. And Rosalie will probably come again.

They are meeting in the labyrinth. But, of them, later. First, I must show here how I became the man they met.

*   *   *   *   *

Two Lives and a Destiny was not only a success in England. It had a big sale in America and was translated into several European languages.

As a result, my name acquired a life of its own. I no longer possessed it exclusively. Suddenly, therefore, I had a background.

All sorts of doors opened to me. I was deluged with requests to write articles on this, that, or the other—on anything, on nothing. I was interviewed. I was asked to lecture. The world suddenly became quite a different place. My publisher, Bickenshaw, suddenly became quite a different person. So different, in fact, that I almost waited to be introduced. Agents wrote to me, enclosing little booklets in which were modestly outlined the inestimable advantages conferred by their services. Hundreds of people who had read the book wrote to me. One correspondent accused me of plagiarising an unpublished work of his own. Every photographer in London wrote to me, craving a sitting—at no obligation to myself. Old school fellows I had forgotten wrote to me, saying they weren't surprised I had written a book because they remembered how jolly good my essays used to be. Scores of people wrote to me saying that their father was exactly like the father in my book. And everyone in the United Kingdom with the name of Trent wrote to me—saying they were distant relatives, and how bad times were with them.

So 77 Potiphar Street was no longer a possible address.

I took a flat. I joined two or three clubs. I went to dinners, parties, country houses. I had a good private income and my appearance was a success. I met all sorts of people—eminent, amusing, influential. And, gradually, I accepted their assumptions about me.

I accepted their assumptions about me. Not one of them was true, not one of them bore any relation to what I was, but I accepted them. How, otherwise, could I meet these people? You lose your background unless you adapt yourself to it. Also, I told myself that all this was temporary. It was amusing to be a celebrity for a year or two. Above all, life had cheated me. Success was a type of revenge. So my real self—the naked, empty Ivor Trent—stood on the bank and watched the successful Ivor Trent swirling round the social vortex.

But although I left Potiphar Street, I kept my rooms there. By now Captain Frazer's experiment had completely collapsed, so I gave Mrs. Frazer money to save them from bankruptcy. This was not generosity. Instinctively I knew that I could only write in this room overlooking the river. That sounds the merest superstition, but it is nevertheless a fact that I have never been able to work anywhere but here. I have tried again and again—always with the same result.

But there was a deeper reason why I retained these rooms. I *knew* that I belonged to the nomads who drifted in and out of this house, for I, too, was a rootless person. I, too, had no place in the world. I, too, was a bankrupt—on a very different level, it is true, but a bankrupt none the less.

I did not see Elsa and I did not write to her. When I returned to these rooms (two or three years after the publication of *Two Lives and a Destiny*) to write my second book, she had gone—and I did not ask Mrs. Frazer if she knew where she was.

I hated her.

That is difficult to explain, but it is essential to explain it.

I had become a man whose external life bore no relation whatever to his interior one. Outwardly, I was a success. Inwardly, I was a failure. I had rebelled against this secret knowledge. I refused to admit this inner emptiness. To do that would be to go into the desert—and wait for a miracle. But I dared not do that.

I rebelled, and the last ten years of my life are the history of that rebellion. My relations with others are incidents in that history. Wrayburn once told me that I had evaded my "spiritual destiny," and that my relations with others "represented my time-killing activities." But he did not know how true these statements were, for I deceived even him.

Only I—and Elsa—knew the truth about Ivor Trent. Only she and I knew the real Ivor Trent, the man who was empty and naked—the man who had made a book out of the débris of his life. To others, I was what I appeared to be. So I turned to these others and deserted Elsa.

I turned to them because I was determined to prove *to myself* that I had power. I would make others acknowledge that power so that it might seem real to me. If they believed in it, I, too, might be able to believe in it.

There was nothing very extraordinary in this decision. How many men are there who, being miserably unhappy at home, devote their finest energies to the creation of a great business in order that outward success shall numb the knowledge of inner failure? Why, what is our civilisation—our pride in "our dominion over Nature"—but one vast conspiracy to escape from the terrible knowledge of our emptiness? More and more we live "outside" ourselves. We blind our eyes with seeing, deafen our ears with hearing. Bigger and bigger grow our buildings, mightier and mightier our cities, in the frenzied hope that outward visible triumphs will so hypnotise us that we shall forget our inward spiritual squalor. Noise, sensation, speed—those are our gods. We, who dare not be silent, dare not think, dare not be still, lest we should see the ghosts we have become.

No, there was nothing extraordinary about my decision to live "outside" myself.

Before the publication of *Two Lives and a Destiny*, I had no choice. I could have gone into the world, of course, but it is one thing to be "a Mr. Trent" and quite another to be Ivor Trent.

I capitalised my background and went into the world. My novel was dramatised and the play had a considerable success in London and New York. Money surrounded me like an incoming tide. I played the part of a successful person, but, underneath, I knew I had run away from myself. I knew that my activities had no centre: they were mechanical, not organic. I was a ghost in fancy dress.

Still, I went into the world. That is, I became involved in chaos. I knew that the structure of society had collapsed. I knew that only a spiritual miracle could deliver the world from its deepening darkness—just as I knew that only a spiritual miracle could quicken life in me. A façade would not save either of us.

So, by a masterpiece of irony, *I did exactly what my father had done*. I presented a façade to the world, behind which shivered my empty and naked self.

Everyone accepted this façade as being the man. Everyone believed that I was what I seemed—that I had a forceful, dominating personality, and all the rest of it. I became reckless in my relations with others. I wanted to prove *to myself* that I had power, and I was determined to prove it.

But there was one person who knew the truth—Elsa. It was why I hated her. She was a nobody, an artist's model, tramping from studio to studio, but she knew the real Ivor Trent whom I was denying. I never wrote to her and she did not write to me. But she *knew*. I had told her everything. And the fact that I had deserted her, without a word or a line, was proof conclusive that I dare not seek to justify my present type of existence to her.

She knew—and the knowledge that she knew was agony. While she lived, I should know that my mask was a mask. Her very existence was a subtle form of blackmail.

The better I became known, the greater my "triumphs" in the world, or with women, the more intolerable the knowledge became that Elsa was not deceived. She knew that the great Ivor Trent was a ghost; a coward who had abandoned himself and her; a fake, like his father, who deceived others with a façade. She knew—this tuppeny-ha'penny starving model in Chelsea knew my secret. And the fact that she was negligible, in the world's eyes, only lacerated my pride more deeply. Had she been my "equal" in any way, I could have endured it. But this nobody, in her squalid room!

While I was at Potiphar Street, writing my second book, Mrs. Frazer volunteered certain information about Elsa. I learned that her life was a pretty impossible affair. Sittings became progressively scarce and she had not literally a penny outside her earnings. Mrs. Frazer was guarded in her account, but nevertheless I realised that Elsa had had to sell herself in order not to starve. I knew the types she encountered, and could guess the rest.

I had no pity for her. On the contrary, I was glad. She had remained "complete," she was everything I was not, everything I needed to be—but the world fêted me and kicked her into the gutter. That fact gave me perverse satisfaction, for it seemed to establish my superiority.

Sometimes I saw her in the street, but, whenever possible, I avoided her. Usually, that was simple, as I only went out at night. Twice, however, we came face to face. We only exchanged commonplace remarks, but, standing before her, I endured terrible humiliation. She was wretchedly dressed, but, although the talons of necessity had gripped and tautened her features, they had not extinguished the light which illuminated them.

I did not see her again after the second of these meetings, and

I never referred to her when talking to Mrs. Frazer. Gradually she became a shadow on the circumference of my memory. If I thought of her, it was only to hope that she had gone away, or married, or that she was dead.

Soon, however, my life became so complicated, owing to the relations I deliberately established with others, that I had no time to think of Elsa. . . .

I am going to reveal the truth of those relationships here. I shall hide nothing. But, first, I must make clear the motive which dominated my actions in every case.

Only a summary can do that.

The discovery that my father's "strength" was weakness—then the inferno of the war—had deprived me of every value I had ever possessed. I was empty and naked. But I rebelled against this inner impotence. The success of my first book made that rebellion possible. I denied the truth about myself and went into the world. I created a personality. I invented Ivor Trent.

But it was imperative that others should believe in him. It was essential they should believe that this Ivor Trent *had power*. That was essential, for, if he seemed real to them, he might seem real to me.

To dominate others, therefore, was my aim. To make them convinced that I had *power*. Power for good, or power for evil—power for this, that, or the other—but Power!

To make them accept this ghost in armour as a man! To dominate them, on some level or other, till my personality was more real to them than their own! To tower above them till they mistook a shadow for strength! To hypnotise them with a mask——

This was Ivor Trent.

F

MRS. FRAZER has just left me.

I asked her how long I had been here. She told me that it is ten days. A week ago last Sunday I collapsed at the top of the steps and was carried to this room.

Then she went on to tell me that the changes I wanted had been made. Captain Frazer had gone to Ramsgate, and so on. This wearied me, and I think she noticed it, for she changed the subject abruptly and gave me an account of a scene which happened last Saturday, and one which greatly embarrassed her.

It appears that soon after two o'clock Marsden, Vera, Wrayburn, Mrs. Frazer and her husband were having a violent discussion in Rendell's room. Rendell arrived in the middle of it, but his appearance in no way abated it. On the contrary, it became more unrestrained till, finally, when everyone was shouting and no one was listening, the door opened and the servant announced that a lady had called to see Mr. Rendell.

Mrs. Frazer described the visitor minutely. It was Rosalie. *And she was in mourning.*

"In she came, Mr. Trent, in the middle of that hubbub! I never felt so ashamed in my life. She looked startled, I can tell you, and I'm not surprised. She was frail-looking, but very beautiful. What she must have thought—and what Mr. Rendell must have thought —I tremble to think. I do, indeed."

"It wasn't your fault, Mrs. Frazer," I replied. "It was your husband's. Anyway, there won't be any more scenes now he's gone."

I passed my hand across my forehead.

"There!" she exclaimed. "Now I've tired you, telling you all my troubles! I shall leave you now and you must have a rest."

"I quite agree, but there's one thing I want first."

"What's that, sir?"

"I want copies of *The Times* for the last week. Could you send out for them?"

"Mr. Rendell takes *The Times*, sir, and as it happens I haven't used the old copies yet. I'll bring them up. It's good to hear you asking for a newspaper. I'm sure I'd never have believed it a week ago."

A few minutes later she returned with the papers. Directly I was alone, I scanned the "Deaths" announcements.

"Vivian . . . after a short illness . . ."

He was dead! Paul Vivian was *dead!* . . .

I remember every circumstance relating to my first meeting

with Rosalie. I had finished a book and had just returned to my flat. Then one evening a Mrs. Laidlaw rang me up and begged me to dine at her house on the Thursday, explaining that her husband had asked a Mr. and Mrs. Vivian to dinner—people they had met on a trip abroad—and now, unexpectedly, her husband had had to go away.

"Do come, Ivor, although it will be dull."

"Why will it be dull?" I asked.

"Because he's a Dreary, but she's rather a darling. Enigmatic—odd! Can't quite make her out. But she's a Lovely—definitely. Do come."

"Very well. I'll come."

I cannot imagine why I said I'd go. I was in no need of distraction, for, two days before, a woman called Vera Thornton had descended on me, who seemed to think I was God and that therefore I could shape her destiny. As I had taken her into the flat, instead of putting her outside it, I did not lack company. Nevertheless, I went to the Laidlaws.

I was in the hall when the Vivians arrived. We stood gazing at each other while her husband took off his overcoat. Her lips were parted, giving expectancy to the beautifully modelled features and this contrasted strangely with the frightened expression of the large very blue eyes.

Then she disappeared, and I glanced at her husband.

I put him down at forty-five, but I was far from certain. He was the type that becomes defined at thirty and changes little thereafter. He was heavy, solid, capable. His appearance told you most things about him. You knew what his parents were like, the kind of life he lived, his opinions, his prejudices, and his virtues. I decided that he was a pendulum, rather than a man, and wondered why that "other-world" woman had married him.

I had one minute with Mrs. Laidlaw before they joined us.

"Well? You've seen them?"

"Yes, I was in the hall when they arrived."

"He's rather like the National Debt, don't you think? But she's joyous, isn't she?"

"I suppose he knows she's going to be very ill very soon."

"Don't be absurd, Ivor! She's *been* ill. That's why they went for that trip. She's had two nervous breakdowns—and the second one was serious."

She tapped her forehead significantly.

"I see. Well——"

"They're coming! I'm counting on you to talk. I can't say *one word* to him. Whatever subject you mention, he always says 'the situation is serious.' Once I asked him if he had a hobby, and he said he was a Numismatist. What's that, Ivor? It *sounds* indecent."

I shall not forget that dinner. I hardly spoke to her, and I do not believe she looked at me once, but I was aware only of her—and the wordless dialogue between us. She sat motionless and silent, rather like a solitary child at a grown-up party, telling me about herself in a language more subtle than speech.

When she said good-bye, she did not look at me.

The next afternoon I rang her up. I recognised her voice, and said:

"Is that you, Rosalie?"

"But—who is it?"

"Ivor."

I heard an odd little sound like a gasp.

"Ivor," I repeated. "I want you to come to my flat—now."

"But—but——"

"Now!"

I gave her the address, then added:

"I am waiting for you."

Half an hour later she arrived.

She made no excuse for coming and gave no explanations. It was some moments before she spoke. On entering the sitting-room, she paused and looked round as if to convince herself that it was real.

I made her rest on a sofa, then she began to talk—rather as if she were continuing an interrupted conversation—and I learned about her parents and the circumstances in which she had married Vivian. Also she told me that she had had two nervous collapses.

I watched rather than listened. Her history was in her appearance—just as her husband's was in his. The difference between those histories was the gulf which separated them. He was unaware of that gulf. She was poised precariously on the brink of it.

Her gifts were those of an emotional genius. She responded to every nuance of feeling, every vibration in the atmosphere, every fleeting mood. It was because she had the potentiality of a great artist that she utterly failed to be a minor one. But she lacked one quality essential to a great creative synthesis—that of Will. For her to attempt an orthodox life was equivalent to a butterfly attempting the work of a bee.

She had lightning transitions from hysteria to inertia; an amazing gift for surrendering to each emotion that welled up in her. In recounting her history, she isolated with unerring flair the one significant detail which made a scene flash into life. Her descriptions were not catalogues of facts. They were impressionistic evocations. You did not hear them. You saw them.

Her beauty was that of a fey child, mysteriously become a woman. The spirit that inhabited her body seemed remote from it. When she was absent, it was her smile, or a gesture, or her rippling laugh which stabbed your memory—never the line of her figure.

After she had been with me for an hour, she suddenly leaped to her feet.

"I must go!"

"Why?"

"He will be back soon."

"You will come to-morrow?"

"Yes."

She came the next day, and the next, and the next.

Within a week we were lovers. Nevertheless, when she was not with me, it was her smile, or a gesture, or her rippling laugh which stabbed my memory—never the white beauty of her body.

Again and again she would lie in my arms sobbing. She clung to me like a child who, till now, had been too frightened to cry.

Endlessly, however, her ever-active imagination tortured her.

Once, when she was dressing, she paused suddenly and pointed to her clothes.

"He paid for these! He's at his office now—working—getting money for me!"

Instantly she identified herself with him. She saw our relations as he would see them. She became hysterical.

"Ivor! *Ivor!* Him—think of him! I shall kill myself! I can't sleep by him, night after night, knowing——"

"Listen to me!"

She stared at me with terrified eyes, her breasts rising and falling as if she had just run a race.

"Our being lovers has saved your marriage. You know that is true."

"Yes, but—*him!*"

"It doesn't matter about him. It matters about you."

"But if—if I tell him!"

"You won't tell him."

"But I may! I *may*, Ivor! Suddenly—without being able to help it. I shall scream—and tell him!"

"You won't tell him."

She came nearer me.

"How can you know?—how can you be so certain?"

"I'll lend you my will."

"Can you do that?" she asked, quite seriously, her voice a child-like blend of surprise and curiosity.

"Yes. If, suddenly, you feel you must tell him, you will say to yourself—I will see Ivor to-morrow and then both of us will tell him. That's what you'll say."

She accepted this as a heaven-sent solution. A moment later she had forgotten Vivian's existence and was laughing at her reflection in the mirror.

But that night at ten o'clock my telephone bell rang.

"Ivor!"

"Yes."

(I had to be monosyllabic, for Vera Thornton was in the room.)

"I'm in a public telephone-box. He had to go out. It was inevitable about us, wasn't it? You said it was *inevitable*."

"Yes."

"You're certain?"

"Yes."

"I knew you were, but I had to hear you say it. I'm certain, too—now. To-morrow?"

"To-morrow."

What Vivian would suffer if he knew! That was the rock round which her imagination seethed. She made his values hers; saw the situation with his eyes. This was her rack, and again and again she stretched herself upon it.

She would devise the most fantastic solutions in order to ease her suffering.

"Ivor! Listen! Perhaps, if he knew, he wouldn't mind. Yes, yes! Wait! If he *knew* that you had saved our marriage, he—might— don't you think?"

I would calm her with a word. It was only necessary to make an entirely definite statement in a tone of authority for her to accept it as if God had spoken.

"If only you would teach me to be strong, like you! Do you know, last night, I laughed in my sleep. He told me so this morning."

"Well, don't let it go any further," I began, but she clutched my arm.

"Ivor!"

"Yes."

"Perhaps I've told *everything* in my sleep! And perhaps he heard —and doesn't mind. Is that possible, do you think?"

Every other day she imagined a new solution. It was curious how, having no consciousness of guilt herself, she suffered agonies of remorse through accepting his standards. Nevertheless, despite this vicarious suffering, the improvement in her health was astonishing. She looked years younger than the woman I had met at the Laidlaws.

One afternoon, when we had been lovers for some months, she made a new suggestion—and a startling one.

"I want you to meet him, Ivor. I want you to come to the flat—often!"

"Why?"

"It—it will seem more—more *regular*."

She was looking at me with great, serious eyes. "You will do that for me?" she added.

"Yes, if you like."

She seized my hands impulsively.

"Why do you love me, Ivor?"

"Because you give me a sense of power."

She laughed and began to talk about something else, but—a week later—I was asked to dine at the Vivians.

Vivian knew I had met Rosalie since the night at the Laidlaws. She had told him that she had run into me somewhere else, and that we had become friends. Consequently the suggestion that I should dine with them was more likely to allay suspicion than to provoke it.

The flat was an extension of Vivian. He had lived in it as a bachelor and, with one exception, it was now what it had been then. Rosalie had merely been imported into it. The exception was her own intimate room which, before Vivian married, had not been used, the flat being a large one. To cross the threshold was to leave one world and enter another.

Vivian's furniture was solid, handsome, heavy. It regarded you with the dull pride of immutability. You were transitory: it was permanent. Each piece had its place and would remain in it. There it stood—a symbol of its owner's virtues.

Vivian regarded other people, not as individuals, but as types. To discover to which type a man belonged, all that was necessary was to know what he did. I was a writer. Very well, then! I was the "artist" type.

Now, with Vivian and his friends, art would have been dismissed as a piece of foolishness had it not been for the fact that certain pictures sold for stupendous sums of money, and certain writers made incomes which were not to be denied. Also, eccentric members of the aristocracy were genuinely interested in art and showed clearly that they did not regard it as ingenious tomfoolery. Vivian, therefore, feigned respect for it while privately regarding it as super-nonsense.

My opinion of him was wholly at variance with Rosalie's, though I did not tell her so. She regarded him as kind, indulgent, unselfish. To me, he possessed none of those qualities. He was a man who was quite certain that certain things could never happen to him. They happened to others, of course—but not to him.

What convinced me of this was the manner in which he referred to Rosalie's illnesses. His attitude implied that his wife ought not to have had nervous collapses. (He always referred to her as "my wife.") He could find no explanation of these breakdowns. She had every comfort, every attention. They went away frequently and she did not lack amusement. Why, then, nervous collapses?

It was plain that he regarded them as disturbances in an otherwise satisfactory and well-organised life. They were the only contact he had ever had with Failure.

"On the second occasion, it was very painful, very painful indeed." He paused and looked round in order to make certain that we were alone. "She used to *scream*—although she was in a first-class nursing home. The one in which Lady Mavers is interested, you probably know of it. I used to say to her—gently, of course—'My dear, you really *must* control yourself.' It was a most difficult time for me. And once—would you believe it?—when I went to see her in the home, she did not recognise me."

I pointed out that she was a sensitive—but I got no further.

"Yes, yes! I know that argument, but it's based on a fallacy. She's deceptively frail-looking. I use the word 'deceptively' advisedly. You may not believe me, but, actually, she's strongly built. Lithe—but strong. She looks far more frail in her clothes than she does—than she actually is."

There he sat at the head of the table, a square, solid figure in old-fashioned evening clothes. He had a ponderous head, shrewd eyes, broad, capable hands. To see him was to know his friends. Everything I learned about Vivian only confirmed what I already knew. I never made a discovery.

Clockwork-regularity was his god. On Wednesday nights they dined at a restaurant, because the servants went out on Wednesday nights. Never did they enter a restaurant on any other night. On Saturday they went to the play, because Vivian did not mind being late on Saturdays as he did not have to go to the office the next day. On Saturday afternoons he had a Turkish bath, because the office was shut on Saturday afternoons. On Sunday from three to five he contemplated his coins. He had a remarkable collection and was very proud of it. He took the same house in the country every summer and went to it every week-end. His wife could stay there from May till September, if she chose. If not, she accompanied him every week-end. Every other year they went abroad for a month. Every morning he left the house at nine-thirty and returned at six o'clock. Every winter he suffered from bronchial trouble.

Rosalie was a prisoner among the prosaic.

On one occasion I referred to the amazing improvement in her health, adding that I took some credit for it as it coincided with our friendship.

"Oh yes, yes! She's quite normal, really. All women have fads. But I always knew that a regular life must have an effect on her. One young fool of a doctor told me that she needed an outlet."

He looked at me with heavy indignation.

"My wife needed an outlet! Did you ever hear such nonsense? Here she is, perfectly well again, and what outlet has she now which she had not then?"

I agreed that a regular life had had its effect on her.

My friendship with Rosalie did not disturb him in the least. In fact, in the winter, when his bronchial trouble asserted itself, he welcomed my presence, and frequently asked me to take Rosalie to the theatre on Saturday nights.

As to the question of possible infidelity, I am convinced it never crossed his mind. To him, she was not Rosalie. She was—his wife. Somebody else's wife might be unfaithful to her husband, of course, but not his wife. Things like that did not happen to *him*.

I half believe that he thought it was my admiration for him which made me such a frequent visitor.

What would he do if he discovered? That was the only question relating to Vivian which I could not answer. Would he merely insist that she was never to see me again—then punish her in secret till the day one of them died? That would avoid scandal. Or would he divorce her, and bang the gates of his memory on her for ever? Would he commit suicide? Murder? It was impossible even to have an opinion. To discover that his wife had a lover would be a calamity so outside Vivian's experience that his reaction to it was not to be imagined.

Rosalie believed that he loved her. I believed that he loved her as part of himself. I do not think he loved Rosalie. But I am quite certain he loved his wife.

I did not care whether he discovered or not. Danger has always fascinated me. It delivers me from that terrible interior weariness. It robs the days and nights of that fearful flat monotony in which everything is steeped in the leaden hue of mediocrity. Danger is the subtlest form of intoxication. It makes the most worthless life suddenly worth the living. It gives meaning to the meaningless. Boredom lies awake in a nightcap, but Danger sleeps with a sword by its side.

At any moment Rosalie might have told Vivian. She lived, moved, and had her being in a state of emotional tension. She had the irresistible impulses of a child. She had, too, a child's craving to share its happiness. Her imagination tortured her by compelling her to regard that happiness as he would regard it. Above all, she had the dream that it was possible for Vivian to know we were lovers—and to share the innocence she felt in that relationship. And, for her, this was not only a dream, it was an objective. It was her belief in this fantasy which enabled her to continue to deceive him. This was why she wanted me to visit their flat. To be there together, the three of us, in a room—seemed to her to be prophetic of the fulfilment of her dream. The three of us—in physical proximity! To Rosalie, that fact foreshadowed a future intimacy in which all barriers would be down.

She was so far removed from Vivian that she could believe that about him! She was such worlds away from him that she could not believe he was what he seemed.

Whenever my telephone bell rang, whenever a wire came for me, or a ring at the door, my mind became a question mark. Often, I was *certain* she would tell him. I have seen the sentence quiver on her lips a dozen times.

Once she impulsively took his arm and mine simultaneously. I could see that her romanticism was regarding herself as a link between us. I burst out laughing, and thereby jarred her back to actuality.

To dominate her so that she would *not* tell him! That was my task, and success almost convinced me that I possessed the power in which she so wholly believed. To steel her with my will! To possess her psychic being! To still her remorse with a word! To rule her ever-active imagination!

And—simultaneously—not to care if she did tell him. Her confession would force me into action. If he divorced her, I would marry her. If he killed her, I would kill him. To be forced to act, to do something—anything! At times I thought that this would be deliverance.

What did it matter to me whether she told him or not? I was living so "outside" myself, so divorced from my centre, that all my actions were unreal to me. What gave them a ghostly appearance of reality was Rosalie's belief in my strength. That belief almost enabled me to believe in the Ivor Trent whom she loved. And, every day, my desire to believe in him deepened, for—every day—the alternative became clearer and clearer.

The alternative was to enter a desert—not unlike the one which surrounded Denis Wrayburn. But of him—later.

Did I love Rosalie? The question is meaningless. When a man is desperately at odds with himself, others do not exist. He is a battlefield of principalities and powers. His relations with others are a caricature of that conflict. He is alone. And the more people he knows, and the more famous he is, the greater is that solitude.

To me, Rosalie was something rare, something unexpected in the modern world—a work of art in a factory. Sometimes I forgot my falsity, my emptiness, in watching her. (Usually, I watched her. I seldom listened to what she said.) At times I felt that she was my childhood—the childhood of which I had been robbed. But, had she guessed that the only link between us was weakness, she would have turned to ice in my arms. For she needed strength, and she believed that I was strong. She needed two types of strength: Vivian's—and what she believed was mine. Vivian's, because the actual world was so shadowy to her that she needed the companionship of one to whom it was overwhelmingly real. And she needed the strength she believed was mine—that is, psychic strength—in order to stabilise her imagination.

She needed the physical proximity of Vivian—and the psychic

proximity of the type she imagined me to be. It was because she realised this unconsciously that she longed for Vivian to share our secret.

It never occurred to her that she was separated from me by a gulf as wide and as deep as that which divided her from Vivian.

She did not know that Ivor Trent was a ghost. She thought he was a giant.

G

DURING the three years we were lovers, Rosalie believed she was the only woman with whom I was intimate. Actually, during the first year, Vera Thornton visited me frequently. . . .

One afternoon—a few days before my first meeting with Rosalie at the Laidlaws'—I was alone in my flat, reading, when I was disturbed by a long peal from the bell.

I went to the door and found myself confronted by a woman of about twenty-one, who was trembling with excitement. She stood, speechless, staring at me with dark fanatical eyes, as if I were an idol in a shrine. She held a bulging bag which was clearly very heavy, for she stood obliquely, so that the pull of her body balanced its weight.

"I'm Vera Thornton," she announced at last, in a voice resembling a gasp.

The name was vaguely familiar, but I failed to place her.

"I wrote to you, if you remember, and—and you answered my letter."

For some reason these simple statements made her blush crimson.

"I remember," I replied. "You wrote telling me about your family. Won't you come in?"

We went to the sitting-room. I was about to suggest she should sit down, when I noticed the absence of the bag.

"Where's your bag?" I asked.

"I—I left it outside."

"Do you mean—outside the front door?"

She nodded, so I went to fetch it, half convinced that I had a lunatic on hand, and half interested.

I struggled back with the bag—which must have been filled with lead to its uttermost capacity—and had scarcely entered the room when she began to speak in a nervous staccato manner, but with great rapidity.

In broken, intense sentences, she literally hurled her history at my head. She told me about her home: her father's promiscuity: the pleasure-frenzied lives of her brothers and sisters: hinted darkly at infamies: described the pandemonium which raged perpetually in the house. Then, with the briefest of pauses, she raced on to detail her scholastic achievements, her sufferings, and the shame she had endured at being connected with such a family.

Exclamations, blushes, angry gestures, served as punctuation in this passionate recital. She emphasised her isolation from this family of hers with ever-increasing intensity. She went on and on. She related her conflicts with her brothers and sisters; their contempt for her standards; her loathing of theirs; and the coarse jokes with which her father had countered her protests.

Finally, she explained that for the last year she had read only my books, knew whole passages by heart, and that they had inspired her to leave her family and come to London.

During the whole of this explosion she did not look at me. When its echoes had trembled into silence, I asked her what she proposed to do in London.

A long tortuous explanation followed, during which she writhed with embarrassment to such an extent that she maintained only a precarious balance on her chair. Nevertheless, I gathered from hints, innuendoes, and side-long glances that she regarded me as a god who would provide her with a destiny—of a highly-spiritual order.

I lit a cigarette and began to pace up and down the room, interested by the knowledge that if all this had occurred when I was about to write a book, I should have got rid of her instantly. But I had just finished one, and so had nothing to do. Also, I had long since tired of meeting herds of people. For some years I had concentrated on individuals. Curiosity therefore suggested exploration.

As I paced up and down I glanced at her repeatedly, noting her powerful regular features, her jet-black hair, her strong over-developed figure. She was leaning forward, her hands clasping her knees, staring into futurity with fanatical eyes. She looked rather like a prophetess who had got the sack and was plotting revenge.

Then, with a view to testing the validity of a theory I had already formed, I began to question her regarding certain parts of her story. Not one of these questions related to her achievements, or her spiritual claims, or her fantastic conception of me. They concerned the members of her family. I pressed for further details about them—especially her sisters. I made her describe their appearance, their clothes and—above all—the types of life they led. Vera had only hinted darkly at enormities, but now I insisted on details.

I got them—obscured by a veil of prudery—but more or less complete. They were not in the least interesting, being merely commonplace examples of the pleasures of dull people with the modern conception of freedom. What was interesting, however, were certain facts which Vera made plain without intending to do so.

Briefly summarised, these were: that her sisters were pretty, attractive, and in great demand; that they ridiculed her preten-sions; patronised her; and generally regarded her as a freak.

In fact, her account of them was an astonishing example of unconscious self-revelation. She made it very clear that it was her pride which was in flaming revolt against her family, not her soul. She hated them, not because of their sensuality, but because they refused to acknowledge her superiority. Her leaving them and coming to London was not the initial deed of a spiritual crusade. It was a melodramatic attempt to convince them of her originality. Her governing motive was to impress them, and so to be revenged for the humiliations they had inflicted.

Secretly, she feared that their estimate of her was the true one. She was terribly afraid that, underneath, she was like them. She was haunted by the fear that what separated her from them was not spirituality, but lack of courage. Her hatred was a secret fear of kinship. Consequently she was determined to prove that she did *not* belong to them.

And she expected *me* to accept her at her own valuation! I regarded her with the contempt that a great swindler feels for a pickpocket.

Nevertheless, I gave her tea and, later, I told the servants some lie about a cousin, so that Vera could spend the night in the flat.

For some days she talked and I listened. I listened to such fantastic nonsense about myself that, more than once, nothing less than murder seemed an adequate punishment. She grovelled before me. I was to be the means by which she would convince herself of her spiritual superiority to her family.

Things could not go on like this. That was definite. By now, I had met Rosalie, and so Vera had to leave the flat. I got her a room and then I told her, in the plainest possible terms, that her Christmas-card conception of me bore no relation to the facts, and that if we were to meet in the future it must be on that basis.

She gave me a superior smile—the kind of smile that is exchanged by members of a tiny community which meets in a basement once a week, and is dogmatically certain that it—and only it—possesses the Key to the Riddle of the Universe. Despite this smile, however, I told her that in no circumstances was she to come to the flat unless I asked her. Then, having repeated that her conception of me was wholly fictitious, I got rid of her.

But that did not stop her writing. My God, those letters! Vera's letters! Someone once said that the spiritual life must be a fulfilment, not a substitute. If ever truth were written, it is there. Those letters—what she believed them to be, and what they were! I began to hate her. I wrote her a line asking her not to write to me. I received three thousand words by return of post, mainly to the effect that I did not know what I *really* was, and that what I *really* was—was what the world *really* wanted.

I had had enough. And I had arrived at a decision. I sent her a note asking her to come to the flat the next night, stressing—for the third time—that if she came she must not expect to find the man she imagined me to be.

She came the next night. I tested the extent of my dominion over her, only to discover that it had no limits. Then I told her she would come to the flat twice a week, and oftener if I sent for her.

For a year she visited me regularly.

During that period I proved a number of things to her in such a manner that even she could retain no illusions about me or herself. Not only did I descend from the pedestal on which she had placed me, but I also forced her to vacate hers.

I humiliated her, physically and psychologically, till no trace of her former conception of me remained. I proved to her that she *did* belong to that family which she so despised. I proved to her that their estimate of her was the true one, and that her pretensions were a façade erected by her pride.

Again and again—breathless, crimson, infuriated—she announced that she hated me and would never see me again—never! And whenever I sent her a note, she arrived at the flat precisely at the hour I had stated.

Her surrender, on every level, was complete and abject. She had no will in my presence—only a genius for obedience. Soon, she had one fear, and only one—that in some mysterious manner her family would learn of her degradation. This fear was so rooted that it was not removed by the statement that they would learn of it only if she told them.

Those are the facts about my relations with Vera. They are not pretty ones, but I am not concerned with prettiness.

To be worshipped for everything I was not—everything from which I had run away—was intolerable. It woke a cold anger in me, an icy determination to destroy. She should learn what she was—as I had been forced to know what I was. She should know what she was running away from—even as I knew. If she wanted to present a façade to the world, it was better to realise what was behind it. It was better to know that it hid a naked empty Vera Thornton, than to believe that it shielded a saint in the making.

So, in the space of a few weeks, I ceased to be a Spiritual Superman for Vera and became a Monster of Vice. (The latter designation was as fantastic as the former. I was, in fact, consistently a ghost throughout.) Originally, she gazed at my Radiance in the clouds, and now she peered at my Dark Shadow in the pit. She melodramatised everything.

But she believed I had Power. Her façade had not deceived me—but mine had deceived her. She was so convinced of the power of my Dark Malignity that at times I too almost believed in it. Almost—but not quite. It threw no shadow on the floor, so I knew it was a ghost.

At the end of a year she said she must have a job. I managed to get her a position in the foreign department of a bank. She left her room and took a small flat in Bloomsbury.

She still came to see me whenever I asked her, but I began to ask her less and less frequently. And, finally, not at all.

H

THE brutality of my relations with Vera temporarily eased the tension created by my association with Rosalie. Or so I deluded myself. Actually, of course, it increased that tension till a collapse was inevitable.

Apart from the ever-present possibility that Vivian would discover our secret, constant companionship with Rosalie was in the nature of an ordeal, for her world was not this one. It was a world of psychic extremity. To meet her was to enter it. To enter it, was to experience its intensity.

Often, when I left her, I was in a state of inner irritability which was intolerable. It was on these occasions that I rang up Vera and told her to come to the flat.

Or, if I did not telephone Vera, I would talk to someone—anyone—and learn all about his or her life till I could steep myself in his or her activities.

There was a girl they called Rummy, who served in the long bar of the Cosmopolitan. I often talked to her, till I had learned everything about her. Then I identified myself imaginatively with her activities till I almost became her. I knew every detail of her life in the bar and at home. I knew her hopes, her fears, her pleasures. I could become her at will—and so be delivered from the heavy chain of my own personality. She was a drug which I used again and again.

But there was another reason why I clung to the madness represented by Rosalie and Vera. That reason was Denis Wrayburn.

I spoke to him for the first time in the station restaurant at Basle. I had arrived at about dawn and had an hour or two to fill in before getting the train to Italy. I went and looked at the Rhine, then returned to the station for rolls and coffee.

I ordered these and was studying the mural decorations, when I heard a polar voice behind me refusing to pay the price asked for the excellent jam provided.

I turned and saw a remarkable-looking individual. I spoke to him and we spent an hour together. Among other things, I learned that he was acting as courier to a rich American family.

I doubt if I saw Wrayburn more than once during the next two years, then—soon after Rosalie and I had become lovers—he turned up at my flat and we met regularly.

I have known hosts of people, but no one remotely resembling Wrayburn. He was disembodied intelligence. He looked like a ghost who had genius—and that is precisely what he was. Only a dying civilisation could have produced him—and he regarded it with the eyes of an undertaker. He was the one man I have met who had to be what he was. No disguise was possible for him. He could present no façade to the world. He was an absolute being.

He frightened me. That is difficult to explain, but it must be explained. He frightened me because I saw an aspect of myself in him. Wrayburn was what I might become. He was what I *should* become, if my gift for writing deserted me. I should enter his wilderness. I should become a ghost with a brain.

Wrayburn was born an emotional outcast: I was becoming one. Elsa represented my real emotional self. I had abandoned her, and I was dying as a result of that desertion. Only by returning to her could I regain the possibility of life. But where was she? And how could I return to her?

No, I should become what Wrayburn had always been. I should enter his spectral solitude. I should haunt the world—a thinking shadow.

I *knew* this would be my destiny, if my gift for writing deserted me. And I knew that, soon, it would desert me. *Two Lives and a Destiny* had been born of vital experience, for Failure is vital experience. The books which followed it had been born of Loneliness—the Loneliness that wears a mask. That, too, for a time, is vital experience. But, soon, I should be incapable of experience. The very roots of my inner life would rot? And then? I knew the worthlessness of books that are born of Observation. They are note-books, masquerading as creative literature.

So, to me, Wrayburn was a prophetic figure.

The fear of becoming like him goaded me to continue my madness with Rosalie and Vera. The fact that such relations would have been impossible for Wrayburn made me plunge deeper into them. By so doing I proved to myself that I was *not* like him. I was desperately anxious to prove that.

Wrayburn usually came to my flat. I visited him several times in a room he had in Bloomsbury, but—later—he moved to a lugubrious house in Fulham, and I only went there once. It had the atmosphere of a crypt.

He met Rosalie fairly frequently at my flat, but Vera only once.

"What do you think of Rosalie?" I asked him once, just after she had left us.

"If you could take *that* woman and Mr. Denis Wrayburn—and amalgamate them into one human being—and bring their different qualities into perfect polarity, you would produce a rough model of a New Race."

After a pause he went on:

"But Rosalie—*not* amalgamated with Mr. Denis Wrayburn—is quite an interesting person. To be her lover would be a notable experience."

He spoke, as ever, in the abstract. Rosalie might have been something in a test-tube.

"And what do you think of Vera?" I asked.

"In regard to the bulging Vera, it would give me a particular and a peculiar pleasure to watch her being tortured every afternoon, from two till four. I may add that the period from two till four in the afternoon is responsible for crime, drug-taking, and the indulgence of every secret vice. God abdicates during those two hours—and slowly re-ascends his throne as tea-time approaches."

The only thing Wrayburn attempted to conceal was his eagerness to meet me—and that was a failure. He never referred directly to his isolation, but his very appearance was a commentary on it. He was so outside life as it is lived that it had no interest for him. He was only interested in possibilities.

He was widely read in occult literature and he believed that I was. As a fact, the only book of the kind I had deeply studied was the one lent me by a priest, which I read in the trenches. Still, I was familiar with the belief that man contained in himself the potentiality of a New Being—and that, by devotion, dedication, and discipline, man could rise to a new order of consciousness.

But this belief in the possibility of a New Race was Wrayburn's eternal theme. He held that, although the mass of mankind was in the kindergarten stage of evolution, every generation produced men and women capable of serving this idea of a New Race. They were prophecies of a new order of spiritual consciousness. They were God's collaborators.

"The New Man is only a few civilisations distant," he would say. "He must arise eventually. He will possess a Cosmic Consciousness. In him, Thought, Will, and Feeling will be fused into unity. That unity will be the Cosmic Consciousness. Compared with it, our present-day consciousness is like the flame of a night-light flickering in a draught."

We met frequently and at last, to my stupefaction, I discovered he believed that I was one of those who are capable of serving the idea of a New Race. He made this staggering statement as if he were enunciating a truism.

Even now I do not know which is the more fantastic—this belief, or the reasons on which it was based.

Wrayburn imagined that I, unlike himself, was at home in the world, adequate to it, and above all that I had real relations with others. He was certain, therefore, that I had Power.

"They can walk down the street with you," he announced, "but they only find me if they go mountaineering."

He saw in me a "great spiritual potentiality." I could be "a link joining the old consciousness to the new."

"You're not half a man, like the rest of us," he once said. "You're a real person. There's Being in you. That's why you can meet all sorts of people—even the bulging Vera."

I said nothing. That Wrayburn, with his almost terrible insight, could believe that the ghost facing him was a potential Superman, amazed and frightened me. Wrayburn, whom nothing deceived, believed *that!*

He believed that the ghost called Ivor Trent had being and . . . .

I

SOMETHING extraordinary has just happened. It is the reason why the last section is unfinished.

I was writing it at my desk in my study, during the late afternoon. I looked up, in search of a phrase, and noticed that the door communicating with the bedroom was open. I was thinking of shutting it when I heard someone moving about.

"Is that you, Mrs. Frazer?"

There was no reply.

"Who's there?" I shouted, more irritably.

The door opened wider and—*Elsa appeared.*

I rose slowly, staring at her.

"You! What are you doing here?"

"I took Mrs. Frazer's place, when she became your nurse."

"Why didn't she tell me?"

"She probably didn't think it would interest you. She knew nothing about us."

"How long is it since I came here?"

"Nearly seven weeks."

She crossed to the window, parted the curtains, and stood looking down at the river.

I do not know how long it was before I said:

"Come here. I can't see you."

She came over to me, then half sat on the edge of the writing-desk. I stood looking down at her.

"Is Rendell still here?"

"Yes, but he is going in just over a week."

"Where? Do you know?"

"To Italy."

Then, after a pause, she added:

"Rosalie Vivian is in Italy."

"Has Rendell met her often?"

"Yes, nearly every day for a month. Mrs. Frazer thinks he will marry her."

Again, there was a long silence.

"And Marsden?"

"He is still here. Hasn't Mrs. Frazer told you all this?"

"No. I haven't spoken to her about the house for a long time. Has Vera Thornton been here?"

"No, but Marsden has met her frequently."

Although I asked these questions, and although Elsa answered them, they had no relation whatever to the real question I was asking—and which she was answering.

"And Wrayburn?"

She did not reply.

"Well?"

"He's dead."

I went nearer to her.

"When?"

"He was buried yesterday. He committed suicide."

"Wrayburn?"

"Yes."

I felt her hand on my arm.

"How?"

"Do you think you'd better——"

"How?" I repeated. "A newspaper—the inquest! Get me the newspaper."

I did not hear her go or return. I found a newspaper in my hand, and flattened it on the desk—but I could not read it.

"You read it," I said to her.

A gas-filled room . . . even the cracks in the floor plugged. . . . Rendell.

"Read again what Rendell said."

Elsa read slowly.

"'I blame myself bitterly for not seeing him more often. I knew he was lonely, but I failed him. As I said earlier, Wrayburn, apparently, had no relatives, but I shall, of course, make myself responsible for the funeral.'"

I do not know how long the silence continued after she stopped reading, but at last I heard her say:

"I must go now."

"Have you talked to Rendell?"

"No."

"See him—tell him about us."

"Very well, and now I must go."

She turned and walked towards the door.

Just as she reached it, I said:

"So you will come with me when I leave here?"

"Yes."

"You will tell no one, and come with me?"

"Yes, whenever you like."

She went out, closing the door noiselessly.

J

NEXT Sunday, I leave here with Elsa.

It will be eight weeks next Sunday since I came to this house: since I collapsed when Mrs. Frazer opened the front door: since I saw *Him* loom out of the fog on the Embankment.

I remember every detail of that Sunday—eight weeks ago.

I left my flat soon after six o'clock. For an hour I had stood by the window in the sitting-room, looking down at the fog-shrouded street. No one was to be seen. Every sound was muffled. The city had become its own ghost.

I stood motionless, watching my thoughts.

I had told everyone I was going abroad for a year to write a book. Rosalie had begged me not to leave her. She was certain she would tell Vivian, if I went. Her fear made her almost hysterical, but I scarcely heard what she said.

For over a year a theme for a novel had challenged my imagination. For months, the bee hive of my subconscious mind had been at work on it. The period of inner elaboration was over. Now I must write it.

I was excited, eager to escape to solitude, but, nevertheless, I was afraid. I knew that, unless a miracle happened, it would be my last book. I had reached a final frontier. I stood at the end of a cul-de-sac.

Also, I had been ill recently. The tension of my nerves had become unendurable. I could feel the foundation of my will trembling.

These were some of the thoughts I watched—as I stood motionless, looking down into the fog.

But they were followed by other thoughts—fantastic projects which flashed across my mind, each offering a final intoxication before I went to Potiphar Street and to solitude.

One suggested I should ring up Vera and tell her to come to the flat. I had not seen her for months. I should hear her gasp of astonishment when she recognised my voice on the telephone. She would indignantly refuse to come—and half an hour later she would arrive.

Or I would ring Rosalie, see her once more, and tell her how wholly I had deceived her. Or I would make Rosalie and Vera both come to the flat, and then I would tell them everything. I would telephone Vivian—and Wrayburn. I would make them *all* come. Or I would ring up people I had not seen for years, who had reason to remember me.

These were some of the projects which flashed and faded in my mind as I stood by that window—eight weeks ago.

But, deeper than all, was the knowledge that I had reached the end of a road—the beginning of which had been my desertion of Elsa.

But the remnant of my will rebelled against this knowledge. My plans were made and I was determined to execute them. My luggage was piled in the hall. I was to leave at about six o'clock.

I remember the church bells beginning to ring out over the spectral city.

Suddenly someone said the taxi was waiting. I started violently, for I had not heard the servant enter the room.

I went into the hall, put on my overcoat, then looked round the flat for the last time. Just as I was going the telephone bell rang. I told the servant to say I was away, then I went down to the street.

I told the driver to take the luggage to 77 Potiphar Street, and to tell Mrs. Frazer that I should arrive at about nine o'clock.

I watched the taxi disappear, then groped through the fog to Piccadilly. Soon after I reached Leicester Square I lost myself in a desert of drifting desolation.

At last, I found myself in the Strand, and, some minutes later, I reached that tavern.

It was empty, but before long two men entered.

Marsden . . . Rendell . . . the sound of my own name . . . the story of *Two Lives and a Destiny*.

I overheard every word they said, as I sat huddled in my corner, too weak to move. Then, directly I could, I stumbled out into the fog and groped my way to Chelsea.

Sentences from the conversation I had overheard drifted through my mind, but they seemed to relate to someone else—some stranger who had stolen my name.

A new consciousness seemed to possess me, a strange terrible clarity which lit mysterious horizons.

And then, at last, I stopped outside the street leading to the Frazers' house.

I leaned over the low Embankment wall and gazed into the vapoury void below, listening to the life of the swiftly-flowing invisible river. In the near distance, the blast of a siren suddenly gave desolation a voice. A moment later, a ruby-coloured light slowly emerged, glowed for a second, and vanished. Then all was still and dark again.

Gradually, a trance-like stupor possessed me. Then slowly, ceaselessly, a sentence began to circle in my mind. It was Marsden's final statement to Rendell.

"He's convinced *that man contains the potentiality of a new being.*"

And then I turned and saw—You!

Your figure was shrouded, but your face was fully revealed. It was the countenance of a new order of Being. I knew that a man from the Future stood before me.

Terror overwhelmed me—then. But I do not fear you—now.

I stretch out my arms and invoke you:—

Come!

I do not know whether you stand on the threshold, or whether unnumbered ages separate us from you. I only know that you *must* be: that you are the spiritual consciousness made flesh: that you are the risen man and that we are the dead men. Yet, in us, is the possibility of you.

We are the Old—the dying—Consciousness. You are the New— the living—Consciousness. We have violated earth. You will redeem it. We descend the darkening valley of knowledge. You stand on the uplands of wisdom. We are an end. You are a beginning.

If you are a dream, all else is a nightmare. But I have seen God's signature across your forehead.

Come!

More and more fiercely we deny our need of you. We say you are a fantasy, a lie, an illusion. We madden ourselves with sensation; drug ourselves with work, pleasure, speed; herd in the vast sepulchres of our cities; blind our eyes; deaden our ears; cling to our creed of comfort (Comfort! the last of the creeds!) sink day by day in deeper servitude to our inventions—hoping to numb the knowledge of our emptiness; striving to ease the ache of separation; trying to evade your challenge; seeking to deny our destiny.

Come!

The martyred earth waits for you. Daily, our darkness deepens. Secretly, all are afraid. None knows what to do. To underpin, to patch up, to whitewash sepulchres—these are the substitutes for action. To shout, to boast, to nickname bankruptcy, Prosperity— this is the substitute for leadership. We have glorified ourselves, magnified ourselves, made gods of ourselves. We have served Hate, Greed, Lust. And now darkness deepens round us. And we are afraid.

Come!

Lacking you, there is no solution to any one of our problems. Possessing you, no problems exist. If it be madness to believe in you, the sanity which denies you is a greater madness.

But we who have lived on substitutes; we who have plumbed the abyss of ourselves; we who have glimpsed the magnitude of man's misery—we do not deny you.

From the midnight of madness we stretch out our arms to you. *Come!*

⋆   ⋆   ⋆   ⋆   ⋆

A shadow seems to fall across the page I am writing. You are here, in this room! I am certain you are here.

I turn, but I cannot see you. I call, but you do not answer.

I rise, grope round the room seeking you, till at last I stand before a mirror.

But the countenance reflected in that mirror is not mine. *It is yours.* A man from the Future confronts me. His eyes transmit a secret wisdom. His forehead is crested with serenity.

THE END

Claude Houghton (1889-1961)

ALSO AVAILABLE FROM VALANCOURT BOOKS

MICHAEL ARLEN	Hell! said the Duchess
R. C. ASHBY (RUBY FERGUSON)	He Arrived at Dusk
FRANK BAKER	The Birds
CHARLES BEAUMONT	The Hunger and Other Stories
DAVID BENEDICTUS	The Fourth of June
CHARLES BIRKIN	The Smell of Evil
JOHN BLACKBURN	A Scent of New-Mown Hay
	Broken Boy
	Blue Octavo
	The Flame and the Wind
	Nothing but the Night
	Bury Him Darkly
	Our Lady of Pain
THOMAS BLACKBURN	The Feast of the Wolf
JOHN BRAINE	Room at the Top
	The Vodi
R. CHETWYND-HAYES	The Monster Club
BASIL COPPER	The Great White Space
	Necropolis
HUNTER DAVIES	Body Charge
JENNIFER DAWSON	The Ha-Ha
BARRY ENGLAND	Figures in a Landscape
RONALD FRASER	Flower Phantoms
GILLIAN FREEMAN	The Liberty Man
	The Leather Boys
	The Leader
STEPHEN GILBERT	The Landslide
	The Burnaby Experiments
	Ratman's Notebooks
MARTYN GOFF	The Plaster Fabric
	The Youngest Director
STEPHEN GREGORY	The Cormorant
THOMAS HINDE	Mr. Nicholas
	The Day the Call Came
CLAUDE HOUGHTON	I Am Jonathan Scrivener
	This Was Ivor Trent
GERALD KERSH	Nightshade and Damnations
	Fowlers End
	Night and the City

Lightning Source UK Ltd.
Milton Keynes UK
UKHW01f2130171018
330727UK00001B/167/P